THE VANISHING RAIDERS

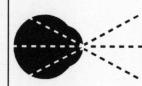

This Large Print Book carries the
Seal of Approval of N.A.V.H.

THE VANISHING RAIDERS

WESTERN STORIES

FRED GROVE

THORNDIKE PRESS
A part of Gale, Cengage Learning

GALE
CENGAGE Learning·

Detroit • New York • San Francisco • New Haven, Conn • Waterville, Maine • London

GALE
CENGAGE Learning®

Copyright © 2005 by Fred Grove.
The Additional Copyright Information on pages 5–6 constitutes an extension of the copyright page.
Thorndike Press, a part of Gale, Cengage Learning.

Thorndike Press® Large Print Western.
The text of this Large Print edition is unabridged.
Other aspects of the book may vary from the original edition.
Set in 16 pt. Plantin.

LIBRARY OF CONGRESS CATALOGING-IN-PUBLICATION DATA

Grove, Fred.
  [Short stories. Selections]
  The vanishing raiders : western stories / by Fred Grove.
    pages ; cm. — (Thorndike Press large print western)
    ISBN 978-1-4104-5377-8 (hardcover) — ISBN 1-4104-5377-4 (hardcover)
  I. Grove, Fred. No man's trail. II. Title.
  PS3557.R7V36 2012
  813'.54—dc23   2012035728

Published in 2012 by arrangement with Golden West Literary Agency.

ADDITIONAL COPYRIGHT INFORMATION

TABLE OF CONTENTS

FOREWORD

I first met Fred Grove in the spring of 1999. *Tucson Lifestyle* magazine had asked me to profile Grove, a local resident who had won five Spur Awards from Western Writers of America, two Western Heritage Wrangler Awards from what is now the National Cowboy and Western Heritage Museum, and the WWA's Levi Strauss Golden Saddleman Award for lifetime achievement in Western literature. Only when I telephoned Grove to schedule an interview, I got hammered with questions, so many, in fact, that I felt as if I were a suspect being grilled by Perry Mason.

Admitting that he had never sought publicity, Grove agreed to an interview whenever I could drive down to Tucson. A few weeks later, I knocked on his door. So full of vigor had been this voice on the phone, so fun-loving but passionate about the American West (once I answered all of *his*

9

questions about *me*), I expected a man in his forties or fifties to answer the door. Instead, a smiling, bespectacled gent in his eighties greeted me with a firm handshake.

I left that house with more than an interview and magazine assignment in the can. I left with a lifetime friend, a mentor, an inspiration, had become fan.

Of Osage and Sioux descent, Frederick Herridge Grove was born on July 4, 1913, in Hominy, Oklahoma, to a family of Westerners. His mother had been born on a Sioux reservation, his father was an old-time cowhand and horseman; one grandfather had served in the Union Cavalry in Missouri during the Civil War, and another worked for Buffalo Bill Cody's Wild West Show.

One of Grove's most vivid memories came in 1923 when a late-night explosion rocked their house in Fairfax, Oklahoma. The Groves later learned that nitroglycerin had been used to destroy an Osage Indian's house, killing two people and fatally injuring a third.

Those grisly murders left a lasting mark on the young Oklahoman. His novels *Warrior Road* (Doubleday, 1974), *Drums Without Warriors* (Doubleday, 1976), and *The Years of Fear* (Five Star Westerns, 2002) deal with the greed-motivated Osage murders during the Oklahoma oil boom that became a national scandal in the 1920s.

His first focus as a writer, however, wasn't Western fiction, but sports. After graduating from the University of Oklahoma in 1937, Grove, still a huge sports fan today, worked at newspapers in Oklahoma and Texas.

"I wasn't interested in Western writing," Grove recalled. "I wanted to write sports, eventually wanted to work at the Tulsa papers. I was interested in reading Westerns, and used to read *Western Story Magazine* every week, which I'd borrow from an old fella who used to work for us."

Westerns, however, began to appeal to him after he left the newspaper business and returned to OU in 1947, this time in the public relations department, and got to know Walter Campbell (better known by his pen name, Stanley Vestal) and Foster-Harris. Grove had also interviewed several Oklahoma pioneers while working at the Shawnee *Morning News* and was a fan of Western novelist Ernest Haycox.

"I started thinking," he said, "Oh, boy, it might be fun to write a Western."

Grove's fiction career started as the pulp magazines were dying, and he never has been the most prolific writer, always focusing on quality, not quantity. He is also one of the few writers capable of jumping from adult to adolescent fiction, and a gifted teller of long and short fiction. Three of his national honors came for short stories — Spur Awards for "Comanche Woman" (1963) and "When the *Caballos* Came" (1968), both found in the Grove collection *Red River Stage* (Five Star Westerns, 2001), and the Wrangler for "Comanche Son" (1961).

The nine offerings in this collection show Grove's range and gift.

Consider the polished detail in "The Vanishing Raiders", published for the first time here. Like an artist with paintbrush and canvas, he adeptly details the landscape of the northwest Texas frontier. ". . . Fort Belknap, instead of an orderly post like Fort Richardson, stood in a shambles of neglect. Ghostly chimneys overlooked a wilderness of mesquite and sand."

Grove often displays a newspaper journalist's wry sense of humor, illustrated by the witty endings of "The Hangrope Ghost" — his first published short story published in *.44 Western Magazine* (9/51) — and "Catch Your Killer", a 1952 offering from *Texas Rangers*.

One of the most interesting tales is "Crow

Bait", which appeared in *Popular Western* in 1951. This chronicle of old-time Quarter Horse racing is a precursor of Grove's series featuring horsemen Dude McQuinn and Uncle Billy Lockhart and their poetry-spouting Comanche jockey, Coyote Walking. Two of those novels, *The Great Horse Race* (Doubleday, 1977) and *Match Race* (Doubleday, 1982), won Spur Awards. Grove's rascally Trifecta of heroes doesn't appear in "Crow Bait", but this story seems to have planted a seed that sprouted years later.

Grove was required to use the house name of Bart Cassidy when "No Man's Trail" was published in 1953 in *Max Brand's Western Magazine* because he had another story, "Town of No Return", under his own name, in the same issue. In "Hush Money" in *Texas Rangers* (5/57), Grove uses the viewpoint of an eleven-year-old boy. Grove has always been comfortable writing about young adults, and in the 1960s became a frequent contributor to *Boys' Life* magazine, which published the award winning "When the *Caballos* Came" and "Comanche Son".

More adult in nature is "Warpath", which appeared in *With Guidons Flying: Tales of the U.S. Cavalry by Members of the Western Writers of America* (Doubleday, 1970) edited by

Charles N. Heckelmann. It is a lean, leathery story about a cavalry officer's distrust of his Kiowa scout.

Two additional stories in this collection make their debut here. "The Perfect Time" is a nostalgic horse story told from the point of view of a reclusive, irritable, J.D. Salinger-type novelist (which Grove isn't), and "A Matter of Blood" allows a Tarahumari Indian prostitute on the border to exact some revenge on a cocksure informant.

Sports writing lost a talent when Fred Grove turned his gaze toward the American West, something for which fans of Western literature are eternally grateful.

If memory serves, *Tucson Lifestyle* paid me $100 for that profile, which didn't cover expenses incurred on my road trip, yet meeting, interviewing, and befriending Fred Grove and his wife Lucile made that excursion one of the most rewarding assignments of my career.

Johnny D. Boggs
Santa Fé, New Mexico

No Man's Trail

Lonnie Ware hurried the gelding down the sloping bank. They splashed across Bird Creek's shallow, rock-bottomed ford, under the cool, crooked arms of the giant cottonwoods. Only an hour ago the major had sent a rider out to the agency beef herd for Lonnie. He was drumming along the twisting wagon road when he saw the long-striding shape.

Big-shouldered against the black tree shadows, the man swung around at the beat of the horse, and Lonnie felt a quick annoyance. It was Turk Tanner, who ran a Caney Trail freight outfit from Kansas to the Osage agency here below the line in Indian Territory. He wore a pearl gray hat, a flag of a tie red as war paint, and the blue suit looked fresh from the States. His trousers were tucked inside hand-tooled boots.

Tanner's bushy eyebrows lifted. "Hot weather for pushin' a horse," he growled.

Before Lonnie could answer, there was a flapping, complaining flutter from the timber and turkeys swarmed across the road. They were fat and tame, Lonnie saw at a glance, one of the Indian-owned bunches he'd noticed around the agency. He halted at Tanner's low mutter.

"Takes a good pistol to drop a turkey." The freighter's yellow eyes lit up with a bright speculation.

"Yeah," Lonnie nodded, not interested.

"Watch me tag that tom." Tanner's long jaws worked and there was a stuttering gobbling. He grinned in heavy-lipped satisfaction as a curious gobbler turned trustingly. With a clawing motion, Tanner swept back his coat, forked up a Colt, and fired. Squawking, the gobbler floundered awkwardly, feathers flying; it flopped and twitched as the other birds scattered, their gobbling a wild racket in the timber.

"Shotgun'd done better," Lonnie said in a dry, steady voice. "About all you get with a Forty-Five is the feathers."

Tanner shrugged. He holstered the pistol and crossed to the downed gobbler. He selected a wing feather and pulled it loose. A flicker of satisfaction in the pale eyes, he stuck the feather in his hatband, one hand preening it. He crimped the hat at a rakish

16

angle, and, when he turned, there was almost a challenge on the broad face. He wore the feather like a badge now, a gunfighter's mark, mocking, scornful, and Lonnie felt a racing caution.

"Take the meat." Tanner's grin was queer, odd. "Help yourself."

Lonnie didn't budge. "Thought you wanted turkey."

"Pass it any day for a fine feather."

"Me," Lonnie said carefully, "I'm kinda particular whose free meat I eat."

He was reining the gelding, pointing down-trail, when brush snapped, crackled. Twisting, Lonnie saw Joe Big Tree. Puffing, bear-shaped body heaving, the old Indian came trotting out from the timber. His long blue-black braids flounced as he waddled to the rim of the road.

"Me see you," Joe panted at Tanner, glaring, accusing. His quick brown eyes settled on the dead gobbler. He pushed forward, pointing a stubby finger. "My meat. You pay dollar."

Tanner's mouth curled. "Woods full of wild turkeys. Free for the shootin'."

"Turkeys tame." Coppery face grim, Joe held out a plump hand. "You pay now. My meat."

"Like hell!" Tanner swung angrily. "You, Ware. Tell this crazy blanket to pull out. Damned if I'll pay hold-up money for wild game."

"These turkeys were tame and you knew it," Lonnie said coldly. "That why you wanted me to take the meat?"

Tanner's face blotched crimson. Lunging, he shoved Joe roughly. Abruptly the old Indian yelled. He clasped both arms around the freighter's bony frame and they grappled, grunting, weaving. Lonnie saw Tanner's furious face as they hit the ground, with the white man on the bottom. They rolled over, and Tanner tore loose and sprang to his feet. His hand jerked up the Colt. There was a dull, sickening *splat* as he sledged the barrel across Joe's bobbing head. On his feet and running, Lonnie saw the Indian roll loosely. Tanner was raging, viciously swinging the gun, when Lonnie dived. He felt a knifing pain as he slammed his shoulder into the man's hard-muscled chest. He heard Tanner's gasp for the knocked-out wind as they sprawled. Lurching up, Lonnie stomped, twisted. Tanner howled and grabbed his wrist. Now Lonnie had the gun.

"Pay up!" he gritted.

"No, by God!" Tanner stumbled up,

tawny, hungry eyes on the gun.

"Well," Lonnie shot back, "there's a way. We'll take this to the major. He'll ride you off the reservation." The bony face was still defiant, mouth hard, set, when Lonnie said heavily: "Freight contracts comin' up soon. Something for you to think about."

"You . . . ," Tanner spluttered. His raging eyes swung to the Osage, up now and rubbing his head. Slowly the eyes wavered and Tanner dug reluctantly for his pocket. Joe stepped over at once. Straight, ponderous, almost haughty, he stuck out a hand and the freighter swore and half pitched the money. Joe caught it with a flat slap of his hand, and Lonnie heard the solid grunt.

Scowling, Tanner spun on his heel and tramped angrily to the road's edge. There he whirled, fists knotted. "You got my pistol."

"It'll be at the horse barn," Lonnie said evenly. He wasn't concerned about the gun. Grim, he watched the big man swinging away, the feathered hat bobbing till the trees hid him.

"Joe, you better keep your turkeys away from the agency," Lonnie said then, very sober. "Tanner might want a new feather. Stick to camp in the Black Timbers up

19

north. Start packin' a gun, too. Might need it."

Joe's massive, brown-hued face was glum, almost melancholy. Frowning, he stared in doubt at the dollar.

"Isn't that enough?" Lonnie demanded. "I figure that dollar was hard-earned."

Joe held up the coin. "Dollar no good . . . lead."

"But you got the turkey."

"Him got away with feather," Joe grunted stubbornly, doggedly. "No pay."

With that comment, Lonnie mounted and turned his horse toward the agency. In siding with the Indian against Tanner, he realized that he had made himself a gun-quick, vengeful enemy. Worst of all, Lonnie had humiliated him. The story would furnish fuel for relishing loafers at the traders' stores, for evening gossip around freight wagon fires, for lonely cow camps on the reservation grasslands. Turk Tanner had been bested, damn him. Lost his Colt to a kid. Reckon you heard about it? Good. He sure had it comin'.

A troubled alarm traveled through Lonnie Ware as he sighted the agency horse barn. Joe could ride in the hills. But Lonnie kept the herd fairly close to the agency, fattening on the high, limestone bluestem. Tanner knew he wouldn't leave. And other men knew it — Tanner's bunch, hard, deadly, loyal in their way. They'd back their boss. Funny, Lonnie thought, how well they prospered. Rode fast horses and spent money freely. There had been hold-ups in the rugged hills. There had been cautious, whispered talk. But nobody knew who did it. Nobody was fool enough to accuse them openly. And Major Laban Miles, the fair-minded Osage agent, wouldn't arrest a man on thin rumor.

Matt French, the horse barn hand, was lolling in the runway and Lonnie handed down the Colt. "Turk Tanner's," he said, wondering how long it would take French to spread the word. "He'll be callin' for it."

French's head snapped up, interested. "You got Turk's gun? How come?"

"Long story," Lonnie cut him off. He saw Henry Swim, the major's chief clerk, step from the shadows of the horse stalls. Leisurely Lonnie unsaddled, pitched hay for his horse, and followed Swim outside.

"Kid," said Swim, low and approving, "you didn't lose any time." His weak blue eyes showed a narrowed excitement behind his spectacles.

"When the major hollers frog" — Lonnie grinned — "I jump. What's up?"

21

"The major. . . ." Swim's reedy voice trailed off.

Three riders were dusting down the road in the direction of the agency, 100 yards away. He shook his head, with no attempt to hide his rank disgust and suspicion, and Lonnie's gaze slid to Jake Ralls, Barney Sparr, and Boots Dillon. They thudded past at a lope, looking straight ahead. Ralls was black-bearded, with small, restless hands. Drought thin, Sparr's lank shoulders hunched lazily. Dillon had a square, stout body and he rode with a swaggering grace.

"Funny to me," Swim snorted indignantly, "how some folks get by. Now me, I gotta work for a livin'." He glanced up the road. "We'll hustle along. Major's waitin' for you and he's a sick man."

"Bad?" Lonnie felt a darting alarm. Miles had given him the job, two years ago, of handling the Osage beef herd. Lonnie had quit one of the big outfits, and he had never regretted the change. By taking part of his pay in calves, he was building a small herd of his own in the high hill country.

"He'll be all right. Only he can't sit up and drive a buggy. Wouldn't be so bad, but payment day's right on us."

"What'll he do?"

22

"He'll tell you," Swim said over his shoulder.

Wondering, Lonnie went up the road with Henry Swim. Nobody but the major handled payments. Escorted by half a dozen armed Indian police, he drove to Kansas twice a year for the money. Because of the police, there had never been any trouble. But now Lonnie was aware of a peculiar stirring, a troubled doubt. Who would go? He thought of Swim and stopped there. The clerk was too old for that kind of business. He didn't know horses; he couldn't handle a gun. And Miles never shifted duties he felt he ought to carry out himself.

They scuffed through the dust past the long wooden traders' stores. Loaded freight wagons groaned past. Down along the creek, Osages from the Big Hill country pitched camp. Squaws setting up skin teepees, cutting brush for the cool summer lodges; Indian kids yipping at a bunched horse herd; paint ponies flashing a bright pattern through the churning dust. Lonnie pulled in his breath. He was a part of this and he knew he wouldn't run. He walked ahead, and, through the towering cottonwoods, he saw the brown sandstone shapes of the council house, the two-storied agent's headquarters. When they came to the second building, Swim paused, chuckling with approval. "He's in there. Can't keep him home less'n we hog-tie him. But the Osages'd raise hell. Well . . ." — Swim turned, angling down the road — "good luck, Lonnie."

Puzzled, Lonnie stepped inside and down a long hall. A door slanted open against the June heat and Lonnie saw Major Laban Miles. He lay on a couch in front of a low window, with pillows propping his gray, shaggy head. A frown on his face, he was writing rapidly on a sheet of paper laid across a brown-backed ledger. He looked up as Lonnie came in.

"Henry tell you?" Miles's soft-featured face was flushed, and he spoke in a mild, weary voice.

Lonnie nodded. "Sorry you're. . . ."

Miles stopped him with a tired wave of his hand. There was a thick, close silence in the room and Lonnie sensed that Miles was searching for words. It was unusual for him.

"Lonnie," the agent said appraisingly, "I want you to go after the payment money."

Swallowing hard, Lonnie pulled his gaze away.

"You don't have to go. You know that."

"Why," said Lonnie, wetting his lips, "I'll go, Major. Guess I grunt enough Osage to get along with your Indian police."

Miles pulled himself up on the couch, uncomfortably, pain creeping through the worry on his face. "Wish it was that simple. But Black Dog's young bucks have been slipping across the Arkansas. Taking ponies from the Pawnees. It's an old game, but it's got to stop. I sent the police to Black Dog's camp. You," he said reluctantly, "will have to go alone to Elgin. The payment is ten thousand in greenbacks. The chiefs will bring their people here day after tomorrow."

Lonnie thought about it. He remembered the forty miles to Elgin. He was feeling the heat now, hearing sounds drifting in from the agency grounds — a camp dog howling, the dry squeal of a freighter's wagon, and a faint rustling movement from the yard. "I'll get a good horse," Lonnie declared. "Pull out tonight. Be back tomorrow."

"I'll remember this." Miles's voice was warm, one of the things you liked about him. "When you get to Elgin, go to the Cattleman's Bank. Hand this letter to Ed Pendleton. He'll give you the money. I was writing the letter when you came in." The gray eyes brightened. "Figured you'd go. Now, you got a gun?"

"You bet." Lonnie took the letter.

"It's a long way, Lonnie. You'll be on your

25

own. You're a dead duck if anybody jumps you in the blackjacks. Watch it." Miles frowned and angrily slapped the ledger. "Country's filling up with men run out of the States. Last time I made the trip, I noticed two bunches of riders. They veered off when they saw my escort. But you shouldn't attract any attention by yourself."

"Won't no grass grow under me," Lonnie promised. "I'll. . . ."

Faintly the noise came again from the yard, a subtle rustling, a soft *crunching*, moving away. Suspicion hit Lonnie and he whirled from the room. Boots booming, he ran down the hall, out on the porch. The broad road showed empty. But as he swung his gaze to the trees, he saw a vanishing flicker among the cottonwoods. Maybe a hat, maybe also a feather.

He was standing there when he heard the major's worried query. "What're you looking for?"

Miles's calling voice, Lonnie realized all at once, had carried distinctly through the window that opened on the porch. With a chilled feeling, Lonnie clumped back inside.

"You're getting jumpy," the major warned, troubled.

"Thought I heard something." Lonnie forced a quick grin. "But nothin' in sight."

Miles's tone was relieved. "Don't take any foolish chances. If you get in a tight, give 'em the money and run. I mean that."

Lonnie walked to the Leland Hotel, ate early, and slept till dark. Afterward, he angled through the timber to the horse barn. He had strapped on a Colt. He carried a Winchester carbine, his coyote gun, and a long slicker. Fastening the slicker behind the cantle, he climbed to the saddle and headed north. Before he ducked into the cottonwoods, he looked back.

A shape slid from the shadows toward the barn. "Hell," Lonnie muttered in disgust, "might as well tell 'em what way I'm goin'." But he whirled the horse, climbing the hills that shouldered the wide valley of the agency. Soon he dipped down through the blackjacks. When he broke out on the Caney Trail, he was going at a rumbling run. He let the horse go for 200 yards before he eased up.

Shadows clogged the road where the timber clumped and he felt the full load of his loneliness; it closed him in and he mistrusted the darkness, the muffled night sounds. Some of his strain went away as he realized that he had nothing to fear for a time. They'd never touch him till he got the money, till he started back.

Lonnie kept moving at a steady gait. His eyes ran sharply along the dim trail. Once he pulled off among the trees to listen. Presently his ears picked up a following drumming, distant, but coming on like horses in a lope.

Tight-lipped, he sent the gelding lunging back on the trail. They were closer than he figured. A chill touched his spine, and in his mind he could see the country as it would shape coming back — broken, rolling, the ragged blackjack timber. Deeper in the night, he passed a stage station, with its outscatter of sheds and corrals. Leaving the trail when it angled northeast toward Caney, he cut north for Elgin.

Several times he halted to listen for the beat of horses, to let his mount blow. While he smoked and sifted the wind for sound, he noticed the sky turning gray in the east. It was streaky daylight when he finally sighted the Caney River, silver-bright through the bordering timber, and crossed the ford. The sun was bronzing up strong as he jogged woodenly down Elgin's broad Main Street.

Tight and numbing, the strain was all through him again. He rode the down-headed horse to the first feed barn he saw. Hungry, he wolfed down breakfast at a place two doors from the Cattleman's Bank. Watching from the front window, he felt his weariness grow. It seemed a long time before a pale-faced, portly man came deliberately along the street, enjoying his morning walk, and turned in at the bank. That'll be Pendleton, Lonnie judged, stepping outside. He was moving to the wide bank door when his eyes caught a shape. Lonnie froze. For Barney Sparr stood across in front of a store. Thin shoulders drooping, he lolled with his lazy gaze split between Lonnie and downstreet.

Drawing in a long breath, Lonnie walked inside. He went over to a clerk and called for Ed Pendleton. When the pale-featured man came up, Lonnie gave his name and handed him Miles's letter.

Pendleton read it with a gathering frown. "By yourself?"

"Yeah," Lonnie grunted, "and in a hurry. I'll need all the daylight I can get 'tween here and the agency."

"Ten thousand dollars," the banker said with heavy emphasis. "Big load for a young man traveling single. Can't Miles wait?"

"No. But I don't want the money right now. You meet me with it at the Two-Star stable in ten minutes. I'll leave from there." Lonnie slanted his head at the street.

"Company's crowdin' me out there." Pendleton's eyes widened in surprise and Lonnie pushed his voice at him. "You can go through the back door. Nobody'll see you."

When Lonnie showed himself empty-handed, Sparr gave him a bold, wicked glance. He was still looking as Lonnie entered the café. Boots pounding the boards, Lonnie stepped to the kitchen, past the curious, resentful cook, and passed through to the alley. Trotting, he traveled to the alley's end and came out on the empty street. Sparr hadn't had time to guess his ruse, but Lonnie realized that he had gained only a few minutes at the most.

At the stable he swapped gear to a racy, Spanish-looking bay gelding and untied the slicker. On edge, sweating, he was watching the door when Pendleton walked in leisurely. He had the money under his arm in brown wrapping paper. Lonnie took the package, rolled it in the slicker, and tied it behind the cantle.

"You sure," Pendleton said worriedly, "you know what you're doing?"

"Right now I do," said Lonnie. Then he straddled the saddle and kicked the bay down the runway and hit the opening in a grunting gallop. Whipping around, he saw Barney Sparr legging it along the street toward a bunch of tied horses. As he felt his horse leap out, Lonnie figured that Tanner had sent Sparr in to spot him while the others waited at the ford. Tanner wasn't fool enough to risk a shooting this close to town. Sparr had been suckered in momentarily, but, instead of facing one man now, Lonnie had three in front and one behind. And he was worried about the Caney crossing. He remembered it as the only ford for a mile each way, and his mind told him that he'd have to find another.

Beyond town, farmers' fences barred any cutting across country, and Sparr was driving at him in a boiling ball of dust. Then about 300 yards from the river, he saw open land and cottonwoods. The gelding was eager and Lonnie pushed him recklessly.

They were among the trees when he slued around. He saw the outlaw's horse raising dust on the road, heard his quick, high-pitched calling shout and the answering yell from across the river. Running through the timber, Lonnie had his brief thought of satisfaction. Tanner and his bunch were posted across the river, waiting, as he had figured they would be. But when he left the trees and raced to the river and swung his head again, Sparr had turned and was quirt-ing after him.

Here the Caney's banks ran sharp and high and crumbling, and Lonnie's stomach fluttered in a sick kind of shock. He slowed down, hunting for a break, but kicked the gelding out again. There was a rushing pounding in his ears as he sighted the bank sloping down ahead of him. As he headed for it, a gun *whanged* twice from the trees. Lonnie ducked and heard the whining hornet sounds. He jerked up at the river's rim, decision hard on his mind. He could jump the horse down now, but, if he did that, the outlaw would be at his back.

"One at a time," Lonnie told himself, and pulled his Colt. Sparr was rushing at him, his gun arm swinging up for a shot. There were two reports, Sparr's, then Lonnie's, clapping together. All at once Sparr sagged; his left arm clamped his right shoulder. In one motion, Lonnie spurred the reluctant bay over the bank. The gelding's front hoofs pawed air for a moment. They hit with a thugging grunt. The animal broke to its knees in the soft sand, pitching Lonnie forward. Wildly he grabbed mane and hung on and raked the horse onward in a faltering, sluggish run, into the summer-shallow water.

Lonnie felt the keen edge of his luck when

he saw the cattle trail slanting up the other side. For a short stretch the bay swam, touched bottom, and they lurched out of it. They took the slope, lunging, straining. Waving him on, the green of the prairie showed through the dark mass of the timber. He heard the yell as he topped the bank.

Riders churned to his left, whirling in his direction now. Abruptly they were driving for him 100 yards away, their mounts drumming a rolling racket on the timber floor. Lonnie's straight-on gaze bracketed three men, unmasked, as he jerked for the carbine. He drove a hasty bullet at a bony-framed man he took for Turk Tanner, and then he was wheeling away. Gunshots beat in his ears. There was a hoarse, frustrated whoop, with Lonnie rushing from the woods and seeing the prairie's open track. Under a bright sky — funny he hadn't noticed it before — he rode at a stretching run.

For the first time he felt a faint security. When he took another look, the horsemen were following at a hard run, but out of Winchester range. It occurred to him that there wasn't a rifle in the bunch, else they'd have cut down on him by now. Catching the labored breathing of the gelding, he pulled up. The horse needed a blow, so Lonnie reached for the carbine. It was a long chance. He raised the sights high and drilled a bullet at the front man. Dust kicked up, yards short. The riders shrank back to a huddling knot.

Lonnie's jaw tightened. Buzzards, he thought grimly, only there wouldn't be any meat. He'd stick to the high ridges; he'd hold them off with the carbine and he knew what the tough bay could do now. And it wasn't likely that Tanner, counting on the Caney crossing hold-up, had fresh horses. When the gelding perked up, Lonnie swung south, figuring he was still thirty-odd miles from the agency. Squinting, he saw the prairie rolling and humped, a broad, muscular chest knotted with rocky hills and blackjack clumps, wrinkled with valleys. He was angling up a hill when he felt the horse tremble and slow, step ahead sluggishly, and halt.

With a grim dread, Lonnie slid from the saddle. Stunned, he saw the left foreleg, swollen below the knee. He touched the leg and the bay edged away. Lonnie's memory leaped back to the jolting jump off the riverbank, the faltering way the game bay lunged across the sandy footing. That had done it, he knew sickly, and his fear was a great lump inside him when he took the reins and climbed the hill. At the top he straddled the saddle again, his mind running over the land as he remembered it. Instead of heading straight south, he'd slant southwest to the Black Timbers, where an Osage band camped. There'd be Joe Big Tree, too, and Joe had a rifle.

Breasting the ridges at a broken walk, dismounting when they dragged up the long limestone hills, Lonnie estimated he had covered five miles when the sun hung straight overhead. The riders came on steadily, keeping a respectful distance. Twice he let go with the carbine to discourage them. He hoped the shots would attract a friendly cowpuncher. But long after the blasts died on the hot wind, he was still alone in a world of prairie, timber-crested hills, and darkened shallow valleys.

He felt a growing nervousness. He crossed a water-low creek and noted deer tracks without interest. The trailing riders were too unhurried to suit him. He had expected them to run at him, once they noticed the lame horse. Yet they hung back, just out of range, and it worried him. Most of the time he rode with his head slanted backward. His eyes burned from the constant squinting; his shoulders ached from the strain of twisting and turning, and his mouth was dry. He went faster as the land dipped.

It was far in the afternoon when he topped a ridge and saw the Black Timbers in the core of a creek-cut valley. Hitching around, he took a quick look before angling down. Suddenly all his dread rushed back. Because nothing moved. Swallowed in the emptiness, the riders were gone.

He watched till his traveling eyes ached, till the land danced in a crazy, jammed-together pattern. Then he cradled the carbine and drove the gelding ahead. They moved downward at a jerking gait to the valley floor, splashed across the creek, with Lonnie's sharp glance taking in the thick timber. He was searching for the square-shaped, summer brush lodges of the Osages. And he spotted the brown, sun-seared tops as he struck across the last stretch of stirrup-high grass.

He scouted for movement among the lodges. Riding into the timber, he expected to see Joe's waddling frame, blanketed squaws, lounging bucks, and romping kids. A chilled realization digging at him, Lonnie reined suddenly. The camp was deserted, so quiet he could hear whippoorwills calling lonesomely upvalley. He worried about the emptiness, till it came to him that tomorrow was payment day at the agency. It was a good bet that the band had gone in early to camp along Bird Creek, to visit and feast and race their ponies across the valley flats.

Lonesomeness rolled over him as he turned down the well-traveled trail. It crooked closely to the creek, cut back, and he saw dense brush. That cautioned him, and for a moment he fought his dread, suspicion, reluctance. But, eager for open country, he hurried the gelding. Brush and low-growing trees clawed at him. His eyes were searching when the bay shied, snorting.

Lonnie yanked him down, his glance swinging. There was a stuttering gobble, short ahead to his right. Jerking, Lonnie caught the flutter of movement and something cold hit him. As his eyes raked the timber, he saw a hat moving, a slanting feather.

Before he could pull the carbine up, three horsemen shaped on the trail, closing him in.

Chilled, Lonnie saw Turk Tanner in the center. Boots Dillon and Jake Ralls flanked him. They had him covered with their pistols, and Lonnie jabbed the Winchester forward, numbly figuring his chances. He could whirl the lame horse, but he knew he'd never make it.

"Git down," Tanner droned tonelessly.

Lonnie heard his own ragged breathing. They had circled him while he had fiddled along, he knew now, dismally. They had him.

Tanner muttered: "Throw it down, kid."

"Come an' get it," Lonnie gritted, voice choked, tight.

Tanner straightened. He threw Dillon a knowing glance. "Move out a little, Boots," he jeered. "He's gonna be stubborn."

Dillon edged his horse a couple of steps, his blocky body swaggering in the saddle. Time was draining fast and Lonnie knew he had to choose.

He didn't have a ghost of a chance against the three of them. But just the same — he swung the carbine. There was a booming, grunting roar in his ears. Off to his right. All at once Tanner was swaying strangely. It happened so fast that Lonnie had the feeling he was paralyzed. Dillon's gun was whipping up, and Lonnie pulled once, a snap shot. He levered in a shell and fired again. Dillon slumped.

Then Lonnie heard Jake Ralls's stricken scream on the heels of another blast. Dimly Lonnie knew that it wasn't from his bullet. Brush crashed, and Ralls was whirling his horse away.

It was over when Lonnie looked around. Joe Big Tree was waddling out from his

38

brush cover, a smoking rifle in his fat, brown hands. His face was wooden. Turning, Lonnie saw that Dillon was down, very still, and Tanner was a long-shaped hulk spilled across the trail.

Bear-like, shirt tails drooping, Joe paced over to Tanner. He nudged the freighter with a curious moccasin. "Me collect." Joe Big Tree's saddle-colored face was almost regretful. "Give 'im back change." With a grunt, he reached down and plucked the feather from Tanner's hat. There was a faint grin in his eyes as he held it out at Lonnie. "You wear him now?"

Watching K Troop straggling up the scarred face of the ridge, Captain Reece Howard felt the welcome stir of wind, hot as it was, off the bleak mesquite country stretching on into butte-broken emptiness. He was thinking of the Texas cowboy's riddled corpse when he hitched around to look down the irregular line of the serpentine column.

They made a menacing sight in the shimmering heat — sullen knots of painted Comanche prisoners, almost naked, clumped among the weary troopers. The Indians rode loose and slumped on their barebacked ponies, the light gone out of them — for the present. Captain Howard thought: *How far do you dare trust an Indian? Any Indian. Even To-hauson, the government Indian scout, who fought plains skirmishes like some kind of primitive game.* Probably it depended, Howard decided with a Texan's far-reaching memory, on whether you had him under your Spencer's muzzle.

With pressed lips, Howard watched To-hauson lope back from the tip of the column.

"H-kou," To-hauson greeted him. "Long Horse no fight Tahannas again. Him satisfied . . . both sides even now." And he held up three fingers.

He wore a blue uniform coat and campaign hat but clung to moccasins and braids. He was erect and stringy and wrinkled, with pushed-out cheek bones and small, round brown eyes in a face weathered and time-lined. He seemed to wear a perpetual grin, and yet it wasn't quite a grin. Or was it? Howard saw the coffee-brown eyes dwelling on the long .44 Dragoon revolver that he wore butt forward with the awkward Army holster flap folded back. It was a Texan's handgun, converted to use cartridges, and the burnished silver star of Texas was screwed into the grip.

Howard turned the old Kiowa's words over in his mind. The cowboy, dead back along the trail, must have been following the stolen horse herd. And two white men had been killed around the ranch corrals. The troopers had dropped three Comanches. *Both sides were even now.*

41

"Tell Long Horse," Howard said through cracked lips, "I will believe him when he takes up a hoe. When he works his garden like a Wichita."

"Long Horse mighty warrior," the Indian argued gently. "Great horse taker. Farm work is for squaws."

"Tell him" — all at once Howard's temper tore loose, and, for a bit, he thought he found an answering flicker in the straight brown eyes — "tell him he didn't look like a big warrior today. He fought like a woman. An old woman."

Howard paused, expecting the Kiowa to speak up. For Long Horse had been very brave in the fight. Long Horse had been the last to retreat when his Sonora pony had been shot from under him; Long Horse had been last to come out of the scattering timber; one trooper carried his arm in a sling from Long Horse's Comanche arrow. But To-hauson's muddy eyes, unchanged, slid to Howard's belt pistol, hung there, flicked away, and slanted back.

"Plenty *tsei* for short gun," To-hauson said. The eyes were bright now. "You trade, huh?"

"No trade," Howard said roughly. "Use your issue pistol." He guessed it was the eye-catching silver star. Nothing drew a heathen's attention like glitter.

"No like Army *ha-zeip-ga* . . . maybe no shoot. *Ka-dei* . . . bad." The furrowed planes in the gnarled face seemed to grin. "Five *tsei*," he grunted. "Fast *tsei*."

Howard shook his head. "No ponies. The white father gives me ponies."

"Maybe so sometime," To-hauson said, and swung his horse away.

Damn him, Howard thought, *he's grinning at me again.* As for the .44, Howard glanced at it and remembered taking it off Grat Solvay when he had caught the rancher cheating in a post poker game. Solvay had started for his weapon, and Howard had beaten him to it. Otherwise, there'd have been a killing. He remembered the hot anger in Solvay's eyes.

Howard began to reflect on how much he should say about To-hauson in his official report. He could see the Kiowa leading the troop across the summer-shallow Red River, straight to the water hole where the spring seeped from sharp rocks. And so when the pony soldiers caught them, Long Horse and the Comanches were resting after hitting the Loving ranch, their tired ponies cropping the short curly buffalo grass with the stolen horses. The fight, brief but vicious, had swirled among the rocks, slashed through patches of scrub oak. Then, pinched in by Lieutenant McCall's brisk flanking movement, the Fort Sill runaways had given up.

Later it was irksome to learn that To-hauson had hastened the surrender by stampeding the Comanches' extra horses. Nevertheless, Howard decided, it would go in the report. Also about finding the cowboy — his belly knifed open, gashed and lance-torn, pin-cushioned with arrows like a scornful afterthought for a man already thankfully dead, the young face crumpled and strangely old-looking, with the skin slipped down from the ripped-off scalp. *Every detail,* Howard decided grimly.

When McCall sided up, Howard lifted his arm, and K Troop plodded along the pitted ridge.

"To-hauson's a good scout," said the lieutenant, hoarse-voiced. "I've been through here five, six times. Never knew that spring was there. Never had time to look."

Howard sent an irritated glance at the sun-peeled face. "He ought to be. Hasn't been too long since he was wearing war paint himself."

As the day stretched out, the heat and the sourness within Howard piled up. *How far do you trust an Indian?* His frame of mind was little improved when they rode in on the hard-packed parade ground where Fort Sill's limestone buildings made their blunt, squared pattern.

His voice hollow, he called to the first sergeant to dismiss the troop. "Take the Comanches to the guardhouse. Let them sweat a while. They'll be glad to eat government rations. Any palavering Long Horse does will be with Colonel Barker."

Reining across to headquarters, he saw a racy, blaze-faced bay gelding at the hitching rack. He frowned: Grat Solvay's horse. Before he went inside, he dropped the flap over the star handle. He wasn't afraid of the Texas rancher, but he wanted no further trouble.

Colonel Barker was scowling, facing Solvay across the desk, his mouth in a compressed worry line. Howard tramped in, immediately recognizing the familiar signs of trouble as he saluted and waited for the colonel to speak.

"So you brought them back?" Barker asked, and, before Howard could do more than nod, the colonel went on: "That's fine . . . but not enough. The Indians are still slipping through our hands like water. Texas authorities complaining again, clear to Washington . . . and now Solvay here tells me Big Bow's Kiowas have broken loose. Passed his place about noon. Headed south in a hurry."

Howard whipped his attention on Solvay. "Sure it wasn't Comanches? The Kiowas have been quiet this season."

"Reckon I know a Kiowa raidin' party when I see one," Solvay drawled, flushing. "It was Big Bow's band."

Grat Solvay moved his blocky body, which pushed out against his wide-beaded belt as he spoke. The round, smooth-shaven face gave him a mild appearance, but Howard knew him as a sharp trader who always got top prices for the mounts he sold the Army from his horse ranch.

"Now you just think the Kiowas been quiet," Solvay said. "Me, I know better. Plenty times they sneak across the river the Army don't know about. Explains a lot of those raids. An Injun loves horses, and the honey's on the Texas side."

Barker nodded in agreement, as if the story were old, and a premonitory feeling rose in Howard. He saw the colonel's narrowed gaze lift. He caught the apology there, and the regret.

"I know," Barker was saying. "You just rode in. But we'll have to go after them.

46

Trouble is, M Troop's out at Camp Augur, and Major Davidson took off yesterday for Darlington Agency. Seems the Cheyennes aren't ready to become Ohio farmers yet. So. . . ." He spread his hands, and again Howard read apology.

"When do you want me to leave, sir?" Howard asked, all the while damning Solvay.

"Take K Troop out first thing in the morning."

"To-hauson, too?"

"Why, yes." Barker looked surprised. "You'll need him."

"How about Sankey-dotey? I'd rather. . . .

"He went with Davidson."

Howard said no more. There were other details, then he turned to go, hesitating as he saw Solvay's eyes rest on his holster. As Howard went out, the rancher followed him.

Both men paused beside the hitching rack in the plum-colored dusk, Howard waiting for what he knew was coming.

Solvay's voice rubbed at him softly. "You'll pick up their trail about four miles due west. Plain as day."

"Cold tracks don't mean much." As Howard spoke, he realized that he should be pleased with the information. "It's not where an Indian was that's important. It's where you find him."

47

"You'll hem him in," Solvay said. "To-hauson will scout him out."

"Depends," said Howard, weary of the big man's circling talk. "We'll be behind when we start, and Big Bow will travel farther in two days than we could in four, time we puzzle him out."

"Oh, you'll get him, soldier."

"You're mighty certain," Howard said, suspicious and curious. "Maybe you'd like to go along . . . help out?"

Solvay grinned and stepped back. "Fighting's the Army's job." He began to turn. "Another thing. You take a man's pistol. . . ."

"You'll get it back when you pay up."

Solvay moved away and swung to saddle, quickly for so heavy a man. His last words were level: "I intend to get it back, soldier."

Howard went thoughtfully to his horse, but he was not thinking about the report he had to write tonight. He was heading across the parade when the parts suddenly came together — bits of garrison talk. Big Bow and To-hauson — the two were old friends. In the old days they had been members of the *Ko-eet-senko,* the Kiowa society of the Ten Bravest. Like blood brothers. To an Indian that meant forever.

To-hauson had taken the pony soldier's blue coat as a scout; Big Bow had clung to the ancient ways, although never — until now — making trouble, raising his voice only when meager government rations ran low and the reservation people had to kill ponies and mules for meat. Now what would To-hauson do? These runaways weren't Comanches; they were his own people. *How far do you dare trust an Indian?*

The troopers formed in the first pale daylight. Howard could feel and see the sulky resentment under the surface. Bone-tired, sleepy-eyed men with tempers on raw edge. Even Lieutenant McCall's boyish features looked cross. All but To-hauson. The Kiowa sat loosely on a stocking-legged gelding, his patience depthless and wooden.

Howard drew erect. "Prepare to mount!" he called in a carrying voice. "Mount!

"Right by twos . . . ho-o!"

As they jerked into motion, Howard saw the scout's eyes travel to the revolver holster. *Damn him,* Howard thought. Did everybody want that .44? He squared around and spurred to the head of the column.

The brassy, yellow sun soon overtook them, a glaring brightness that chased the coolness away, and Howard knew they faced another blistering day.

Within an hour he saw To-hauson pull up

and gaze down, beyond a long rock-crusted ridge.

It was a hoof-scarred trace, running in a scuffed, chopped-up pattern to the south, as easy to follow as wagon tracks. With the awareness of a man riding late, Howard started to go on, but the Kiowa lingered, his furrowed face intent. He slid down and bent over, peering.

Howard rode back, calling impatiently: "It's plain enough!"

To-hauson grunted. "Big bunch." And returned to his deliberate study of the tracks.

"Well . . . what is it?" Howard demanded. His intolerance of delay mounted. These were tracks that any fuzzy-cheeked recruit could read at a glance. Yet To-hauson, who knew the country better than any white man alive, was pondering over the obvious, holding up the march.

At last the Kiowa mounted. Howard searched the brown, crinkly face. Sarcasm roughed up his voice. "Those *are* horse tracks, aren't they?"

To-hauson's puckery mouth spread into what seemed a dim grin. The Indian said: "Captain's eyes are good."

Howard turned away, disgusted and suspicious: *Was the scout stalling?* He led the troop southwest. Gradually they passed from rolling, sweeping grass country into a broken web of tumbling ridges and ravines dancing crazily in the smoky heat.

As the day passed, Howard grew more uneasy with To-hauson's frequent delays. Often the Kiowa stopped to read sign, while Howard held the column and fretted angrily. When the light faded and darkness caught them, they found water and camped — still north of the river.

Flat on his back, Howard listened to the night noises and smelled the closeness of horseflesh, sweat-soaked saddle blankets and leather. Around him the troopers grumbled. *They have a right to,* he thought.

Lieutenant McCall came by and said: "We'll cross the Red in the morning. Been slow today."

"Too slow," Howard said. "A schoolboy could read this sign from the saddle." He said it loudly, for the benefit of To-hauson, who squatted nearby, a narrow wedge in the dark. "And if we catch Big Bow," Howard continued, "it'll be too late. By then he'll already have his Texas horses and scalps."

To-hauson said nothing. Howard pushed up on his elbows and stared at him. It was one thing to tell an Indian to his face that

51

he was wasting time; it was something else to bring it out before others and cause loss of face. A Kiowa had a fighter's pride. But the silence ran on.

After a while the Kiowa said: "Maybe big fight damn' quick. To-hauson maybe need good gun. You swap? Ten *tsei.*"

Howard felt his face go hot and stiff. He heard McCall's suppressed chuckle. A few feet away, a trooper laughed, only to snap it off abruptly.

"No swap," Howard said curtly, ending the talk. He lay back and presently, recalling the trooper's laughter, decided it was good for a weary troop to be able to laugh, even at his expense.

Faint daylight broke raggedly across the up-and-down land as Howard heaved into the saddle. To-hauson soon faded away in the vastness, a shriveled, bony man looking grotesquely small when his large-framed cavalry horse topped the backbone of a ridge. Now the hills dipped, and near noon, through a broad cut in the bluffs, Howard saw the silvering streaks of Red River. A ripple of alert movement jerked along the line of troopers, a jangling of iron bits and equipment.

Howard saw To-hauson drop back and waggle a scrawny arm, but the Kiowa was waving up the river, away from the crossing.

Hot, quick anger sawed through Howard. He let his horse out, running him hard toward To-hauson. When the Indian lifted slack, lazy eyes, the captain couldn't keep down the suspicion in his voice.

"The river's that way," he said, jabbing a forefinger. "You're leading us away from the crossing. That's all broken country up there." All his banked-up uncertainty whipped through him. "No Kiowa runaways on this side, and you know it. No ponies. . . . No Tehanna scalps."

"Plenty *kadl-hih,*" To-hauson said, shifting deliberately and staring northwest.

Howard looked that way and found black moving masses far out across the wavering heat waves. "Buffalo!" he snorted. "Big Bow's not after meat. He wants ponies."

"Big Bow hungry." The intricately wrinkled face was fixed, quietly defiant. "All Indians hungry. No *kadl-hih* 'round fort. All gone." Then To-hauson made a gripping motion, bony fists knotted.

Wearily Howard understood. Hide hunters' rifles had thinned out the buffalo. On a long scout into the Staked Plains he had seen the hide crews' camps, the piles of drying hides. And he had told himself it was all for the best — with the buffalo gone,

Comanche and Kiowa raiding parties couldn't travel on empty bellies to plunder the Texas ranches.

Howard swung back, looking. "You're off the trail here," he declared. "Don't tell me that Big Bow didn't cross the river."

To-hauson clapped heels to his horse and rode to the wide cut where it flattened toward the river. Howard loped after him.

"You look," the Kiowa said, and pointed down.

Howard stared at the churned, hoof-slashed earth. Sure enough, the sign angled away upriver. He turned stiffly. "All right. We'll follow it after we've watered."

Long afterward, with late shadows beginning to blot the frowning ridge lines, suspicion still remained a hard core in his mind. But, oddly, To-hauson was no longer delaying over the cluttered tracks. He moved as he had after Long Horse — a shrunken-faced gnome scouring the ravine tops and bottoms, his restless gaze darting and swinging, and K Troop thudding behind. Where they halted again, Howard heard the men's low droning. Just where was the Indian taking them?

McCall pulled over, bringing the dank odor of horse sweat. A question stood in the red-rimmed eyes. "To-hauson smells something," the lieutenant said. "You figure Big Bow's close?"

"He'd sure as hell better be."

McCall sent him a look.

Howard said: "To-hauson had better be sure whose side he's on. I never saw better ambush country in my life." *How far do you trust an Indian?* he wondered yet again.

The day was turning dusky when Howard smelled smoke, faint on the lifting wind. After a few minutes he caught it once more, pungent now.

Suddenly he wanted To-hauson back here where he could watch him, under his revolver muzzle. But the Indian was well out in advance, a sliding, dipping shape in the half light.

Howard halted the troop, not liking this place. It was too still, too dark; it was no position for a stand. Behind him a horse shied heavily, kicking up a racketing echo. It stirred McCall's growl: "Damn it, Haines, hold him in."

From the mouth of a ravine a horse took shape, and Howard could see To-hauson drifting toward the command. The Kiowa stopped and pointed. "Over there."

"How many?" Excitement pounded through Howard, and a trace of remaining suspicion. It looked too easy.

The Kiowa's parchment hand cut a circle. "Maybe big bunch, maybe little bunch. Back in timber." The forefinger drew an air picture. "But plenty *tsei*."

"Hour's twilight left," Howard said, half to himself. He felt only half assured; he judged the ravine as he freed the clumsy pistol flap. "McCall, I'm going in with half the troop. Hang back and bring up the rest after me. To-hauson, you stick right with me."

He thought he saw the Indian grin. McCall moved off, and soon the column began to shift and rustle. To-hauson didn't stir. His attention was fixed on Howard. Rather, the captain saw, on the starred pistol grip.

To-hauson said suddenly — "Fifteen *tsei* now." — and looked up.

Howard gave him the edge of his anger, and then he was spreading the troopers, deploying them in a short line. He led them forward at a walk, his senses turned keen.

The ravine enclosed them with flanking cedar-braked slopes. They were deep into it when Howard sighted horses in the thin timber up a back-cut clearing. The Kiowa saw, too, for Howard caught the eagerness glittering in the black eyes.

Smoke, drifting on the wind, eddied down the ravine. It prompted Howard to slow for a better look. A hoof cracked against rock, like a shot in the stillness. Eyes straining, Howard picked up a stirring at the clearing's edge. A long-haired man was bent over a cooking fire. The man straightened and took a sudden, searching look, wheeled, and ran, his hoarse yell carrying. Immediately the camp sprang alive in blurs of motion.

Now Howard was bawling, and the troop charged up the incline in a tangle of hoofs and racket and boiling dust, the troopers rising and falling violently with the broken footing. There was a booming big-caliber blasting up ahead, and around Howard cracked the lighter rattle of K's carbines.

Howard kept calling: "Come on . . . stick together!" He kept looking for old To-hauson — where the hell was the heathen? He saw horsemen clumped in the timber, heard a rallying shout. A knot of riders broke fast from the trees; they slashed through the clouding dust at a dead run for the far side. The troopers shifted toward them, carbines banging. A trooper fell; Howard glimpsed the dim whiteness of the man's face going down.

A screeching whoop rose above the boiling noise. It was To-hauson, the captain saw — To-hauson spurring for the horse herd in the timber. And all at once riders boiled on

Howard's left, driving straight for the troopers' over-shifted line. To-hauson swung back, too late. Howard saw him cut off; Howard himself was deep in the pivot of a confused, horse-turning wheel of drifting black powder smoke and snarling lead and the crack of gunshot noise. He saw To-hauson's horse stagger and go down, saw the Kiowa leap clear. To-hauson was fumbling frantically with his pistol as he ducked away from a charging, eye-rolling, blaze-faced horse.

Automatically Howard broke from the confusion and rushed in. An Indian in a white man's greasy shirt loomed before him, rifle swinging. Something exploded in Howard's head; the sky turned black and spun. He felt himself fall. The flinty terrain leaped up at him, and pain sogged through him as he slapped the ground. Half blind, with blood rolling in his eyes, he shoved up and felt the pistol come heavily and awkwardly into his hand. Close upon him men and rearing horses cut indistinct leaping shapes.

He felt sick inside; his senses swayed. A trooper spilled beside him, his loose carbine clattering down. Blood blurred Howard's vision; he could not find a target. Dimly he made out a blaze-faced horse whirling, heard To-hauson's challenging whoop.

Just a few feet away the old Kiowa stood like a post, brave and helpless, snapping his empty pistol. Howard felt a stab of admiring respect. The shadows were thickening swiftly. To-hauson threw the pistol savagely at a shaggy man running up — a warrior's last fighting gesture. Then To-hauson was wheeling toward Howard, kneeling down, grunting at him: "You trade now?"

It happened in a fast whiplash of action, a split interval of time; there was a swarming smear of black in Howard's eyes and he pitched the Colt. Dimly he knew that To-hauson caught it.

But To-hauson didn't wheel on the shaggy rifleman. He crouched, and the muzzle came forward, pointing toward Howard. Howard's eyes widened. To-hauson drove a shot past Howard's head; the echoes beat hard against Howard's ears. Howard rolled toward the carbine and grabbed it up; he was turning again when a body slowly pitched at his feet.

To-hauson was swinging back toward the shaggy man, and now Howard, half blind and astonished, had presence enough to raise the carbine and snap a shot at the shaggy man. To-hauson's pistol shot rang on the heels of Howard's, and the shaggy man went down. Howard jerked spasmodically and looked at the man who had fallen behind him, and his eyes went wide open.

It was Grat Solvay, dead.

The fight swirled away. Behind him, Howard heard To-hauson's quiet grunt: "Good Tehanna, now."

Howard got raggedly to his feet. The shaggy man was stretched out. To-hauson was staring down the ravine, and Howard heard it now, the coming-on racket of McCall's detail in hard gallop. Around him the firing had pinched off. There was a ragged after volley. Through a slowly dissolving haze, Howard saw troopers herding stragglers toward the clearing. The stragglers were white men, every one of them.

The knowledge crashed through Howard. "To-hauson!" It was a roar.

He got a broken grunt from the Kiowa. Howard smashed his voice at the Indian: "You tricked us, damn you. This isn't Big Bow's camp. These are white men. That's Grat Solvay. You led us into the wrong camp!"

The carbine hung emptily in his hand, and he saw the Dragoon revolver knotted in To-hauson's fist. The Indian seemed to grin at him in the dusk.

Lieutenant McCall wheeled up on horseback, out of breath. "Captain, they're horse hunters . . . *tame* horse hunters. Thieves. Enough good Texas-branded horses back in the timber to mount five troops. Except for an Indian renegade or two, the whole crew belongs to Solvay's outfit."

Howard let loose his grip and dropped the carbine. He was swaying slightly on his feet. He put a level stare on To-hauson. "Where's Big Bow?"

His eroded face wreathed in the familiar puckery expression, the Kiowa made the sign for buffalo — the curved forefingers close to the side of the head. He made the sign for hunt — the first and second fingers held up like wolf's ears. Finally he made the sign for see — the same fingers pointing front and to the right and left.

Weariness settled across Howard in a wave. "I know," he said. "Big Bow hungry . . . Indian always hungry. . . ." He caught himself before going on with the singsong talk.

To-hauson cut a quick sign. "Big Bow hunt buffalo. Solvay take Big Bow's trail, then turn off." He made the pointing-around sign for camp or teepee.

"Solvay's ponies wear iron shoes," To-hauson said. "To-hauson him turn off same place."

Something, Howard knew, that a green trooper should have noticed.

McCall said: "Maybe this explains some of the border ranch raids. It sure explains how Solvay supplied his horse ranch."

To-hauson shifted his feet. His grooved face took on a sad look. "Solvay steal short gun from Tehannas," he said. "But me" — he signed — "me honest all time." With reluctance, he held out the Dragoon revolver toward Howard.

"You horse thief," Howard said. "Like hell, you're honest." He heard McCall chuckling, and he said: "Keep it, damn you."

To-hauson drew the gun back hastily and looked at it in wonder. Howard glared at him. And when To-hauson looked up again, the captain decided he was truly smiling.

They angled wide around Painted Rock's outscatter of frame houses and sheds, and headed for the towering cottonwoods beyond town. Two bone-weary riders, three heads-down horses, and a loaded pack mule. Most of the small-bore outfits, Buck Jensen remembered now, camped here along the cool creek when they drifted in for the fall fair races. It was cheaper than the county barns and the grass was good.

Almost furtively Buck's eyes went first to the tent camps pitched across the bluestem meadow. With a narrowed, squinting concern, he studied the men and their horses for a time. Satisfied, he turned to Keechi Joe, but his voice was strained.

"We'll try it," he said reluctantly, "but I'm going to town for another look. Nobody knows us here. It's been six years and we didn't have Humpy then. Camp on the other side of the creek, away from the others. Better walk Humpy around, loosen him up."

"Humpy, him ready to run," Keechi Joe grunted, grinning. Suddenly eager, he slid from the saddle, a shrunken old full-blood, bowlegged and wrinkled, with a nose hooked like an eagle's beak. Beady, tobacco-brown eyes peeked from a seamed, high-boned face. Stepping over to the bay horse haltered to Buck's gelding, he looked up, hopeful, pleading. "We run 'im tomorrow, huh?"

"Afraid to risk it," Buck said in a worried tone. "That sign up the road said the big race is day after tomorrow. So we keep Humpy under cover till we're ready. We just show him once here. That means we got to play for the big one. Hell, Keechi, we're damn' near broke."

"Hungry, too." Keechi Joe ran a gnarled hand across his lean middle and there was a thoughtful, mournful expression in the stern face. "Injun sure could use money with painted pictures. Get 'em grub. When we eat, huh?"

"We got bacon," Buck reminded him. "A little flour."

Grunting, Keechi Joe took the bay's rope halter and Buck watched the animal's lazy movements in pleased wonder and not a little pride, stirred by a nagging worry. If somebody recognized Humpy, they'd have to run for it again.

You didn't alibi a bank robbery and expect a marshal to believe you. Not when you rode the evidence.

After two years, it was still hard to believe that Humpy could really scamper. Sleepy-eyed, bored, he was anything but a short sprint horse in appearance. He had a mustang's long tail, shaggy black mane, and he was short-coupled, tough. But what got you was that damned sway back. Why, it hurt a man just to look at him.

Buck had never failed to hear snickers when he rode Humpy out on a track, his own half-pint frame almost lost in the warped hollow of the bay's back. But it wasn't so funny when Keechi Joe shrilled that Osage whoop, and Humpy broke like a bat out of brush. For an Indian pony that Buck had bought as an oddity, Humpy had kicked dust at far better-looking competitors.

There was a chilled nervousness working along Buck's spine as he rode into noisy Painted Rock. Crowds flowed along the boardwalks, and wagons, buggies, riders, and kids, loose for a holiday, clamored and jammed the street.

He felt a quick relief as he pointed for the fairgrounds, thinking he'd guessed right, dodging down into Indian Territory from Kansas.

Leisurely he jogged past the stables, swung back for a second look. Then he tied up and watched the milling crowd for half an hour. His mind made up, he walked across to the fair headquarters building. It was crowded, smoke-thick, loud with talk, and Buck saw the stooped, rail-thin man as he edged up to the race secretary's desk. With a steady hand, he wrote in Humpy's name for the wind-up feature and paid the fee. It all but cleaned him out, but there was enough left for a small side bet.

Swinging around, he noticed the interested flicker in the gray, skinny man's eyes, and with a start he saw the star sticking out from under the calf-hide vest. And the big Colt was handy, strapped down.

"You running tomorrow?"

Suddenly Buck had the cold feeling again. "Nope," he said. "The big one . . . last day."

He was stepping away when the man's voice cut in curiously: "Got a good horse?"

"He'll scatter dust." Buck stiffened, suspicious.

"Aw," the marshal spoke up good-humoredly, "I'm just the law around here . . . Simp Crawford. A homemade betting commissioner on fair days. But don't let it bother you. It just happens that horseracing is my meat." The weathered face crinkled in a tight grin. "Of course, now, I'd take a tip on a fast horse for my friends."

"My horse'll do," Buck said, feeling his tension easing. "He's. . . ."

"Watch that Moco horse or you'll eat dust," a voice drawled.

Buck whipped his gaze around. A slim, blond man, his face reckless, wind-scoured, stepped over. He made a grimacing expression. "I ought to know," he complained. "He made Old Red look like a plow horse."

"Old Red," Crawford supplied with a wink, "was the 'puncher's choice till Moco day-lighted him yesterday. And I mean the boys got cleaned proper, a month's pay. Ted Haley here is hunting a new favorite. Something crossed with forked lightning and a tornado. He'd kinda like to recoup."

"Hold on to your money," Buck said coldly, "and keep looking." With that he sauntered outside, glad to be out of there. As he rolled a smoke, he felt the tight strings in his stomach loosen up. Hurrying, he started working through the crowd. Something crossed his vision, and he jerked to a halt, froze. The big man stood about ten feet away, broad mouth open in surprise, eyes narrowed. Buck got a quick hold on himself, straightened. He took a step away.

"Hey, Jensen!"

With a sick dread, Buck faced Spade Barlick, wondering if the hoarse shout had carried inside to Crawford. Buck had never liked Barlick, and he cared less about seeing him now.

"You . . . here?" Barlick exclaimed, staring. "You got a horse?"

"I've always got a horse," Buck told him evasively.

Barlick's expression was tight, hard. "Dammit," he growled, "you know what I mean. Is it that sway-backed bay?"

He towered over Buck's spare frame, a knotty-shouldered, flat-nosed man with cunning, close-set yellow eyes. Coarse black hair showed raggedly under the brim of his hat.

"Maybe," Buck said, grim, stubborn.

Barlick spread his soft, pulpy hands. "You got me all wrong, old friend." His voice was coaxing, persuasive. "I don't carry grudges, even if you did clean me in a couple of races with that freak road-burner."

"I beat you fair!" Buck squared around. "What the blazes you want?"

68

"That's easy. Moco . . . my new Quarter horse . . . is favored in the feature day after tomorrow. He's a cinch unless. . . ." The face, dark and heavily jowled, creased in a smirk, speculating. "Unless you enter that bay runt."

"He's entered," Buck blurted, "and he'll run the legs off anything you ever beat the hide off of! Why don't you call the marshal? That'd win you a race."

There was a throaty roar from the grandstand, the cry of a holiday racing crowd, and, cutting through the swelling racket, Buck heard hoofs thudding.

"Old friend," Barlick said, "my horse is in the next race. See you later."

"You mean" — Buck caught the strained surprise in his own voice — "you're not saying anything?"

"I said you had me all wrong, didn't I?" Swaggering, Barlick turned and clumped rapidly toward the barns.

Still puzzled, Buck trailed over to his horse. He knew from past experience that Spade Barlick gave you nothing without strings attached. One word from him and the thing Buck and Keechi Joe had been running from would catch up with them.

Tight-lipped, Buck remembered the whole sorry mess of a few months back. With

Humpy running like a wild stud winding home country, Buck had money that folded. He had taken Barlick a couple of times, plus side bets. Then Humpy was stolen from the horse trap outside town. It was a slick, wire-cutting job.

Thinking again of the theft, Buck swore and let his eyes slide to the stables where horses were being led out for the next race. Oddly the valley-backed Humpy was found loose near camp the night after the robbery. By that time Buck had learned that whoever had cleaned the bank of $10,000 in new greenbacks had run off from a posse of galled townsmen on a sway-backed bay horse. With the only animal of that description in the country, Buck and Keechi Joe had hurried south — foolishly, perhaps, but when you couldn't beat a frame-up, you had to run from it.

Barlick's broad bulk emerged from a stall door. He was leading a chunky, gray horse, powerfully quartered. Squatty, face cruelly twisted by a broken nose, a little man waddled out. Buck recognized Chalk Deal, Barlick's strong-armed jockey. As Deal hit the light saddle, the gray's eyes rolled, went wild, and Buck could see the trembling muscles. Snarling, Deal jerked the reins and the horse reared.

"Damn you!" Barlick shouted in alarm. "Ease 'im up! Want to lose this race before it starts?"

Buck heard Deal mutter something, and, with the gray still skittish, they moved toward the track. The little tableau interested Buck and he followed. When he had elbowed up against the railing, four horses were dancing nervously toward the starter. There was one ragged, false start, with the eager gray breaking too soon. Yanking savagely, Deal hauled his mount around. When they came forward again in a tight clump, the foursome lunged across the line.

All at once Buck felt a rider's admiration for good horseflesh and a reluctant respect for Deal. For the iron-handed little man slammed his horse to the front and held him there. As they stretched past the stands, Buck saw Deal's thick arm whip up, down, quirt flailing mercilessly. When they hit the finish line, better than 200 yards away, there was wagon room between Moco and the runner-up. It wasn't even close, Buck saw, and Deal hadn't needed the bat, damn him.

Hands clenching, Buck turned away, sobered, troubled. Barlick, he realized, had a real sprint horse now, and Chalk Deal was just the man to beat the last ounce of speed from him. He knew, too, that Barlick held another whip, if he wanted to use it.

Doggedly Buck rode back to camp, but it was the race he had in mind at sunup. Together he and Keechi Joe walked the barebacked mustang through the thick, wet grass. Buck picked an open stretch, sheltered from view behind the tree-lined creek. When the Humpy horse was warmed up, Buck said: "The other outfits'll be working out soon. I'll let him go a piece."

Keechi Joe's answer was a toothy grin, and Buck brought the bay around, with the Indian playing the starter's rôle. As Buck drew even, Keechi Joe yelled: "Go!"

Then he whooped, catching Buck by surprise. It was a screeching, piercing yowl, almost terrifying. Humpy's indifference vanished and Buck felt the stringy muscles bunch under him, felt him lunge and bound. In a few stretching jumps, he was driving. At fifty yards the grass was a green blur in Buck's wind-whipped eyes. Humpy was still picking up at 200 yards, but Buck eased him off, satisfied.

Loping back, he caught a sheepish look in his partner's muddy-colored eyes. "Keechi," Buck complained mildly, "that was some workout. You made Humpy take off like he'd been hit in the rump with buckshot. And that danged whoop . . ." — Buck swung his gaze — "could bring us visitors."

"Humpy, him Injun pony," Keechi Joe grunted. "Whoop make 'im run fast. No whoop, no run, Injun no eat!"

Buck felt himself grinning. "No call to worry about that," he said. "Anything hearin' that screech of yours would never forget it. Me, it still gives me nightmares."

They were walking through the crowded creek timber, letting Humpy cool, when Buck heard a horse crashing against brush. Jerking, he saw a rider break from cover. Buck ran a few steps, then hauled up. A hot resentment stirred in him as he watched the rider rush out of sight, realizing that they'd been spied on.

Keechi Joe's bony brown face was grim. "Injun whoop too damn' much. Him watchin' Humpy, huh?"

"Forget it," Buck said with a casualness he didn't feel. "Some ranch hand passin' through."

But friendly riders, he reminded himself, don't run from you. He stuck to camp the rest of the morning, watching the town road, while the Indian went to Painted Rock for tobacco. He guessed he was a fool for staying here, now that Barlick had spotted him and acted so damned peculiar. But a $300 purse is a heap of money when you're a one-horse man and flat busted. Deep down inside him, though, he knew that wasn't his real reason. He wanted to whip Barlick once more, and he was tired of running.

It was late afternoon, with the shadows thickening through the gray cottonwoods, when Buck noticed the dust clouds. It wasn't Keechi Joe, who always rode at a shuffling gait. These were wind-lifted puffs, kicked up by a horse in a hurry. The visitor was a broad man, rolling easy in the saddle. Too late, as Spade Barlick trotted up to the tent, Buck thought of the pistol in his bedroll. Grim, quiet, he stood with hands hanging knotted at his side.

Barlick's gaze took in Humpy, shifted, and Buck glared back. "He's looking good," the big man said, stepping down.

"He never looked good in his life," Buck said, a bite of sarcasm in his voice, "and you know it."

"Still going to run him?"

"He's entered."

The shrewd, yellow eyes appeared to be studying the tent top behind Buck, but there was something cold in them, calculating. "I got a damn' fast horse," Barlick growled softly, and let the words sink in. "There's plenty of doubt in my mind that you can beat Moco. Why take that chance?"

Suspicion burned rankly in Buck, and he squared his jaw pugnaciously. "If you're so cock-eyed sure," he snapped, "what're you worried about?"

"Five hundred if you hold that bay back a little tomorrow."

Gulping, Buck jerked with shocked amazement. $500! That was almost double the purse.

"Here it is." Barlick slapped his hip pocket. "All yours."

With a hungry craving, Buck thought of the money. The thick-necked man smiled, and Buck realized that his own eyes had given him away, bared his need. And why not?

With something to go on, he and his Indian partner could keep drifting, cross Red River, and fade into the sprawling Texas country. Yet something told him in a tiny voice that a man couldn't run forever, that there had to be a stopping point.

Jaw hard, he straightened. "I'll go on making mine the slow way," he said coldly. "Keep your filthy money!"

Barlick didn't budge, but Buck caught the flinty glint in the shallow eyes, the almost imperceptible swelling of the thick shoulder

muscles. He felt a real physical fear as Barlick paced over, towering hugely. And with a
dull terror he saw the bulge of a shoulder
holster under the vest.

"Run that horse right!" — the growling
voice was harsh, threatening — "unless you
want to rot in jail. And don't get any ideas
about running off. I want your horse in that
race and I want him held up."

Buck saw the wide-lipped, snarling face
through a reddening haze. Desperately he
swung, thin arms pumping. He felt his fists
thudding futilely against the hard chest.
Then Barlick swung with surprising swiftness for so ponderous a man, and Buck saw
the closed fists looming like square wedges.
There was a meaty, whacking sound and
something exploded in his head. He was
falling, full of a racking agony, and the world
was spinning blackly.

Pain throbbed like hammer blows in his
head. He tried to focus his eyes on the shifting green pattern of the cottonwood tops
rustling high overhead. He discovered that
he was flat on his back, that he ached all
over. He caught Keechi Joe's grunting voice,
low, matter of fact: "Barlick . . . him been
here, huh?"

Groaning, Buck rolled up and felt of his
puffed, touch-sore jaw. "How'd you guess

it?" he said in thick disgust. "He wants us to throw the race. Or he'll turn us in. I told him to go to hell."

"Mebbe so we go to jail." The Indian's face was thoughtful, resigned. "Bad time. Ain't winter yet. Too damn' hot."

Buck wobbled to the creek, doused himself with water, and came back. Like something long forgotten, it came to him then that he hadn't placed his bet. But first he took the pistol from the bedroll, slipped it in his saddlebag. He was cinching up when he noticed that the old full-blood hadn't moved. Keechi Joe was gazing off across the meadow, frowning in thought.

"What's eatin' you?" Buck straddled the horse and stared down. "I'm the guy that got clipped."

"Purty pictures on money."

"Like those Kansas greenbacks?" Buck asked him with a sore jaw. "Yeah, we could use some."

Ted Haley was the first man Buck saw in front of the fairgrounds office. He came over at once, and Buck saw that he was excited. Buck started to go inside, but Haley caught his arm, held on.

"How's your horse?"

Buck shrugged. "He'll do, I guess."

"Don't give me that stuff." Haley's wink was sly. "He'll do, all right . . . and then some!"

Buck shook his arm free. "What're you drivin' at?"

Haley shifted his gaze, hesitating. "Listen," he stammered, "I have to tell you. I saw you work him out this morning. That was me in the timber. He's mighty fast . . . I got a tip."

"Who?"

"Well" — Haley grinned — "it's kinda funny in a way. Him telling me. That new fellow, Spade Barlick. The loud-mouth. He said you had a fast horse, so I went to see for myself. Reckon I saw plenty."

Understanding began to ravel through Buck, and he muttered: "What are the odds now?"

"Barlick's givin' three-to-one. I took him and so did the boys on my word. Anybody with a loose dollar is backin' your horse."

"You tell 'em what my horse looks like?"

Haley's laugh was quick, loud. "Sure. They think it's funny as hell. Be a good joke on Barlick if you win, after him tipping us. And you'd better. It's a long walk home."

"Crawford say anything?"

"Naw. He's too busy watching Barlick bankroll Moco."

All of a sudden it made sense, complete

sense, Buck thought. By tipping off Haley about Humpy, Barlick had stirred up betting against his own horse. It was money that he would rake in if Humpy lost. It occurred to Buck that Barlick was sure of himself, damned sure.

"Haley," Buck said, rubbing his jaw, "grab me a little of that three-to-one money." As he passed his over, he was thinking that he was in this up to his neck now. If he won the race, Barlick turned him in to Crawford. If he got Humpy off slow, holding him back, there was $500 waiting for him and an open trail south. Decision was a hard ball in his stomach as he returned to camp.

It was still there, a tense, knotted reminder, as he and Keechi Joe trotted in the next afternoon with Humpy lazying behind. Theirs was the third race, Buck remembered.

He had stayed away from town as long as he could, and it was thirty minutes till race time when he tied up at the barns. Barlick wasn't in sight, but Ted Haley was there, grinning at Humpy.

"Circus is comin' to town." Haley laughed. "Gonna warm him up?"

"He trotted in," Buck said without apology. "He's ready as he'll ever be."

"Wait'll the crowd sees him." The cowpuncher's laugh was a loud, cackling guffaw, and suddenly Buck didn't like it.

While they waited, the cry of the crowd broke from the stands as a race finished. Barlick was pacing from the barn, Chalk Deal siding him, leading Moco. Barlick and Deal talked for a time, then Barlick motioned and two men stepped from the shadowed stalls. Buck stiffened, and slowly, reluctantly he swung his leg over the light saddle on the sloping, comic back.

"Humpy, him ready," Keechi Joe's gaze was centered on Barlick. "What you think, Buck?"

"Not much choice."

Tight inside, Buck loosened the reins, wet with sweat in his hands now. It was time to move on and gently he clapped naked boot heels against the bay's thin sides and Keechi Joe followed.

Spectators stood four deep at the track gate. Buck pulled up, waiting for the rider ahead of him to go through. Then boots tapped behind him and he hitched around.

Barlick was glaring up at him. The two strangers, rough and flat-faced, flanked him.

"Remember!" Barlick's hoarse voice was a challenge. "Run that scarecrow right. No damn' tricks. Act smart and you'll get more than a jail ride." He touched the left side of his vest where the holster bulged, and Buck was conscious of a hemmed-in helplessness. "Starter's my man, too." Barlick's raw, whispering voice grated.

The gatekeeper was yowling for him to come in, and Buck turned. But Barlick held Humpy's bridle. The big man licked his thick lips.

"You ain't fooling me with that Injun," he snarled. "I've heard him whoop at the start. So he'll be deep in the crowd when the race starts. We'll see to that." He jerked his head and the two men sidled over to the Indian. "Keep him away from here till they break."

"Lay off that Indian!" Buck protested. "Damn you. . . ."

Hard-eyed, Barlick spun away and Buck saw the puzzled, helpless look on Keechi Joe's bony face. The Osage tried to push up to the gate, but the tough pair shouldered him off. Nobody seemed to mind. The gatekeeper's insistent shouting was pulling him forward, and in an odd kind of daze Buck found himself on the track. Vaguely he remembered it was a 300-yard race. Chalk Deal cut the corner of his glance, swinging the gray across. For a time there was a confused milling of high-strung horses and tense-faced jockeys. A low-slung, speedy-looking dun caught Buck's eye. He tabbed the horse for future trouble.

At first he heard only the murmuring sound of a crowd settling down for the big race — the low babble of voices, vendors squawking, a vast restless stirring — and hoofs thudding around him. It started slowly with a ripple of snickers from the railbirds. Next somebody laughed; it seemed to catch at once and others took it up.

"Crow bait! Where's the glue factory?"

Buck felt his face grow hot and stiff. He glared at the upturned sea of grinning faces. And Keechi Joe — Buck strained for sight of him, knowing it was useless.

"Git that hoss over here!"

It was the starter whooping at him. Reining over, Buck saw the other horses, five with Deal's gray. Instinctively he pointed Humpy toward the starting line. But Deal was having his troubles now. The spooky Moco bolted down the track. Sawing cruelly on the stout reins, Deal strong-armed him back, headed him around, and somehow they were all clumped together, moving forward.

Humpy was coyote-quiet, too quiet, Buck realized. He sensed that the scrawny bay outcast was waiting for something — something that wasn't going to happen: Keechi

Joe's prodding whoop.

"Crow bait! Somebody give 'im a plow!" That was white man's yelling, Buck knew, and meant nothing to the undersize Indian pony.

A black anger cutting through him, Buck hunched forward, got set. Grim-mouthed, he felt a blazing rage and a certain pride, too. You couldn't let a good horse down, and suddenly he knew he had to show this snickering crowd — and Barlick. He had known it all along.

"OK, Humpy," he said gently.

Deal was close on his left, next to the railing. On Buck's right the eager, squatty dun was trembling. They bunched forward in a nervous knot. The crowd had turned bone-still, waiting.

"Go!"

Like a gray streak licking out, Moco had broken first. And it rushed over Buck that Deal had cunningly sprung the gray a fraction of a second before the starter yelled. Humpy was lunging under Buck's hands, but late. For there was no screeching whoop. Neither was there a call back from the starter's gun, so closely had Deal timed his move. It struck Buck what Barlick had said about the starter.

Deal opened daylight and Buck was shouting hoarsely at Humpy. With the gap closing slightly, Buck heard the rushing, oncoming threat from behind. From the rim of his eye, he saw the dun come even, burst ahead, driving for the gray. Within fifty yards Buck knew that he was in a three-horse race. He saw the dun closing on Deal, saw the little man's whip arm already slashing. Tenaciously the dun seemed to hang there, but Buck had Humpy rolling for the first time.

Dimly Buck heard the howling thunder from the stands. Stretched out, head low, straining, Humpy was pulling up on the fading dun. Buck closed in and they were running side-by-side, the big horse game. Slowly Humpy's head was jerking in front, and Buck passed the dun in a brownish blur. But with a sinking realization, he knew that he couldn't catch Deal. Then he heard it.

It started high-pitched, screeching, strung out in a whooping, carrying yowl, and Buck was aware of a thin, amazed hope. It was Keechi Joe's howl, Buck knew. It shrilled across the tumult of the crazy-gone crowd, terrifying, barbaric. It sent a shuddering shock through Humpy, and Buck felt the abrupt, leaping change in the little horse. Through a dusty, filmy haze he glimpsed Deal on his left, just ahead, his whip flashing. Humpy was charging toward the gray's sprinting shape, moving away. And Buck was thinking that Keechi Joe's yell did it.

He saw Deal's shortened stirrup suddenly close up, heard the flat, vicious slap of the whacking bat. With a deadening slowness, he was working Humpy to Moco's sliding shoulders. Deal swung his wide-boned face sidewise, astonished, and went back to the whip, swinging furiously, desperately.

For a moment the gray was drawing away. Like he was trying to leap from under Deal's lash. But Humpy was sticking, straining forward. In a fast-closing image, Buck saw the men at the finish line, grouped to one side. Then the *thunk-thunk* of Deal's whip was lost in the primitive screaming of the crowd, and Buck was howling wildly at Humpy.

It seemed a long time before Humpy quit running, before Buck thought to ease him off. Woodenly he pulled at the short reins, gradually slowing his horse and turning him. There was a question in his mind, a fear of lateness when he angled back down the track.

There was a man running toward him, calling. It took Buck a second to recognize Ted Haley.

"You son-of-a-gun!" Haley was shouting.

"You did it . . . by a head!"

Buck grinned mirthlessly and thought of Keechi and the two toughs and Barlick. People were yelling at him now, wanting him to stop. No laughing, either. Buck loped the lathered Humpy to the gate. It was open and he cut through the thinning crowd, halting when he came to his tied saddle horse. He slid down, tight muscles protesting, feeling the need for haste. He took the pistol from the gelding's saddlebag, stuck it in his belt. Boots beat along the hard-packed runway behind him.

He wheeled around, facing the red, raging face, the accusing eyes of Spade Barlick.

"You!" Barlick was swinging his arms. "You double-crossed me!"

Buck stood very still. Somewhere boots were pounding. Barlick's hand was sliding toward his shoulder. Dismally Buck thought of his own awkward slowness. He saw the heavy hand jerk clear in a smooth, practiced motion. Fumbling for his pistol, Buck realized that he wasn't fast enough. He heard a shout, almost like a whoop.

Off to Buck's left, up close, there was a flat, booming report just before Barlick's finger clawed the trigger. Buck saw the weapon jar back, felt the air blast of the bullet whip over him.

But Barlick was down, the pistol spinning from his hand.

Colt smoking, Simp Crawford was running over, Keechi Joe dogging him like a hungry hound smelling trail. Barlick sagged, looked up, a stunned alarm showing in his pain-glazed face.

"There's your man. . . ." Barlick's words came jerkily, with effort. "Buck there . . . he's Jensen. Your bank robber with the sway-backed horse."

The marshal made a brief, angry sound, and Buck straightened. It was over now, he realized, and he let his cold gun tilt down.

But, strangely, Crawford didn't seem to notice him. Good humor wiped from his time-bitten face, the marshal scooped up Barlick's gun.

"The shoe don't fit," he panted angrily. "You're comin' along." His loose, wrinkled cheeks flared out as he groaned: "Dammit, I got to haul you clear back to Kansas an' I don't hanker for long rides any more."

"You old fool!" Barlick snarled. "You want him . . . Buck Jensen!"

"You damn' near got away with it." Crawford's voice was indignant. "Betting stolen money. Had everybody fooled but that Injun. He remembered the pictures on that new money you were flashing around at the office yesterday."

So that was what Keechi Joe was doing in town yesterday. With a dazed feeling, Buck understood. They were off the starvation trail for good. No more looking back. No more running away.

He saw Keechi Joe nod. "Purty pictures, too," the old Indian grunted regretfully. "But white man, him always want too damn' much."

"Yeah," Buck said, grinning, "but that wasn't me yelling for Humpy to go."

HUSH MONEY

Tom Worth reviewed his instructions in detail as he took the beaten path toward town. He wasn't to linger after he left Landow's store, which meant passing up Simon Rolling Thunder and his dogs outside Rhiner's butcher shop. He wasn't to stop more than a minute at the express office, and not at all in front of the Palace pool hall where the roughnecks collected.

"You will," Kathleen Worth had said, her blue eyes fixed on him, "march straight home. Remember, I won't have you trailing that dirty old Indian. You're almost eleven now, Tom. Old enough to do as you're told. Understand?"

"Yes, ma'am. I'll roll my wheels."

"You'll what?"

"Hurry, I mean," he amended, already moving and realizing once again that women didn't savvy freighter's talk. In his haste, he neglected to shake the screen door two, three times to ward off the flies.

Only this was early June and the scrubby blackjacks beckoned, cool and green, and it came to him that it wouldn't hurt none to prowl some on his way. Like yesterday, when he'd saved that wagon train of poor, helpless womenfolk, bug-eyed kids, and greenhorn men. When Red Cloud hisself, after he'd given up, admitted just one man could 'a' done it — and that was Texas Jack. Other times he might be Yellow Hawk, chief of the Osages, smoking up a war party against the Pawnees, because he ranged mighty far once he got stirred up.

Angling off the path, he held a dog-trot for several minutes. Shadows formed black patches under the crowded trees, and, where sunlight trickled through, the sandy earth looked yellow as California gold. Not far distant the new oil field grumbled, making noises he'd grown to listen for in the few months since his family had come here. A steady, comforting sound, beating good in your ears after you'd shifted around so much, from town to town.

He came to a wagon road, rutted and twisting. Across it the timber massed. Smoke smell hung in the morning air. It grew stronger as he legged ahead, and he stopped half curiously.

He spied the hobbled horses first; they looked tuckered, their saddle-marked backs caked with dried sweat. One, the bay, had a fine blazed face. The other was all mouse-colored, just plain horse in Tom's appraisal. Two men squatted back from a low-smoldering fire built between sandstone chunks that supported a blackened coffee pot. Emptied cans, unwashed tin plates, flung-down saddles and horse blankets completed the careless clutter.

A hurry prompted Tom. He started on, but the nearest man jerked to attention. He rose smoothly and Tom checked up, at the same instant fighting a sudden desire to run.

This man was raw-boned, with small, quick eyes and a black forest of beard stained yellowish-brown by tobacco juice. His pistol wobbled as he straightened. His pouched-out jaw worked briefly. "What's the matter, kid?" he asked in a liquid drawl. "Ain't you ever seen white men before?"

Tom didn't like the amused tone. "Most folks don't camp in here, that's all."

"Any law against it?"

"Nope, but the freighters like it along the road. Water's closer."

"We ain't freighters. A man can bed down where he takes a notion, can't he?"

"Guess so," Tom replied.

"Vamoose!" It was the second man, growling and inclining his head townward. He was blocky as a tree stump, scowling and cranky. The wide, beaded gun belt circling his vast middle strained to the last notch. His blunt fingers tapped a gurgling pipe, its strong stench fouling the clean woods, causing Tom to draw in his nostrils.

When Tom hesitated, the man growled again: "I said vamoose!"

At once Tom turned, jogging fast, relieved to go, and yet annoyed that strangers should pitch their dirty camp here.

Coming presently up the wagon road, he found Rocky City before him. A sort of funny, nowhere place to move to, he figured, although not minding. These scrub buildings everybody called a city; what was really just a boom town sprung up around Landow's old trading store. But there was a longing within his mother when she talked of Reedville.

A right nice little town, she said. Clean streets, neat store buildings, pretty houses, and gentle elms shading the walks. Yellow grain fields rolled like waves in the summer wind, instead of blackjacks and lonesome prairie. The town where Tom and his mother had lived while his father was away from home so long that time.

He was slowing, fascinated by the sights and greasy smells, his ears throbbing to the din of heavy machinery pounding in the oil field. Yonder more wooden derricks than he could count reared toward the clear, bright sky. At night they looked on fire, like torches, which his father said was just waste gas burning.

He gave them one more scanning and trotted between slow-moving freight wagons to the supply yards, so loaded down with stacked pipe, bull-wheels, rig timbers, and such you'd think the ground would bust, and across to the express company office on the opposite corner.

Going in, Tom saw his father behind the long counter, in vest and black sleeve guards up to his elbows. He did not look around, and Tom's interest strayed to the squatty iron safe. He knew it held plenty of money, having watched his father open it, and there was an old single-action .45 close in a drawer.

His father kept gazing stiffly out the murky glass, as if he hadn't heard. You could see he was just faced that way, gazing into space, his face troubled. Then he turned and his face smoothed.

"What is it, Tom?"

Although he was given to leanness, he had

the strong wrists and capable hands of a much larger man. Carried his head good, too, Tom thought. But his face was too old for a man his age, and his hair, white as cotton along the temples, and his slate-gray eyes, sometimes showing a stored-up bitter caution, made you wonder if maybe he'd lived and done things he'd never tell a boy, not till he got man-size, anyhow.

"I'm going to the store," Tom told him.

"Well, tell your mother I won't be home at noon."

Tom eyed him with disappointment. "Y'mean Mister Hines . . . ?"

"Tom!" His father shot him a warning glance. "See you at supper." He turned to the counter, his curt movement a dismissal, as Adam Hines, the company agent, entered briskly.

He had a long unsmiling face. Now he nodded in his precise manner to Tom. Folks said one sure thing about Mr. Hines. He never wasted words or money and he wasn't the easiest man to work for.

Mumbling a greeting, Tom went out and walked slowly past the Palace and the noisy oil field workers around the door, smelling the damp, close odors from inside.

Long-eared hounds whined before Rhiner's butcher shop. By that, Tom knew Simon

Rolling Thunder was in there. Tom's father said you could set your watch by the time Simon bought meat, since he came to town every day to feed his dogs. Even on Sunday, when Rhiner's was closed, he loafed on the plank walk, soaking up sun.

Tom eased through the pack, ducked into Landow's store. Afterward, leaving with his groceries, he found Simon outside Rhiner's. About him, his dogs wrangled, leaping for the chunks of meat Simon tossed.

Tom took a long look, for Simon was no ordinary Indian. Maybe the richest in the world. Leastwise, the way Tom's father told it, all the oil in the county belonged to the Osages. Not that you could tell Simon was rich. He wore a bandanna around his broad head, his red flannel shirt hung loosely, the tails flapping, and his trousers were rusty with age.

Of a sudden the dogs lunged together, snarling, their sharp cries overriding all other sound.

The next thing Tom knew Mr. Landow appeared in his doorway. "Simon!" he called sharply, gesturing. "Can't you feed those dogs somewhere else? They're raising an awful racket."

Simon's mahogany eyes blinked. He nodded good-naturedly and dangled red meat above the dogs. Instantly they leaped after him, and Tom's curiosity carried him after them. Between the Palace and the express office Simon halted, turned, and pitched, and the pack rushed in.

In front of the Palace one man stood apart. If there was any expression on the dark, craggy face, it was one of sullen boredom. Tom noticed him mainly because he wore a gun on his hip. Also, fancy-like, a wide-brimmed hat, yellow-topped cowboy boots with Levi's tucked inside, and a dirty blue shirt, instead of oil-spattered clothing and high-laced oil worker's boots.

It happened swiftly, as Simon lobbed a piece of meat. A scrambling dog struck the stranger's yellow boot, throwing him off balance. He caught himself, quick as a cat, and wheeled on the dog.

Tom read a sheen of touchy anger in the large, bulging eyes. He saw the pistol flash upward. There was one shot, another, and Simon's hound howled and tumbled.

Tom never remembered running, but he was, his arms loaded. With a sense of shock, he bent down. One glance was enough. His skin went cold, prickling. He was flinching, hurting inside while his stomach turned. He swiveled his head and ran against Simon's

gaze, the coffee-black eyes glinting dangerously.

"Tom Worth! Get away from there!"

It registered on Tom that his father was
shouting somewhere, but he couldn't budge
for the life of him. Couldn't rouse his
wooden body or tear his fixed eyes from the
man's bulky pistol.

"You shot my dog," Simon said dismally,
which wasn't how Tom expected a real full-
blooded Indian to talk when he got stirred
up. Not pounding his chest or making signs.
Then Tom felt powerful arms grasping him,
and his father was pulling him back.

"Ran into me, didn't he?" Tom heard the
stranger say.

"You shot him." Simon's persisting voice
rose a notch, stronger. "You pay me."

"Pay . . . for that flea-bit mutt?" Suddenly
it became a crude joke. The stranger's
laughter rolled, except it lacked any funning. Until now, Tom hadn't noticed the
closeness of the bulging eyes, how thin and
mean the mouth curled.

"Now," Simon muttered, and extended
the broad platter of his hand. "You pay me
now."

In return, the stranger mocked him with
his eyes, while keeping his pistol level, as
much as telling Simon to collect if he was

mean enough. The crowd stayed put, not coming any nearer.

Simon moved forward one stubborn pace. The stranger waited. All at once Tom knew nobody was going to stop it.

"No, Naves! No."

Tom heard his father's tight voice. He saw him in fast stride, as a man might rush in before he thought, the skin around his mouth white as he stepped between them. "Don't be a fool, Simon," he said, the words piling out. "Better get out of here. Take your dogs."

"But he ain't paid," Simon protested.

"And he's got a gun . . . you don't. Go on, I tell you!"

His father gripped Simon's shoulder. For a moment Tom wasn't sure what the Osage would do. Simon stood erect and unmoved, glaring. At length his glance, centered on the pistol, lifted grudgingly. With a reluctant slowness, he stooped and gathered up the dog's body, cradling it, and shuffled into the street.

But it wasn't finished. Tom realized that darkly as his father turned.

"You had no call to butt in," the stranger said coldly, holstering his weapon. "I wasn't gonna shoot him. Pistol-whip him, maybe, if he climbed me. That's all. Way I see it, I did the town a big favor. Got rid of a public nuisance."

"No more nuisance than your loose gun."

"Loose gun?"

"Yes. You'd have shot Simon. Same as you did the dog."

"That's mighty strong talk," the stranger said. "And I'll show you're wrong. Look, my gun's up. I won't use it." He shifted his feet, suddenly raising his fists. "Come on. You an' me."

Tom's father kept his arms down, but his hands were knotted.

"What's the matter?" There was no answer, and the baiting voice came again, harsh with contempt. "I know, you're afraid to fight. You're all bluff. You're yellow. Hear me? You're yellow!"

Still, his father said nothing. He stood there, tight-lipped, stiff, his chest rising and falling.

Tom felt himself shrinking to an inner numbness, unable to understand, and all the while it deepened that his father was backing down and the entire town could see.

Without a word, his father made a sudden movement and shouldered through the crowd. As he followed behind, Tom couldn't miss the stilled faces of the men, Mr. Hines among them. And, last of all, he saw some look aside in embarrassment.

"Tom," his father murmured when they reached the office door, "never mind telling your mother. I will tonight."

Boots striking the walk drew Tom's eyes to Cab Morgan, who ran the blacksmith shop. A bushy-browed man, friendly and massive. Looking broad in his leather apron, and unaccustomed to running.

"John," he asked, breathing fast, "what's this all about? Anybody hurt?"

Tom's father spoke in a few crisp words.

"Wouldn't have happened if we had any law in this town," Morgan said. "Wait'll we get ourselves incorporated. Hire us a marshal." He was peering at the milling crowd as he spoke. "So that's the gunny in the blue shirt, big hat? Don't place him around here. You know him?"

"Never saw him before."

Not until he was lengthening his strides toward home did it occur to Tom that his father had called the stranger's name, this man nobody knew.

During supper his father appeared to have forgotten the morning. He talked little, frowning while Tom's mother spoke of the railroad spur being built to connect Rocky

City with the main line, of more families moving in. It was old news, yet tonight her enthusiasm made it take on added importance.

Tom squirmed in uncomfortable silence.

"Rocky City might be a real good town," his father agreed. "If the wells don't play out and the market holds. A lot of things can happen to a boom town, Kathy. Not many last long."

Undaunted, she held her pleased, musing expression. "Why, only yesterday you were talking about the new wells west of town," she reminded him teasingly. "How they extended the field. I'm just thinking of what might be and what it means to us."

"I know," he said without expression.

"If the town grows, Tom can go to school regularly like other boys. Not just a few months each year." She paused and Tom caught the earnestness in her long sigh. "We'll have church buildings. There'll be paved streets like in Reedville, new stores, a bright red depot. We can stay here . . . grow up with the town. Be somebody."

"Kathy," he began, and the frown edged into his face again. "I hope everything works out. But let's not count on it too much, just in case."

Her face darkened and, for several moments, Tom saw the same uncertainty between them. She rose quickly to clear the table.

Dusk fell. His father lighted the hall kerosene lamp, his face unreadable as he turned up the wick and a yellow glow filled the room. Later, John Worth dried the dishes for his wife and you could hear them in the kitchen, speaking of everything except that morning.

By late evening Tom decided his father had no intention of telling. He carried the realization to bed and was still awake when a knock sounded at the front door. Cab Morgan's voice boomed through the house. His heavy body made the floor creak.

"John," he said, "we've called a special meeting of the merchants Sunday night. Eight o'clock sharp. Over Landow's store."

"Meeting?"

"Don't you figure it's time we organized?" Morgan shot back. "This morning showed that. Why, you might've been killed, John. Aw, I know how you feel, eatin' crow in front of a crowd, even after he put up his gun. But I don't care what people say, you had good reasons or you'd have fought him," he finished with some sympathy.

A stillness followed. Tom found himself upright in bed, straining to hear.

"Who had a gun?" His mother's words were half swallowed, dragged up from her throat. "John, you didn't tell me."

"I was going to, Kathy. Later. I didn't want to worry you."

"Sorry, Missus Worth," Morgan interrupted hastily. "I thought you knew. I'll run along. Can we count on you, John?"

"I guess so, Cab."

Morgan clumped out. His heavy boots rapped across the yard, faded in the night, before Tom's father spoke again.

Tom heard his father's voice.

"Duff Naves is in town. He had the gun."

"Naves? Oh, no!"

"He came to the office this morning. Hines was out. Later, he shot one of Simon's hounds. That's how it started."

"That old Indian!"

"Wasn't his fault. I thought Naves was going to shoot him. Then, when Naves offered to fight me, I backed down."

"He's caught up with us, just when we thought. . . ."

She did not finish, and Tom's father, pacing back and forth on the creaky floor, said with a firm gentleness: "You quit fretting about it. He can't send me back. I served my time for mixing with his bunch."

Without a sound, Tom slipped from his

bed to the door. His mother was slumped in a chair, her hands wadding a handkerchief. What held him rigid, though, was the sight of her face — the sickened shock there.

"What did he say?" she persisted in a voice much dimmer than Tom had ever heard.

"Just passing through the country."

"That all?"

"He didn't say much."

"He wants something," she said, an ancient knowledge within her. "Why else would he come here? Remember, he fixed it so you took the blame before. Oh, John, why can't you turn him in? He's an outlaw. He's killed men."

Tom's father stopped, in the grip of a powerful emotion. "And have him tell Hines that an ex-jailbird is handling company funds?" He shook his head savagely. "No, I can't do that. Besides, there's no law in Rocky City."

She stared up at him, her face white. "What can we do?"

"We'll have to wait and see, Kathy. But I know one thing for certain, I'm mighty tired of running."

On numb legs Tom went woodenly to his bed. Drawn tight, his mind spinning, he lay awake long after the house darkened and there was no sound save the wind off the blackjacks. He pulled tighter, loaded with an overwhelming fear and shame for his father. He beat his balled fist into the pillow, wet against his face.

A knot began to form in the pit of his stomach, and it was still there in the morning when his mother called him to breakfast.

Later, Tom straggled behind as they walked through glassy sunshine to the open-air church, no more than a short row of seats shaded overhead by a framework of blackjack brush. Sitting on the rough bench, he was soon aware of the Reverend Mather, long-haired and showing need of a week's board somewhere, warning of Rocky City's increasing wickedness. There was a rough element drifting in, he shouted. Decent folks would have to stiffen their backbones. . . .

Tom's mind wandered. He was suddenly alert as the preacher, waving his scarecrow arms at the climax of his sermon, called on everybody to have courage when enemies camped around. And to Tom, the Reverend Mather's penetrating glance appeared aimed straight at his father.

His own face reddening, Tom stole a sidelong look. His father had that faraway expression, like in the office. He wasn't even listening. And as the people filed out after the services and his own family's turn came to shake hands, Tom thought the Reverend Mather took extra long today.

Once home, his father shed his coat and went to the woodpile behind the house, snatched up the double-edged axe, and began chopping so fast you figured he had a hate against the scrubby logs.

"Tom," he said, after a minute, breathing deeply, "I know you're wondering about yesterday. Wondering why I didn't fight."

"I'm not . . . a bit." Tom tried to make it sound right. The moment he blurted it out, however, he knew he'd failed. Loyal, that was all, and miserable.

The gray eyes studied him. "Honest, now?"

"Yes, honest," Tom declared in a loud voice, too loud for conviction.

"You wouldn't be much of a boy if you didn't wonder why," his father said, and buried the blade halfway. He left it there, his knuckles like white knobs around the handle. "I'd do the same in your place. Just remember this, sometimes it's harder not to fight."

Afterward, he labored without let-up, making the chips fly, splitting and sizing the logs into stove-length pieces, cutting enough to cook Sunday dinner all summer. At intervals he rested and gazed off in his detached way.

Called to dinner, he ate slowly, lingering over his meal. At last he stood and took up his hat.

"Working today?" Tom's mother protested.

"Big week coming up." He smiled dryly. "And you know how Mister Hines is."

"Too well. But he won't be there . . . it's not that." Into her eyes edged a gleam of fear.

"It's nothing unusual. I worked last Sunday. Remember? Tom, you stay within call."

Upon reaching the screen door, his father slowed his steps and he looked at them with an intentness that was approving and also curiously sober. Something fast ran across his face. He was gone, then, and, glancing through the window, Tom could see him striding up the path toward town.

Not long afterward, Tom drifted outside into the warm, still afternoon. He stood a moment. And when the woods called, as they always did if you watched good, the branches seeming to wink and signal all at once, he made tracks.

Inside the shadowed coolness of the black-boled timber, he was Texas Jack once more, this day on the Santa Fé Trail. Sure enough, what looked like a whole tribe of screeching Pawnees dusted up on their painted ponies, all raw to fight. So he tended to that business right off and rolled his wheels, in no great hurry now. He chased antelope and shot himself some buffalo whenever the fancy struck, which was anytime because Texas Jack did as he pleased.

Somehow, though, the game lacked its old appeal today, and for the first time the thought began in him that maybe he was growing up. His mind kept going back to yesterday morning.

He was dog-trotting, circling, when he made out the flutter of movement along the road. A hat and next a tall shape. A few steps farther he turned motionless, his mouth dropping open, watching his father stride down the road from town.

Tom started to call out. But the impulse died almost as it welled up, squeezed down by a peculiar unease that thinned to caution, formless and vague.

His father stepped to the timber's edge and peered in uncertainly, as if he expected somebody but wasn't sure. He gave a sharp, plaintive whistle.

Time dragged. Tom's heart tugged at the wall of his chest, thumping high, and he realized it wasn't right, spying this way. Yet, when he thought of leaving or calling, he could not act. Meanwhile, his father fidgeted, thrusting hands inside his pockets and kicking his boots at the ruts.

At that moment dried branches snapped. His father straightened, stiffly waiting, and Tom saw horses in single file, bulking high. In front rode Duff Naves.

Everything in Tom seemed to tighten. Behind Naves came yesterday's surly campers, still dirtier and unshaven in daylight. The bony, quick-eyed man astride the fine blaze-faced bay, which irked Tom deeply, and the cranky, thick-bodied man aboard the dun. The polished handles of their pistols cast greasy glimmers above the worn holsters.

For no reason at all, Tom caught himself remembering the Reverend Mather's sermon. About enemies camped in close, and he called on the strength he needed suddenly and did not have.

Naves's swarthy face shone with a brittle satisfaction. He growled at Tom's father, who nodded heavily and turned up the road. The horsemen followed.

Something warned Tom to stick to cover as he trotted behind, drawn by a mixed urgency of fear and puzzlement. When the timber scanted out to prairie and Rocky

City loomed, he took hesitantly to the road. From a distance back he saw Naves dismount and walk beside his father. Together, they went past the storage yards. The campers, leading Naves's horse, reined out of view at the corner.

Tom stared a moment, in relief. Nothing was wrong. The campers were riding off. Scattered wagons and people marked the street. Not so many on Sunday afternoon, nevertheless, they provided a comfort, just the sight of them. Everything looked in place, even Simon Rolling Thunder hunkered on his heels in front of Rhiner's butcher shop, which was closed for the Sabbath. His restless hounds ranged the walk, again and again sniffing hungrily at Rhiner's door. Simon seemed to be dozing on the sun-drenched street.

The next instant Tom froze, his gaze pinned to the express office, watching his father unlock the door and enter. Pressing close behind was Naves.

A sense of wrongness stabbed Tom as his skinny legs carried him to the supply yards. Heaving for breath, he scrambled to the end of a rack of pipe, scanned the street, then pulled back instantly.

There, in the mouth of the alley, the campers slouched in their saddles. And yet

Tom sensed an unmistakable vigilance beneath their indifference. Something in the way their attention kept swinging to the corner.

The fear that Tom had almost driven from his mind moments ago stirred again, growing. He dreaded to look at the express office, and, when he did, quickly, the feeling seemed to surge and swell. His dry throat contracted as understanding crashed through him.

His father was letting Duff Naves rob the office, while Naves's men waited with the horses!

Sound erupted without any warning. There was a gun booming, its deep-throated roar hanging muffled along the quiet street and turning Tom cold.

He saw Simon's head jerk up, saw him jump to his feet and break into a lumbering run for the express office, his hounds racing playfully with him. Just before he reached the door, it jolted outward and a man sprang through.

Tom recognized Naves. He carried a lumpy sack. His pistol glinted in his hand. He half spun on the closing figure. Simon grabbed.

Naves's gun hand rose swiftly and chopped, the barrel taking Simon across his upflung arm before his face, and, as Simon reeled backward, he shrilled to his dogs. Naves was free, only to come against the lean shapes crowding underfoot. He kicked and cursed.

Now Simon, crying out in Indian, lunged like an aroused brown bear. Naves slued around with his pistol, this time to kill.

Tom flinched at a single ear-splitting blast and waited for Simon to buckle. Instead, Naves jerked strangely. His sack dropped first and his pistol right after, making a hollow *whap* on the plank walk. Then he clapped both hands to his chest, twisted back, and fell.

Tom stared. He was scared to death and sick. Movement pulled his eyes sideward.

His father stood swaying in the powder smoke doorway, gray-faced, that old .45 still leveled on Naves. He flicked Naves a quick look and limped toward the corner of the building.

In an instant Tom remembered, even before he heard the pounding racket and glimpsed the blaze-faced horse charging forward. There came a flash of flame from the rider's pistol, but Tom's father didn't go down. His own gun was bucking and suddenly the horse swerved off, riderless, and the third man was swapping directions, racing his mount out of town.

It was over by the time Tom ran across. His father stood, hard as a post for several moments, still defiant, strung tight. And that was the part Tom always remembered best, better than the gun battle. Him rooted there, kind of gaunt and great, with a terrible light in his eyes, with blood sopping high along his trouser leg and powder smoke blooming around him.

All this before he clawed suddenly for the support of the building, missed, and crashed into the arms of Simon Rolling Thunder.

An awkward hurry seemed to come over Cab Morgan and Adam Hines after a minute in the cramped lamp-lit room that smelled like a doctor's medicine case.

"You won't run in any Fourth of July sack races, but you'll be there," Morgan boomed, and started to go.

"Let me know if there's anything I can do," Hines murmured.

From his station by the foot of the bed, Tom saw a frown crease the lean, pale face on the pillow. "Wait a minute," his father said curtly.

They halted.

"There's something I want you to hear. Especially you, Mister Hines." He swallowed, and Tom saw the sudden search of his glance upon his mother, then felt it himself, as if his father needed strength.

Morgan and Hines eyed each other. "It can wait," Hines replied agreeably, turning.

"No, it can't." Tom's father raised himself so abruptly that pain pinched his face. "You're going to have to hear this!"

Hines regarded him a moment, once again the old Mr. Hines — all business, brisk, disapproving.

"I see you're determined to talk, John. However, there's nothing you can tell us about the hold-up, or why Duff Naves happened to pick an off-trail place like Rocky City. We know because Naves's wounded friend has been talking his head off."

Surprise built in his father's eyes, then plain dismay. "So you already know?" he said.

"Most of it . . . enough. Naves's price to keep still to me was for you to let him rob the office. So you played him the hard way. Even took his insults in public. And now you want to tell me the very thing you fought to stop." In the next moment, the long, strict face of Mr. Hines switched to a surprising meekness. "Good heavens, man! Maybe it mattered once, but not now. Come along, Cab. We'll be late for the meeting at

Landow's store. Let's get up there before some fool passes an ordinance against loose dogs."

And suddenly they were gone from the room.

For a time nobody spoke. Then Tom's mother said: "Everyone's been asking about you, John. Simon Rolling Thunder was here."

"Sorry I missed him."

"You were sleeping. I . . . I told him to come back." Her tone quickened his gaze. "Tomorrow," she said. "He's coming for dinner."

"Why, that's fine, Kathy," Tom heard his father answer. "We'll be here. We're going to be in Rocky City a long time."

Sheriff Lee Rand rode inside the pole corral behind the sheriff's office, dismounted stiffly, and watered his horse at the planked trough. He was jerking at the cinch when he heard the strung-out undertone of men moving along the street. He peeled off the saddle and sweat-crusted blanket, slipped the gelding's bridle, and hung up the rigging. Then he stalked to the office, and hauled up abruptly, grinning widely to himself.

Lumped in a chair, Charlie Big Sick was fast asleep, snoring in snorting, raveling gusts, his long braids sliding as he nodded. It was the middle of June, but he had wrapped an orange-striped blanket around his broad body. A blood-red rooster feather reared from the round-topped hat. One brown hand gripped a beaded buckskin bag and looping his neck was a rawhide thong anchored to a cow horn, year-yellowed, worn smooth. Between his knees was a carved hickory cane.

All mighty proper, Lee thought, for an Osage medicine man. Even to the string of fish hooks rimming the rattlesnake hatband. As Lee's boot heels scraped, the snoring snapped off and the old full-blood stirred, blinked, mild eyes the muddy sheen of strong coffee.

"Catfish bitin'?" Lee asked gently. Big Sick's determined but futile wooing of Salt Creek's catfish was a standing joke in Antelope Springs.

"Sign no good." Big Sick licked thick lips in a high-boned, Roman-nosed face. "But me catch 'em yet." He was grinning now.

"Yeah," Lee grunted, his good humor gone. "Your luck's about like mine." Watching the front door, he realized what was coming — Tracy Bullard. He had sensed it for weeks. He had read it between the lines of Trinkle's weekly newspaper — Kate Trinkle's now that old Tom had passed on — the *Oklahoma War Chief*. He could feel it now in the deliberate tramp of boots, in the rising mutter of men's voices.

With a straight-backed dignity, Tracy Bullard swung inside first, and Lee straightened. Bullard was a thin wedge of a man, angular and loose of joint, with a slack-jawed face and the jumpy, bargaining eyes of a traveling horse trader.

In his Prince Albert coat and plug hat, Bullard cut a fine figure among the town's tobacco-chewing, booted gentry and blanketed Osages. Only a year ago he had drifted in from back East and opened a law office. A convincing talker, he had soon established himself as a manager of men, and awed citizens had elected him mayor.

"Heard the news, sir?" Bullard's voice was soft and low-toned, but it carried a challenge. He stood stiffly erect. Behind him, Lee saw men gawking, and he caught the stubby shape of Duff Shaner, the Black Dog Hills rancher.

"Been beatin' the brush," Lee said. "But I got an idea."

"Well," — the mayor thrust out his chin — "they did it again. Only this morning, sir. Caught poor Johnny Strack coming through Wildhorse Gap. Cleaned out the Big V outfit's payroll. Manhandled the passengers." Bullard scowled and his voice trailed off, half choked. "Johnny's dead . . . shotgunned twice. A most brutal act. . . . Folks are beginning to talk . . . even Editor Trinkle."

"Too bad about Johnny." Regretfully Lee was thinking of likeable, reckless Johnny

Strack, who had yowled the Salt Creek stage from the Osage country to the Kansas line town of Yellow Hand. "He's been helping. Rode with me when he wasn't driving. We looked hard. No luck, but they'll make a mistake yet. Wait and see."

"Wait!" Bullard threw up a protesting hand, his face to the crowd, sneering, outraged. "As spokesman for the good citizens of Antelope Springs, I demand action. Not tomorrow . . . but today . . . now! Eight hold-ups in three months and you say wait. Damned if we will . . . you've got to do something!"

Angry growls chorused from the packed crowd, and Lee saw Duff Shaner step forward, a hint of stored-up trouble in his square body. For Shaner was Lee's opponent in the coming July election, openly chosen and backed by the Honorable Tracy Bullard.

"Lee, him damn' fine sheriff."

It was Charlie Big Sick's deep, grunting voice, and Lee turned. The Osage's hands were knuckle-ridged on the hickory cane, his eyes stoutly defiant.

Lee said — "Thanks, but stay out of this, Charlie." — and whipped back. He had a closed-in feeling, a rankling resentment against second-guessing, complaining town-ers. Lee had been without a deputy for weeks, and, knowing it was bad politics, he had scorned the gesture of a city-manned posse as slow, awkward, useless. In this stretching land of rock-rimmed ridges, bluestem prairie and timbered hills, a man could hide forever from noisy, bungling riders. And Tip Wall, his deputy, still wouldn't straddle a horse. It was a funny sickness, Lee thought, that kept a strong man abed so long.

"Bullard's right," Shaner announced. "If this keeps up, Antelope Springs'll be ruined. People got a right to protection." He swung thick, sloping shoulders. "We'll get it after the election."

This was his little piece for benefit of the crowd, Lee knew bleakly, and it rang true. Black-browed with work-toughened hands, Shaner looked hard, capable. He had a restless way of turning his muscled fighter's body. He was making an impressive show.

Lee's voice was dry, bitter. "Nice speech . . . and maybe you'll get the chance."

"He will," Bullard cut in roughly. "You've had yours. You're already a dead duck." There was a pleased expression in the pale eyes when he turned, calling: "Let's go!"

As Bullard wheeled, Lee saw Big Sick still

hunched in the chair. His nut-brown, wrinkled face was mask-like, fixed. He seemed to be gazing beyond the grumbling men. Then Lee noticed the hickory cane. It slanted out like a brown snake in front of Bullard's boots. There was a scuffling sound, and he fell in a spread-out, awkward sprawl. Instantly he whirled up, sputtering, face crimson.

"You . . . ," he roared at Big Sick, "you did that!"

"Huh?" Big Sick's head tilted. For a second his eyes showed a flashing hardness, then he pulled back the cane. "White man's foots too big," he grunted, peering down in concern. "Watch where walk next time. Maybe bust medicine stick."

"You red. . . ." Bullard's bony fists knotted, his careful dignity lost in the furious wash of a whiplash anger. His arm jerked back.

Before Lee realized it, he was lunging. He caught the raised arm, twisted, heard Bullard's yell. "Get out!" Lee ordered. "The whole damned bunch!"

Bullard was struggling, his face pained, and Lee let go so suddenly that Bullard fell backward against a man. It came swiftly to Lee that he had made the worst possible play here. But his own built-up anger was goading him in wild, gusty impulses.

"Clear out!" he repeated harshly.

"I wasn't going to hit him," Bullard argued.

A red-faced townsman raised a blunt, clenched fist. Duff Shaner was moving over, but Bullard waved him to a halt.

"We'll go," Bullard growled through his teeth. "And you, sir . . . you'd better start looking for a new job."

Bony shoulders upthrust, Bullard whipped out of the office. The others followed, shuffling and grumbling. Shaner's leathery face was a frozen picture of malice.

Watching them go, Lee realized that more than a county election was at stake. Raw, rank murder had glinted from the chilled surface of Bullard's flinty stare. For Big Sick, too. And Bullard was smooth. With Shaner siding him, it could get rough for a man caught deep in the timber, boxed in a rocky cañon. And there was something else — a half-paid-for ranch in the hunkering, grass-rich hills. Worth fighting for and the reason Lee had buckled on lawman's irons to pay it off. Solemn, he swung around, but he couldn't hide his grin.

"Funny," he said, "how clumsy some folks are."

"Luck still bad." Charlie Big Sick shook

his broad head regretfully. "No break neck."

Slowly, ponderously the Indian stood up, catching the bright blanket around him. There was a rugged and enduring quality about the old man that Lee had always liked. He was a rooted part of the blackjack-studded hills, immovable, like stone. But Lee caught a troubled glimmer in the straight, unblinking stare.

"You," Big Sick grunted, "you got to catch 'em now."

Soberly Lee watched the full-blood pad away, the cane tapping. Big Sick was right — dead right. But it would take some extra good bait. Lee stepped outside and saw that the crowd had broken up, drifting to Bullard's office. This was reservation country, bone dry, and Bullard kept a bottle handy for the politically faithful. Lee was crossing the street, thinking of thick-armed Tip Wall, when he saw a flutter of skirts in the doorway of the *War Chief* office.

Kate Trinkle saw him at once, checked herself, and he went across to her. There was a question in her wide-spaced eyes.

"You heard?" Lee asked.

She nodded. "I was going to see you. This means more trouble, Lee. You want to make a statement for the paper?"

Straight-faced, Lee considered her, feeling

a traveling uneasiness. He guessed the trouble was Miss Kate thought of herself as a newspaper editor first, a woman last. Like old fire-eating Tom, she took editorial duties seriously. Much too seriously for somebody with the biggest gray-green eyes Lee had ever seen, and a full, rich mouth that stirred a man. Ink smudged the tip of her small chin, wind whipped her copper-colored hair, and Lee caught the clean scent of soap. She moved slim shoulders impatiently, with a twist. She took a restless breath and Lee saw the soft swell of her blouse.

"Why," he said patiently, "just say I'm doing the best I can. Like the one-legged man in the foot race."

"That won't do." Her face was severe, almost reproachful. "People want to know how you intend to correct the situation."

"Correct it?" he flared. "You sound like Bullard. Just tell 'em fearless Lee Rand is still on his stick horse, riding the ridges, beating the brush" — her eyes were stormy, but he went on — "that he hasn't made a capture since the Peabody boys burned down the schoolhouse."

"Want me to print that?"

"Sure. Go ahead."

Kate spoke with quick exasperation: "Lee,

you're a thick-headed, stubborn. . . ." Her voice broke off.

". . . mule's the word," he cut in.

"It's getting worse." Her face turned grave, serious. "I'm just trying to help. You know what happened to Johnny Strack. That's the first killing . . . that starts it. It's a wonder there haven't been more. They pistol-whipped an old man today when he tried to hide a ring. The passengers gave me good descriptions."

"Yeah." Lee shrugged. "I know . . . three men wearing flop-brimmed hats, red bandanas for masks, shotguns . . . jeans . . . shirts . . . boots . . . spurs . . . hands . . . feet."

"You're making fun of me." Her voice was sharp.

"Anything but," he said grimly. "That description would fit a hundred men. Nothing to go on. All I can say is, I don't believe in big talk. Better do something first, but they tell me my time is running out."

"I'm worried," she said, frowning. "The government is making a payment next week to the Osages. It's for part of the tribe's Kansas land. It'll be in cash and come by stage to the agent's office here. It means a lot of money in the merchants' pockets. Yet. . . ."

"Might be a good idea to run it."

All at once she was indignant. "So everybody will know?"

"That's why it's a good idea."

"You're not telling me how to run my paper, Lee Rand. You can't even handle your own office!" Her head snapped up and she whirled around abruptly, and, with her eyes flashing indignation, she walked away from him.

Lee moved down the street, heading for the two-room house along the creek where Tip Wall, his deputy, lived. As he came up, he saw a horse fiddling in a corral, heard the *tunk-tunk* of axe blade against wood, the strokes steady, powerful. They quit suddenly, and, when Lee stepped behind the house, a broad-backed man was stacking wood. The man looked up, a sheepish grin on his bearded face.

"Hello, Lee," he said.

"Looks like you're feeling all right again." Lee grinned, eyes on the two-bladed axe, the pile of fresh-cut chunks thick as a man's leg. "Hope you're ready to ride. I need you."

Tip Wall dropped his chin and coughed faintly. It seemed an odd weakness in so powerfully built a man. "And me still with the miseries," Wall complained, his voice strained. "Just trying to toughen up so I can

126

ride." He was slow-moving, slow-talking, and Lee had found him sullen at times, yet reliable in a stolid way. His head was a blunt, bushy-browed wedge resting on thickly muscled neck and shoulders.

"Hear about Johnny Strack?"

Wall shook his enormous head. "Nobody ever comes here but you."

Lee told him about the robbery and Wall muttered: "That's bad . . . killing."

"That's not all," Lee snapped. "If we don't come up with something soon, we're out of a job."

Wall was staring, an uneasy look in the shallow eyes. Groaning, he picked up an armload of wood. When he straightened, there was a dogged expression in his wide face. "Nothin' I can do," he grumbled. "Maybe in a few weeks."

"Time's runnin' out." Resentment was running through Lee, and he said coldly: "Too late then. I figure a man able to swing that hog-killer can hold down the office. Help a little."

"You . . . you doubting that I'm a sick man?" Wall stiffened and a meaty hand slid across a piece of stove wood.

Lee felt his muscles grow rigid, saw the streaky wildness in the eyes. "A sick man . . . no." Then Lee said it, blurted it out: "You're faking!"

Wall's lips were working. His hand clamped onto the chunk of wood as he threw down his load.

Lee saw the swinging club. He ducked, heard the swift, vicious *swish* pass his face. Wall whirled, came at him, wild-eyed, muttering, feet stamping. And Lee knew. "Remember, you're sick!" he yelled.

Something smashed and tore into his shoulder, rocked him back. Wall's broad body was dancing crazily before his eyes. He lunged and drove his fist into the hard belly, heard the quick, throaty grunt. Lee's left arm seemed numb, useless. Wall was whipping the club again. Lee threw up his right arm. As he moved, the world seemed to explode. Daylight faded. His feet couldn't find bottom. He was struggling up, but he couldn't see through the closed-in darkness.

Light broke raggedly across Lee's eyes later when he groaned and awoke, flat on his back. He stirred. Pain whipped through his left shoulder and arm in steady, pulsing waves. His head throbbed, felt knotted, swollen. His shirt was ripped and bloody. It came to him slowly that it was almost dark. The fight, he remembered, had started in full light. Teeth clenched, he pushed up on his right hand, looked around. Tip Wall was gone. So was his horse from the corral.

With a grunt, he wobbled up, head whirling. But it took a while before he could get up and walk. He kept thinking desperately of the Army cot and bucket of water in the back room of the office. Dragging toward town, he realized that he didn't want to be seen like this. It was pride and it was business. A beat-up sheriff already down on his luck wouldn't draw sympathy in hard-crusted Antelope Springs. There would be questions that Lee couldn't answer, and something far back in his mind told him that he'd need plenty of time.

When he came to the first row of board houses, he angled in behind them, cut down a can-littered alley. Evening's first lights blinked like yellow, groping fingers. They made a flickering, wavering pattern to his glazed eyes and the rough ground kept rolling under his feet. It seemed a long time before he heard the growing murmur of Main Street. Then the corral loomed up, the shape of his horse high-shouldered in the half light. The gelding's head moved. Against the barked poles, Lee caught the rustle of loose hay being nuzzled. He was reaching for the blacked-out rear door of the office when it occurred to him that he hadn't thrown in the hay.

He fumbled awkwardly for the edge of the cot, found it. Pitching forward, he heard a cautious grunt from the corner. Fear touched the back of his neck. He tried to lunge up, but his muscles were all water.

"Maybe you hurt?"

Relief swam through Lee as he recognized the low-toned voice of Charlie Big Sick. A match scraped and Lee saw the old Indian's leather-brown eyes, questioning, troubled. Charlie lighted a coal-oil lamp.

"Ran into a chunk of hickory," Lee groaned. "Tip Wall was swinging it." He saw Big Sick digging into his buckskin bag. After a moment, he pulled out a handful of brown, wrinkled leaves.

"You sleep," the Osage ordered. "Me fix. You beat up purty bad." He drew a long-bladed knife from under his blanket. With quick slashes, he cut off Lee's torn shirt. Through bleary eyes Lee saw him fashioning wide strips. Shuffling, the full-blood waddled over to the water bucket on the low wooden bench and soaked the cloths. Lee jerked when Big Sick layered the bruised shoulder and arm with the leaves, bound them loosely with the dripping bandages into a cool, soppy poultice.

"What's this?" Lee grumbled.

"Big medicine," the Indian grunted, pleased. "Work on Indian . . . white man, too."

All at once the room was swaying strangely. Big Sick's blanketed shape seemed to turn and tilt, out of focus. "We're going fishing, Charlie," Lee heard his own voice, high and hoarse, with the swirling, streaky blackness shuttering him in again. . . .

It was daylight beyond the cheap, cracked window shades and Lee was staring at the ceiling. He kept remembering the ghostly, towering form of the old Indian scuffling across the thin flooring. But Big Sick had gone. And clear in Lee's mind was the mean cut of Tip Wall's bearded mouth as he swung the murderous sledge. With it, Lee felt an urgency, a sense of lost time. The shock traveled slowly through him. This was press day for Kate Trinkle's newspaper and maybe he was already too late.

Frowning, Lee half turned on the cot, expecting a sickening rush of pain. His arm responded stiffly, with an ache that flogged his entire body. Sweat dampened his forehead. But he could move. He sat up and stared down at the crudely bandaged arm in pleased amazement. Big Sick didn't prescribe according to the white man's medical books, but there was a looseness in the arm and shoulder muscles now. And he was hungry. Cautiously he stood up, looking around him.

He saw the scarred bureau by the washstand. Dizziness hit him again when he rummaged for a clean shirt. Afterward, he stepped out into the blazing sun, blinking. He hooked the swollen left hand in his belt, yanked down the hat to cover his bruised face. Slow-footed, he angled down the street to the printing office. He felt the hurry in the place as he went inside.

Miss Kate was reading a galley proof on the office counter. In the rear, a stoop-shouldered printer was hand-setting type. She looked up reluctantly. He saw her eyes take him in, widen with astonishment.

"Lee!" she burst out. "What happened?" The concern in her voice turned him awkward, and his weakness slid back.

"Horse fell on me," he said, trying to appear casual. "You gone to press yet?"

"Just getting ready . . . soon as I read these proofs."

Lee swallowed hard, knowing she'd storm. "I wish you'd run that story about the Indian payment," he said quickly.

"I thought we went over that," she answered in a low, stubborn tone.

"Listen," Lee argued. "You didn't give me a chance to finish." Kate stood very straight, her mouth firm, and he noticed the smooth, white column of her throat. "It sounds crazy, but that money is bait. They'll read about it in the paper. It'll bring them out in the open where. . . ."

". . . they can get it," she snapped. "I won't do it!"

"But I'll stop 'em!"

For an instant, he saw an odd change in her eyes. A brief uneasiness, but there was mockery there, too, and suddenly he was fighting a resentful anger.

"You wouldn't stand a chance," she said, and he was aware of her steady stare. "You can't ride and it's only two days till the payment comes in."

"We'll see," Lee gritted. He was turning when a tall, bony figure filled the doorway.

With a wide sweep of his hand, Tracy Bullard lifted his shiny plug hat and smiled grandly for Miss Kate. Lee felt a grudging annoyance at the courtesy. He started to move on, but Bullard's eyes were scanning his bruised face and Lee flushed.

"Why, Sheriff!" Bullard said. "You've been hurt."

Miss Kate spoke up before Lee could answer. "A horse fell with him."

"You mean on him," Bullard said skeptically. "I'm sorry to hear it, sir. Particularly at this time. With you in the middle of a campaign and hunting the hills for criminals. But you still have help. There's Mister Wall."

"Used to," Lee growled. "He's gone. Left town."

"Oh." Bullard made a clucking sound. "Too bad, sir."

"Don't sir me! You know damn' well you're glad I'm short-handed."

Bullard pulled back, startled. He swung his glance from Lee to Kate and back again. "Why," he sputtered, straightening, "I was simply expressing my regret."

"Sure," Lee said with loud sarcasm, "and I'll bet you can tell me where Wall hid out."

"I don't understand. How would I know . . . where?"

"Duff Shaner's ranch." It was a wild guess, Lee realized, and Bullard's expression didn't change. Lee faced Miss Kate. "Maybe you'll run that in your paper."

Her face flamed and he knew that he shouldn't have said it. Sore in a hot, raging way, he turned his back and went outside. He walked to the office, weak, disgusted, hurting. Soon hunger rolled through him and he plodded to a café, ate hurriedly, and came back.

When Charlie Big Sick shuffled in, Lee growled from the cot: "It's no use. Won't be any fishing party . . . no bait." He wondered why he even mentioned it to the Indian who was too old to help, yet it felt good to talk to somebody who'd listen. Big Sick looked puzzled, and Lee said: "Indian payment was coming in. All cash. I figured a story in the paper would flush out the outlaw band with the greeners. I'd planned to be on the stage when it left Yellow Hand. But Miss Kate won't oblige. Thinks it's better to keep it quiet. Maybe she's right."

"How you catch 'em?"

"Charlie, I'm through. It'll be up to Shaner . . . later."

"Maybe."

Big Sick's grunting voice came drowsily to Lee. He was almost asleep when the Osage went out, the cane tapping. It floated in Lee's mind that he'd have to go on trying. That the only style he knew was to ride the fat off a horse. About dark, he heard the Indian's rapping approach. He stayed only a few seconds, and Lee, too bone weary to talk, drifted back to sleep.

Lee got up long after daybreak, his feet dragging with dread when he thought of another pounding ride. He was belting on the heavy gun when he saw the newspaper.

It was spread out by his hat and he wondered why he hadn't noticed it before. "Now Charlie's even delivering the paper," he muttered. He was grabbing the hat as his eyes caught the headline. The heavy black lines jumped in his vision: **INDIAN PAYMENT DUE THIS WEEK**. There was the story under it, just as he'd asked Kate to run it.

The gun slapping against his thigh, he crossed to the *War Chief* office. Only the bent-shouldered printer was there, and Lee felt a twinge of disappointment.

"Where's Kate?" he asked.

The printer looked up from his type case. "Gone. Early this morning."

"Where to?"

"Said somethin' about hiring a fast rig." He grinned indulgently. "You know Kate, she's tight-lipped."

As he rode away, it kept drumming through Lee's mind that things were shaping up now. He'd ride to Yellow Hand, board the stage tomorrow morning. He realized the plan was far from foolproof. What if they didn't take the bait? But the story had said $15,000. That was a fat fortune out here, where you rode your heart out for $20 a month, biscuits, and bunk. With a hard, jaw-tightening soberness, he thought of laughing Johnny Strack. Lee remembered to pick up his carbine, to jam his brush jacket with shells, before he tramped stiffly to the corral. He'd already lost half a day's ride.

Topping the first long-running ridge, it struck him as odd that Big Sick hadn't been in today. Funny, how the old Osage got around. "Maybe," Lee chuckled to himself, "he's out fishing."

Night's hazy, blue-black shadow had begun to dissolve and a cooling wind brushed down the last line of the hills as Lee caught sight of Yellow Hand. It was a one-street town on the flat back of the browning prairie. He had eaten a cold supper at a relay stage station, rolled in his blankets, and, in a few hours, had struck out north. He had made it just in time, too, he realized. Already, Hank Bristow, Johnny Strack's relief, was hustling up four horses from the back corral of the livery barn. Lee rode over where Bristow was hitching up.

"You've got another passenger," Lee said.

"I like company," Bristow said dryly. He was short and thick and square-shouldered. "Anybody with a gun."

Lee grinned. "I can push if you get stuck." He stabled the exhausted gelding, pulled off saddle, blanket, and bridle, and rubbed him down with some hay. Then, climbing aboard the stage, he threw the sweaty gear in the top rack. He slid the carbine between them. When Bristow trotted the coach to the express office, the fat agent came out of the office. He tossed up a black metal box. Bristow caught it deftly, let it *clang* down at his feet.

"Look sharp," the agent said with an old man's plain worry.

"Reckon I know." Bristow laughed flatly. "We got passengers, too." He was staring across at the hotel, still waiting. There was a steady tapping noise, and Lee swung around.

Enormous in his draped blanket, Charlie Big Sick was shuffling across the planked porch. His feathered hat jerked as he took the steps. Lee saw a half grin on the copper-hued face.

"You . . . here?" Lee asked, amazed. "How come?"

"Fishing." Big Sick rolled his muddy eyes at the sky and the string of fish hooks rattled faintly on his hat. "Sign about right. Looking better all the time." As Big Sick clambered inside, grunting, the stagecoach sagged on its leather braces.

Lee snorted as Bristow said: "One more."

Angrily Lee looked around. Kate Trinkle was hurrying down the porch steps. Her eyes were bright with a held-in excitement as she came up. "You, too?" Lee glowered down at her.

"Charlie told me," she said defiantly. "You can't stop me. I bought a ticket."

"There'll be trouble," he warned her. "Get back to the hotel. You tell her, Hank."

Head high, Kate went to the stage step, climbed in. Hank Bristow shrugged, pained, disgusted. "Women!" he growled. He swore at the leaders. They lunged and the stage rolled from Yellow Hand in a churning, kicked-up dust.

Back stiff against the seat, Lee was thinking ahead bleakly to the timber crowding the rutted road where it scarred the great-humped hills. Those were places where Bristow would have to slow down, with a man sticking out on the high seat like a shooting gallery duck.

When the passengers got out to stretch at the noon relay stop, Kate kept her back turned to Lee while he helped Bristow change the horses. Soon they were rumbling across rolling prairie. In the distance, Lee could see the beginning of the black, ragged timber on the slopes, and he felt a growing dread. Before long the grade steepened abruptly.

Bristow laid a troubled glance on the thickening timber.

Lee shifted his carbine. "Hit 'em a lick!" he yelled.

Bristow's whoop rang with the whip, and the four horses plunged up the wooded hill. They racketed up its stony footing and crossed a clearing. Lee breathed easier. Maybe he had guessed wrong, better if he had with Kate and the old Indian along. Here the land buckled and tossed, the road bending, looping.

All at once, Bristow raised his voice. "Get down!"

Lee felt a stunning jar. There was a loud *crack* as the wheels struck again, bounced high, and fell with a lurching jolt that shook Lee violently. He had to let go the carbine to hang on. Bristow was cursing in his ear, sawing furiously on the long reins. Over his shoulder, Lee saw the cut logs strung across the road behind them and, twisting around, the piled timber short ahead blocking the stagecoach. At the edge of the blackjacks three riders waited, shotguns slanted. Too late, Lee saw his carbine rolling loosely around his feet. Now Bristow had stopped the stage.

The horsemen moved in close. "Get out!" a man called. He was broad in the saddle, with blunt hands. He jogged his greener at Bristow and Lee. "Get 'em up . . . high," he growled. The others spread out. They wore long brush jackets, flop-brimmed hats, red bandannas across their faces.

Sick all through, Lee saw Kate and Big Sick step out stiffly. Kate's face looked white, scared, but still stubborn. She gave Lee the sharp edge of her condemning eyes.

"Throw that box down!" the heavy man called up to Bristow.

He hesitated, looking up. Lee, remembering Johnny Strack, grunted helplessly: "Go ahead, Hank. I'll get it back."

With a dogged reluctance, Bristow nudged the strongbox out with the toe of his boot. It dropped close to the front wheel, bounced back under the braces. The big rider cursed nervously.

"You," he ordered, jabbing the shotgun at Big Sick, "get under there and drag it out!"

Deliberately the old medicine man stiffened, glaring. "White man go to hell," he grunted. "Indian money."

"You mean was," the rider jeered.

"Go . . . cut out the talk," the middle horseman broke in with authority, voice muffled behind the mask.

His partner swung down. Holding the reins, he clumped to the stage. When he straightened up with the box and shotgun cradled in his arms, he was very close to Big Sick, contemptuously close. Silent, stone-faced, Big Sick stood with his hands brushing his hat.

Lee caught a glimmer in the muddy eyes, the sudden decision tightening the thick mouth. Lee knew then that he had to say something, anything.

"Hold on!" he hollered. "You. . . ."

The big man was turning to his horse as Lee yelled. Lee saw the two riders jerk his way. But Big Sick's hand had flicked out. In a motion astonishingly fast for so huge a man, he skinned off the fish hooks, tagged them on the tail of the gunman's brush jacket as he stepped away, eyes on Lee.

The outlaw hit the saddle and suddenly screamed in pain. Box and shotgun flew out and the horse spooked, bucking wildly. The rider lost his one good stirrup, grabbed for leather, missed. He bounced off in a rolling tangle, the bandanna sliding down. Lee saw Duff Shaner's pain-twisted face. Then the boss man was swinging on Big Sick, and Lee saw his chance.

Lee ducked low, digging for the carbine. He swung it up, squeezed the trigger, heard the slug *thud*. There was a booming roar in his ears. The rider was swaying. His arms slacked and the gun spilled down.

"Duff . . . Tip!" A voice shouted — Tracy Bullard's stricken, pleading voice.

But Tip Wall was spurring away, and Duff Shaner was wobbling up, a pistol in his hand. Lee's bullet hit him in the chest. He pitched forward, knees buckling.

He didn't get up.

All Lee could hear was the fading beat of Tip Wall's horse on the stony slope. "He won't be back," Hank Bristow said.

When Lee looked down, Kate was staring up at him. Her face was still white, but there was something there that he hadn't noticed before.

"Next time," Lee said to her in a half-swallowed voice, "you won't be so stubborn."

"Maybe," she said stubbornly, "you'll just have to get used to it."

Ponderously Big Sick was shuffling past Tracy Bullard's recumbent form, over to Duff Shaner. With a grin, he picked up the strongbox. Then he stooped, his hand jerking. When he stood up, he was dangling a string of fishhooks.

"Me catch 'em," he grunted, pleased and proud, and Lee knew that Antelope Springs would be telling this story for many years to come. "Two fish . . . plenty big."

A MATTER OF BLOOD

Riding into San Miguel at this hour, he found the narrow streets deserted. Wood smoke from piñon fires laid a sweet scent across the crisp evening air. The hoof beats of his gaited saddler sounded unusually loud in the stillness. A scrawny dog ran out barking and quickly slunk away from the sharp hoofs.

At a small adobe house near the end of the street, he saw that her lamp burned in the window. Good. She was alone. He was tired after being in the saddle most of the day. She would be glad to see *Don* Antonio Ramón Gallegos, son of a *hacendado*. It was his superior air, he supposed, a man of his blood, why men deferred to him and women were impressed with him.

He rode around to the rear of the house. Dismounting, he opened the gate of a low shed and led his mount in and gave it water in a bucket from a barrel, unsaddled, and tied the horse to a halter at the feed trough under the shed. From a pile of corn in a corner, he took an armful of ears and left them for the horse. Then, picking up rifle, pack, and saddlebags, he went out and shut the gate behind him. Strolling to the gate in the wall that enclosed the rear of the house, he rang a little bell hanging there, rang it four times. He must let her know of his coming. *Don* Antonio had manners.

Smiling to himself, he opened the gate and stepped inside.

As he expected, Elena was waiting on the patio, which was ablaze with flowers. A brightly plumed parrot squawked nonsense from a cage under the low *ramada*. Her one pet. Why not a cat or a dog? That god-damned parrot. He couldn't stand it. She had trained it to say "Forgive me, Holy Father" and "Jesus loves you." Absurd.

He crossed over, and she said: "*Don* Antonio" — she was always quite respectful — "you are back sooner than I expected. Why?"

"My work," he replied mysteriously, a little irritated that she should ask about affairs that didn't concern her. That was a woman for you, any woman — always prying. He'd told her nothing. That way, he took on added importance in her credulous eyes. Actually he was only an unofficial scout for the Sonoran government, paid only when he had valuable information. He was to meet a company of *federales* early in the morning and guide them to where the notorious Indian bandit, El Lobo, was said to be camped in the foothills of the Sierras some miles away. A location he had learned by chance from a drunken bandit in a *cantina*.

"I need to be up and gone by daylight," he told her. "I have a long ride ahead of me."

"Meanwhile," she said, "the night is young. I will feed you and then. . . ."

She kissed him on his bearded cheek without particular passion and led him inside. Despite the wear of her profession, Elena had managed to look years younger than she was. Possibly, he'd thought, because she was a devout Roman Catholic and confessed regularly and therefore assumed she was forgiven. She spoke often of the "Heavenly Father" and the "blessed saints," talk which always left him uncomfortable. She wasn't a good-looking woman, her features were too flat and plain for beauty, but her voice was soft, and she was dark-haired, with the blackest of eyes and a clean, sturdy body, and she knew how to take a man in her arms and make him forget the rigors of a long ride across the desert with the rhythm of her tireless strength. Her passion was steady and endless and workmanlike, of even more duration than his own, which he did not like to admit.

Elena was a full-blooded Tarahumari Indian, not a drop of Spanish blood in her, which would have elevated her to a *mestizo*. She endured life without complaint in a harsh land of desert and mountains dominated by those of haughty Spanish ancestry. He had never heard her laugh, but she was always evenly pleasant. Always the same. He prided himself on his macho image around women. To that, in late years, he had built on the rather mysterious air he'd adopted, which further intrigued them. One time a drunken whore in Bavispe, stepping beyond the bounds of manners with her upper-class customers, had asked him: "What do you do? Are you a secret agent of President Juárez?"

How he wished he were! He'd knocked her across her crib. "Don't ever ask me what I do. I cannot say. It is forbidden." Which it was in a way; in another it was all show. He was just the only son of a wealthy *hacendado,* a minor actor in the cast of characters changing the face of Mexico. Not a major player, as he wished. That would all be changed tomorrow, when the *federales* caught El Lobo and his band. Well, let them think what they wished. It helped create the important image he fancied.

Now Elena took him into her bedroom, past a tiny altar in the corner with a statue of the Virgin Mary, and laid out his things with care. Somehow the mere sight of the altar always bothered him. It was uncanny. He was not superstitious. But he stepped past it fast and did not look again. When in bed with her, he studiously avoided it, as if the Virgin Mary were watching him and questioning his faithless way of life.

"I have some warm supper left," she said. "Come on."

He took a bottle of tequila from his pack and followed her to the little kitchen. Like the bedroom, it was neatly kept. There she poured water into a pan on a bench by the door and handed him a bar of soap that smelled of cheap roses and a towel. He washed the dust from his face and neck and hands, dried, and opened the tequila, and set it on the small table, already neatly set, waiting for her to pour the drinks, which she did, and handed him his glass.

"My house is your house," she said, and downed the hot tequila as if it were a drink of spring water, her Indian face showing not the slightest reaction.

He blinked at the fiery stuff and swallowed hard, forcing it down, somewhat amused at her. He had never seen her drunk. He wondered if she had an iron stomach, in contrast to most Indians he'd seen, who drank the vilest mescal until dead drunk, then became inert mounds of flesh sprawled outside *cantina* doorways or in the street. Was that because Elena had one purpose in life, which was to survive it as an Indian? She was, he admitted, a strong woman of much inner strength, yet of lower status put on earth to serve her superiors.

They drank some more, Elena never changing her expression. Now and then they would talk of earthy things: whether the river was up or down, and would the Apaches come again this year when the moon was full, and would the people of San Miguel have good corn and bean and chili crops, only to have the river flood the fields during the summer rainy season? Most of the time, however, they just sat there and drank.

Then she put food before him and, in her own subtle way, urged him to eat, although by now the drinks had taken away the edge of his hunger and his thoughts were only of her in bed. If he didn't eat, she said, he would be sick in the morning and couldn't make the long ride. With the drinks, he thought she would ask him where he was going, but she did not. *She knew her place.*

He ate, not to please her, because he wouldn't have an Indian telling him what to do, but because he knew it was best for him, the beans, the tortillas, and the odd-looking squash. No beef, as he was accustomed to at the *hacienda*. Her food was plentiful, but not as tasty as he was used to. She cooked like an Indian, and Indians were not good cooks. In the mind of a Spanish-blooded *hacendado* such as himself, the owner of acres as far as the eye could see, many *peónes* tilling the soil and gathering the crops, Indians would eat or drink anything. Why? Because they were primitive people without the finer sensibilities of the Spanish and other Europeans, such as the Italians, without art or music. He didn't like the French and would not include them because they had tried to install Maximilian as Emperor of Mexico, but President Juárez had taken care of that. Yet the Indians were still here; they had survived Spanish torture, rape, and disease. They would be here forever because they were part of the cauterized earth, and because they were the color of the earth. He stopped himself. The drinks were making him philosophize too much.

After supper, they had another drink, and another, and then she led him off to the bedroom. Without making a fuss, she removed his clothing and boots, and, when he was naked, she led him to her bed.

He was drunk and getting sleepy, but he still wanted her. When he opened his eyes at her touch, she stood naked beside him. In the sallow light of the lamp, her skin was indeed the color of earth. His eyes lingered over her. At that instant she struck him as a benign Aztec goddess, towering over him, and he might have been a *conquistador*.

She broke the spell by slipping in beside him and taking him in her arms and sweeping him away on a buoyant journey that never seemed to end. Finally he slept.

Hours later, it must have been, that something woke him. A faint sound in the room. He turned over and saw her kneeling at the foot of the altar, naked except for a rebozo over her bowed head. A candle cast a cone of amber light. She was murmuring words he couldn't catch, perhaps in her Indian tongue, her gentle voice remindful of a dove's cooing.

He drifted off to sleep again, feeling a deep contentment. Several times he felt her body by his.

Sunlight streaming through the little window onto his naked skin jarred him awake. He sat up with a jerk, his head pounding. It was late, too late. He should have been in the saddle at daybreak, riding to his rendezvous with the *federales*. Why had she let him oversleep? Hadn't he told her he had to leave at first light? No excuse for that. Another example of Indian stupidity.

She lay sleeping beside him, faced to the wall, her long, gleaming hair spread over her like a black veil, her breathing even and serene, a picture of peaceful sleep.

The sight aroused his anger. He kicked her buttocks. "Get up!" he shouted at her. "I have to go. Make me some breakfast *pronto*."

She woke at once and said nothing, impassively revealing neither surprise nor hurt anger at the hard kick.

"I told you I had to be gone by daylight!" he shouted at her again.

She said nothing, but shrugged into a loose dress and padded on bare feet into the kitchen.

Groaning, he sat on the side of the bed and held his bursting head with both hands, thinking the *federales* would consider him untrustworthy, just the spoiled son of a *hacendado,* instead of the responsible person he wished them to see, with vast political opportunities in the future as Mexico changed under Juárez. He tried to summon some plausible excuses for being late: sudden illness, a lame horse, lost his way, and discarded them at once. It would be obvious that he had a dreadful hangover. His horse couldn't be lame or he shouldn't ride him at all, and he couldn't have lost his way because he knew the countryside better than the *federales,* to whom he had given the most exact directions. No. His only recourse now was to ride as fast as he could and hope the *federales* were still waiting. After all, they couldn't find El Lobo's camp without him. He would make no lame excuses; that would make him look weak. If they asked questions, he would only shrug and lead them on.

By the time he had dressed and washed, she still didn't have his breakfast ready. He was about to shout at her again and call her deserved vile names when she told him to come to the table. She poured him strong coffee, which he drank in gulps, and served him generous helpings of eggs with green chilis and fresh tortillas. The usual fare she'd always prepared for him. Indian food.

Yet somehow heartening this morning. His monstrous headache receded. He ate wolfishly.

Rising from the table, he quickly gathered his pack and saddlebags and rifle and came back to the kitchen and put a single *centavo* on the table. It was niggardly, not nearly enough for all the generous hospitality he'd enjoyed. He knew it; she knew it. But to him she was only an Indian, a whore to boot, beneath him because of his vaunted Spanish blood. The way he looked at it, he honored her merely by coming here.

She glanced at the *centavo,* but showed not one flicker of disappointment or anger, her plain Indian features as unreadable as stone, symbolic of her strength. She would have expressed no more emotion if he'd left her nothing. For what could she have done about it? Nothing. Neither would she beg. He knew that, also.

There was not even a good bye between them as he lurched out. No word, no touch, no gesture, although he had been here a number of times before. Inwardly the pittance of the one *centavo* incensed and hurt her to be treated so shamefully, as if she were dirt and far beneath his polished black boots. But the *alcalde* would be here during *siesta,* when the village grew quiet and not many were about to see him come to her house. He was a kindly man, fat and genial, always laughing, always generous, a relief from *Don* Antonio's cruel stinginess, done to remind her of her proper place and his proud Spanish blood.

This was her life, which she had survived by will and a strong body and, above all, her devout faith, which had sustained her since she'd run away as a thirteen-year-old slave from a wealthy *hacendado* in southern Sonora. Many times, looking back at her early survival, she had divined that God had made up with mercy and guidance for what the young innocents suffered. She loved the Holy Father and she loved the Virgin Mary and sweet Jesus. Her favorite mind-picture, one that rose before her often when she was alone and gave her strength, was of Mary and baby Jesus, a scene she dearly loved. They would all be with her always. She was not afraid.

In a secret place in the wall behind a picture of Jesus, she put money away now and then for when she grew old and could work no more. She would place the *centavo* there for safekeeping. Sunday she would give it to the church to cleanse her soul. The mere thought made her feel better, and her anger and hurt vanished.

At that moment, as *Don* Antonio moved past the parrot's cage, the bird suddenly squawked: "Jesus loves you!"

Startled, he cursed it with fervor and hurried on.

Elena, watching, allowed a little smile to crease her impassive face. For her it was a very big smile. *Don* Antonio had talked in his sleep of leading the *federales* to El Lobo's camp and of the acclaim he would receive. Although she was awake at dawn, she had let him continue his drunken sleep. Later, she had purposely delayed his breakfast. El Lobo, the notorious Indian bandit, would be gone by now, safely into the rugged Sierras. The *federales* would be displeased with *Don* Antonio because he was late and the bandits had escaped.

God was merciful in many ways. Sometimes life was just. She smiled again.

THE HANGROPE GHOST

Chris Frazier left the yellow-grassed prairie and dipped downgrade along the slanting wagon road to Rocky City. Below the rim of the round-top hills, the wind was shut out, and he felt the sharp edge of the sun boring against his back. Rounding a bend, he saw dust boiling ahead, heard a dog's thin yelp.

Whimpering hounds roamed the road, trailing a shuffling, thick-set man, and Chris recognized Joe Big Cloud. Despite the steamy heat, a red bandanna was knotted around the Indian's head. He wore a blue flannel shirt, with rusty trousers hitched up loosely under the flapping shirttails. Pulling even, Chris called — "Howdy!" — and waved.

Big Cloud's broad head tilted slowly, the copper face shiny with sweat, expression-less. *"H-uh,"* he grunted and jerked straight. Down the road Chris felt himself grinning. He hadn't expected more of a greeting, for

Big Cloud couldn't talk. He was dead. The liveliest dead Injun in America.

Rocky City's Main Street was almost brooding under the summer sun's harsh glare. High-fronted buildings shielded the boardwalk from the wind-whipped prairie. In front of the tree-shadowed trader's store, ponies stood heads down, switching flies. And in the doorway of the flimsy bank building Chris saw a tall man whose flinty gaze covered the street.

Mayor Del Evans waved from his one-room law office and Chris reined across. Evans was hunched over a paper-littered desk. Bookshelves cramped the place. An old Sharps buffalo gun slanted against the wall and a few fat shells reared up on the desk. Evans had taken the gun in on a fee, Chris remembered.

As Chris swung down, he noticed the big man angling up the street. He was swaggering a little and now Chris saw the two tied-down holsters. The man had paused at the store, peering up, searching. Suddenly his hand blurred and a gun exploded. It was a darting draw, made with a swiftness you'd remember. Ponies spooked back as a bird fluttered down and plopped in the street. Chris felt a growing resentment at senseless killing. Then he saw Evans's gray, woolly head canted from the office door.

"What's the ruckus, Chris?" He stepped out, thin and stooped, wrinkled face squinting in the brightness.

"Somebody got a bird. Hard up for a target, I'd say."

The big man had moved past the store, ignoring cowpunchers, townsmen, and Indians gawking from the stores. Evans grunted in disgust. "Anything that moves is a target for Sid Breen. He's the new marshal. Pinky Adams had to quit. Gettin' too old."

Down the street, men still stood in doorways, gazing at the tiny bundle of feathers in the dust. But Chris noticed, too, that nobody ventured out or raised a protesting voice. Breen's slow, arrogant prowl seemed answer enough.

"He's comin' here," said Evans. "Stick around and meet our new city lawman. All guts and guns. He's got the town buffaloed. They're even afraid to fire him." His tone was mocking, bitter, and Chris sensed the old man's indignation. As mayor of Rocky City, Evans necessarily combined an erratic law practice with the call of gratuitous civic services. In a land where the ability to recite statutes was looked upon with slack-jawed awe, he was considered the local authority

160

on legal matters. He was fair and always gave the Indians a square shake. A deputy marshal years back, hard-handed ways riled him.

As Breen paced closer, Chris saw that he was even bigger than he had first thought. Sloping shoulders wedged thickly on a wide-boned frame and he walked with a deliberate arrogance.

"Hello, Breen," Evans said tonelessly. "Looks like you still have your shootin' eye."

"I've always got it," Breen agreed, and moved on.

A moment later, dogs yipped up the street and Chris turned. Joe Big Cloud and his pack were dusting into town, the long-eared, curious hounds sniffing the strange smells. Chris counted about twenty and noticed a gaunt-ribbed female with a pup wallowing behind on stubby legs.

Breen halted. "Now who'n the hell's that?"

"Just an old full-blood," Evans drawled. "He happens to prefer dogs to people. I guess he's got good reasons."

"Damned nuisance, them hounds," Breen snapped. His voice was rough, and Chris caught an odd irritation in the black-browed eyes. "They're disturbin' the peace around here." Breen stood very still, deliberating. "Oughta be run out of town," he growled,

161

and, when Chris swung around, he saw the thick lips curl with a thin amusement. The wide shoulders jerked and a rough hand slid toward a holster. The pup yelped once as the slug struck. Then it rolled into the scattering pack and fell dead. Big Cloud whirled, the dark eyes glinting dangerously. Breen flipped the gun with satisfaction, holstered it, grinning with a sly, wicked pleasure.

Anger stirred Chris, and his voice was flat and hard. "You didn't have to do that, Breen. He wasn't botherin' anybody. If you want gun play, pick on somebody who packs a gun. Not a poor damned outcast Injun."

"Yeah?" Breen whirled, scowling. "You're like all of 'em in this damned town," he complained. "Hire a marshal, then you want him to go easy. Hell, that ain't my way. I say a bunch of wild hounds is a public nuisance." He turned back to the Indian, jerking one hand. "Get that mangy litter out of town. Bring 'em back and I'll shoot every flea-bit mutt in the pack."

Big Cloud was motionless. But Chris read the puzzled hurt in the black eyes glaring from under the bandanna hood.

"Go on!" Breen exploded "Move!"

"He don't understand much white man's talk," Chris cut in. "Anyway, he's dead . . .

he can't talk."

Breen pivoted around, a stolid disbelief flushing the thick face. "What kind of crazy talk is this?" he demanded.

"Nothin's crazy about it," Chris said. "Years ago he had a fit and the Osages found him stiff in his teepee. They took him out on a hill, buried him Injun fashion, piled rocks around him. He came to and walked back to the village. But the tribe wouldn't have anything to do with him. Once they bury a man, he's dead."

"That's why he likes the hounds," Evans put in, enjoying Breen's bewilderment. "They stick by him and he feeds 'em what he can shoot. Damned good shot with a rifle, too. Old Joe's like a lonesome ghost prowlin' the hills. His own people won't talk to him. He's listed on the tribal rolls as deceased. Just comes in for tobacco. Maybe a little meat, if the huntin's poor. Always comes by the office. I'm his guardeen, as most folks say, or administrator."

From the corner of his eye Chris saw Big Cloud lift the blood-smeared puppy. But when he saw Breen watching him again, his expressionless face changed abruptly, leaving a cold, gleaming hatred. Then Big Cloud turned and scuffed down the road with a contemptuous, high-headed dignity, the restless hounds trailing.

"He'll be back," Chris said.

"Let him," Breen grunted. He draped his hands on the wide gun belt. "Next time he'll go back lonesome."

"Maybe . . . but ghosts don't scare."

Breen whipped straight and there was a dull, killing glare in the boring eyes. Chris still felt the remembering malice in the darkened gaze after the marshal had swung away, pacing slowly back toward the store.

"Listen, Chris," Evans pleaded. His gray face showed a worried soberness. "Watch yourself in town. You never pass up a fight, but don't cross Breen. I don't mean hide from him . . . that isn't your style. But you don't even pack a gun. . . ." His voice trailed off. "If you did . . . well, he'd kill you before you could lug it out. Last night he busted up a harmless little card game."

Chris shrugged. Afterward, when he walked to the store, the big man wasn't in sight. He ordered supplies and a shipment of barbed wire to be hauled from Elgin on the Kansas border.

"Be here in two weeks," the clerk told him. "You'll need a big wagon."

Chris nodded and moved outside. He was thinking of the new fencing regulations ordered by the agency, when he glanced across the street. He halted at once, stiffening.

Breen stood in the thin shadows, huge shoulders angled against a door frame. Staring through the shimmering heat waves, Chris felt the crawling, murmuring silence of the empty street, and an odd chill ran along his spine. There was the same steady flare again in the upslanted eyes and he found himself watching the wide hands, the low gun holsters. He was aware of his own unarmed condition, and Del Evans's low warning was a grimly cold caution. Then the big man stepped deliberately to the plank walk, passing on to make his swing to the other end of the street.

"Remember what I told you!" Evans called as Chris rode past the office. He grinned. "You're a cold-jawed cuss, but I want to keep you around."

"You don't have to tell me, Del," Chris answered, and wondered at his own soberness.

A yellow moon hung over the black-timbered hills when he rode up to the low-slung ranch headquarters. The crew had eaten and he caught their low talk drifting across the windless night as he walked to the cook shack to dig into supper's leftovers.

Sid Breen's powerful frame receded slowly from his mind. Grudgingly he admitted that Del was right. He'd be a fool to open the ball against the big man. But, he reflected, chewing slowly, you couldn't run from any man if he wanted trouble. No matter what your chances were. Del hadn't mentioned it today, but there was a reason why he never packed a gun any more.

He frowned, the food suddenly tasting flat in his mouth. He pushed up from the table and crossed to the house. He went to his gear-cluttered room, lifting the tall chimney from the coal-oil lamp and lighting it. The amber glow touched a scarred gun holster and belt hanging on the rough wall. He stared solemnly, feeling alone, remembering old scenes and a kindly, rugged, seamed face. The gun had belonged to Ben Frazier, his father, and Ben had fired it last.

An ancient bitterness, never healed, rolled back, and he stepped and jerked the holster down. Rubbing the worn leather, he was seeing old things, old places, as they used to be. Ben feeding and talking to the Osages. Listening to their complaints of short rations, sickness, dwindling game. His own hatred for hide hunters and poachers. Hunters had been sneaking across the reservation boundary, slaughtering deer and

166

turkey, and Ben, alone, had jumped a well-armed party.

Chris had found him afoot, reeling. And the Colt hadn't been fired since, at Ben's request. "Trouble," he'd told Chris in this same room. "A gun means trouble. Hang it up, Chris, for keeps."

The promise had been kept. Now. . . . Breen's amused face shaped again, hard and taunting, then faded slowly. Ben was right, Chris thought grimly, and Del Evans, too, with his old man's wise insight. He straightened, hung up the holster, and went outside to join the crew.

Rains had greeted the wild, rough hills, breaking the sticky summer heat. It was a bright, soft-winded day with all the prairie's smells fresh, heavy, pungent. Chris Frazier let the eager team set its own gait as he followed the rocky road to town for the load of wire. He figured to be back by noon so the crew could start that afternoon stringing wire across the bluestem grasslands leased from the agency.

Briefly he remembered Sid Breen, then dismissed the thought to regard the grass, quail whistling along the road, cattle grazing as dark moving blots against the cool green of the broad-backed land. Rattling down Main Street, he waved at Mayor Del Evans bent over his desk, and drove to the trader's store. The wire had arrived, and, with the puffing, round-faced clerk helping, he loaded the wagon. He was in the wagon seat, pulling the team around, when he saw that the clerk was still standing, his gaze riveted on the far end of the street.

Chris's eyes followed, took in Del Evans, halting in the middle of the street. Sid Breen striding across from the other side. Past them, Joe Big Cloud slowing, swinging around, with his shuffling dogs. Breen's hand lifted, a blunt, menacing wedge. Evans didn't move, and the marshal's head bobbed in short, furious jerks. Chris whipped his startled team into a run.

He saw Breen's thick arm whip up, chopping powerfully, and Evans sprawled, crashed on his back against one of the dogs. Its quick yowl of pain cut across the running rumble of team and wagon. Breen whirled at the racket, feet spread wide in a gunfighter's crouch. With a blind, sawing fury, Chris yanked the team back, raising dust and he was down and running.

Seeing Chris jump from the wagon, Breen whirled. Evans had pushed up.

"Stop it!" Chris shouted.

Instead, the big man took a long step and

clubbed Evans across the face. Big Cloud tried to wedge in between them, and Breen cuffed the Indian hard, ripping the bandanna loose. Big Cloud staggered, knees buckling him into the dust. Breen turned back to Evans and kicked viciously. Chris heard the sharp-toed boots slamming into ribs with meaty, sickening sounds.

Red haze danced before Chris's eyes as he plowed into Breen. He felt the man stagger, felt the powerful shoulder muscles knot as he whirled. For a moment Breen stared, the thick lips flattening. There was a killer's gleam in the cold eyes when he swung.

Chris saw the blow coming, and stepped aside and hit him in the belly. Breen grunted, swore angrily, and bored in. Chris ducked and slammed into him again, feeling the hard belly muscles sag. But still Breen came rushing in, swinging. His knuckles raked Chris's face, jaw.

Half blinded, Chris sagged to his knees, sucking in air. He lunged, crashed a solid blow to Breen's dodging head, and Breen went down. But Chris was too sick to follow through. Then he saw Breen jerk up, lash out. Too late Chris threw up his hands and tried to twist aside. The boots caught him full in the chest; there was a crushing pain, a roaring in his head. Through a streaky blackness he saw Breen rear, gulping wind. Breen's gaze steadied, decision working quickly across his bruised features. His hand moved for his gun as Chris heard Evans's weak, ragged call. "Keep that hand away, Breen! You've had your fun!"

Breen's hand twitched, hesitated. "He's got it comin' to him, by God! He butted in . . . you, too. You been talkin' behind my back, tryin' to get me fired."

"More than talk," admitted Evans, pulling up with a painful slowness. "The truth, Breen. You're too damned mean for this town."

Breen was still glaring, full of the will to kill, as Chris stumbled up. His head was clearing, and from the tail of his bleary vision he saw Big Cloud on his feet, silent, watching, the dogs whining.

"Don't touch Del again," Chris heard his own blunt voice say. The sickness was quitting his bruised stomach and he was surprised at the fight he still felt.

Breen laughed. "You stuck your nose in the last time," he said, and Chris caught a flat, final challenge in the taunting voice. "Now," Breen growled, "you'd better be packin' a gun when you hit town next time. I'll be here . . . waitin'."

As Breen wheeled and swaggered down

170

the street, Evans's low protest broke in: "Don't let him bait you, Chris. Can't you see it? He's itchin' for a gunfight. Anything to prod a man to draw. He jumped me, figurin' you'd take a hand. If it ain't you, it'll be somebody else, anybody. Now play it smart and stay away from town a while. This'll blow over."

"It won't." Chris shook his head. A dull certainty settled in him and he was thinking of the gun hanging in the ranch house. "I'll see you, Mayor," he said, and walked stiffly to the wagon. Evans was watching him with a bleak, slumped regret when he racketed out of town. He drove the team hard, whipping them down the level stretch and up the rough grade till the animals slacked against the steep pull.

Once he topped the crest of the hill, Chris eased up with the hard realization that Ben's promise was gone in the dust and blood of a swirling, wicked street brawl. He could never match Breen in a gun showdown, but there could be no other way, for he liked Del Evans. And he pitied Big Cloud, helpless, cast out by his own superstitious people and bullied by a white man.

It struck him as a strange fittingness that first Ben, then he, should scratch out the same way. Both caught taking up another man's fight. He was afraid now, and yet he wasn't afraid. It was the sure, straight course he knew the fight would run that rankled him, even hit his pride. He knew Breen's gun would fire first, because the man was faster. It was that simple. Driving through the noon brightness, he wondered if Ben had had the same awareness when he had ridden alone against the hunters.

The crew was waiting, six men, and he felt the temptation to ask them back with him. They'd slap leather and like it. But Breen's fun, he decided, wasn't worth a dead cowpuncher. "Start stringing it, boys," he said easily. "I'll be back later," and he went inside.

He buckled on the gun belt and felt the holster's unaccustomed weight. In his hands now the Colt was cumbersome, cold, strange. He slid it back and waited till the ponies' clatter on the rocky road pinched off, till the wagon's rattle died, then saddled up and rode away.

It was deep in the afternoon now with the sun lowering, the shadows fingering out. Rocky City, he sensed, was waiting for more than cooling dusk before it stirred. Where was Breen? Chris saw the livery stable was idle as he rode slowly down the silent street. Del Evans stood at his office door, old and stooped, with one thin hand pressed against bruised ribs.

He looked up, searching Chris's face. "Figured you'd be back," he said, his voice dull, lifeless. "He's down there . . . around the store."

Chris was passing on when Evans spoke up with a sharp and bitter desperation: "Don't get yourself killed over me. I don't matter."

Deliberately Chris shut out the voice, and his eyes took in the high-fronted shape of the store. He halted and scanned the dusty stretch with a troubled dread. Then he stepped down, letting the horse's reins trail, and moved ahead.

He felt his heart slugging against the tight wall of his chest, felt the stringy jerkiness of sore muscles. He swung his gaze across the deserted benches fronting the store, then back to the bank building. There was a flutter of movement inside the door. Swiftly the shadows broke, formed, and Sid Breen bulked at the entrance. Chris froze, his eyes tearing at Breen, standing so easy and relaxed, blunt hands hanging low, ready.

Chris's belly was quivering as he stepped to the center of the street. Might as well get it over with. He felt awkward, alone, and a chill raced up his stiff back. Breen appeared to uncoil, like a man playing a long-familiar game. His boots rapped the splintery walk, the tread sure, heavy, coming on. He reached the dusty rim of the street, and Chris stared back, watching the darkened face.

"That's far enough," Chris said. His voice sounded half choked, strange.

The marshal hauled up, eyes mocking. "Your mouth's still big," he sneered. "But we're through talkin'."

"Any time," Chris said. He was tense, waiting.

He saw Breen's eyes half close, saw the thick shoulders twitch slightly. But Breen's head had slanted up, the eyes wide with amazement as feet padded rapidly behind Chris. Breen's hands opened, the fingers fanning out, then slid for his guns. As Chris dug desperately for his own holster, the world exploded in his ears. It whoomed, roaring, rolling, and he smelled gunpowder, acrid, bitter.

The Colt still cold in his sweat-slippery hand, Chris froze, staring. Breen was sway-ing oddly. His glazed eyes looked stunned, bewildered. Blood was blotting the wide shirtfront. With a dim understanding, Chris whirled.

Big Cloud stood a few paces back. A big rifle, Evans's buffalo gun, Chris realized, was flat and smoking in the square, rough hands. Big Cloud's face was so much stone. But for a moment, the eyes were bright glowing coals. Turning, Chris saw that Breen was down, face buried in the dust, gun arm flung out.

A man moved on the edge of Chris's vision — Mayor Del Evans.

As cowpunchers and blanketed Indians ran from the store, Evans halted, looking down at Breen. Then he spun around and stared at Big Cloud with a startled expression of concern. He spoke in an overloud voice: "Breen was shooting at you, too, wasn't he?" Half defiantly, his glance whipped around. "Why, you're hit!"

Somebody made a strangling sound in the crowd, and Chris saw Big Cloud's face go blank. His eyelids snapped shut. The heavy Sharps clattered down. Big Cloud fell suddenly, ponderously, like a great brown bear, hands clapped across his round barrel of a chest.

For a moment, Del Evans gazed bleakly at the old Indian's silent shape. He swallowed hard. Eyes searching, he gestured at four Osages bunched at the crowd's edge. "Take

Big Cloud away," he said in a loud, flat tone. "Bury him again. This time it oughta take."

The Indians stood rooted, reluctant. When two men hurried from the store lugging a door, Evans waved the Indians over. Chris caught something urgent in the motion. Finally a tall brave edged the door alongside Big Cloud. Together the Osages lifted the lumpy bulk aboard and, grunting, moved down the street.

Chris followed at a stiff-legged walk. He looked down and felt a quickening interest, because there was no blood smearing Big Cloud's blue flannel shirt. When Del Evans closed in beside him, Chris turned with a question stirring his mind. But the mayor of Rocky City didn't appear to notice. He was looking straight ahead, the ghost of a smile creasing the corners of his wrinkled mouth. A whining dog trotted up. In one swooping lick, it ran a hot, red tongue across the thick face on the board.

One muddy-brown eye slitted open cautiously. "Sure nuff dead now," Big Cloud grunted happily, and winked. Then the copper-colored face was fixed again.

Chris felt himself grinning as he met Del Evans's defiant stare. Del was the law here — white man's law, anyhow. Chris got it. With Big Cloud dead by both the law of the

white man and the red, he should find right
happy hunting in the hills.

THE PERFECT TIME

My name is Christopher Barker. You've probably read how over the years I've been the recipient of numerous national awards and monetary prizes for my novels of the old West. Yet how I've never once given an interview, apprehensive that my studied remarks would likely end up garbled by some hurrying, rattle-brained reporter, the sort who would say — "Between you and I." — at highbrow cocktail parties because he thought that sounded more intellectual. And how, likewise, I've often turned down invitations to appear on ribald television talk shows for fear I'd be asked to bare intimate details of my quiet life, such as my sexual preference, which I can assure you is irrelevant at eighty-one. Thus the wish to guard my privacy has forced me to become a reluctant recluse, regarded as an eccentric.

But as I realize I'm getting on in years and every man comes to the end of the trail in time, so to speak, and the question is still bandied about in the public prints as to what inspired me to write so movingly about the West that used to be, I feel the moment has arrived for me to take pen in hand and tell you of my beginning.

We called him Blue. As the years passed, we called him Old Blue. Yet he never seemed old to me until the last time I saw him. I can't remember when Blue first came into my life, but he is so vivid in my memory to this day that he must have been there in my earliest thoughts, waiting to be saddled, ready to take me to faraway places and a mystery sometimes hidden behind the wooded hills. His alert eyes look out from the dimness of a box camera snapshot taken at the ranch; in their depths his infinite patience seems to live yet.

When I arrived in the family, he'd already endured teaching my older brother and two sisters to ride. After myself and a younger brother came a noisy niece and nephew. Blue educated us all with unswerving tolerance, never failing to bring everybody safely home. A three-passenger load was not uncommon, counting other ranch kids. If their antics became unbearable, he'd simply stop until order was restored and the chastened urchins pleaded and urged him to go on.

His beginnings were vague, without pedigree. Figuring Blue must surely be of noble heritage, I asked my father. I remember how he smiled down at me and said: "All I can tell you, Son, is that he showed up in a band of range horses I bought across the Arkansas River and drove home in Nineteen Ten, the only blue roan in the bunch." And, then, to please me, he added: "Oh, sure, he's a good horse. You can tell just by lookin' at him."

Because of his dependable nature, Blue was destined to live out his years as a kid horse in the blackjack hills of southwestern Osage County, Oklahoma, and, when the kids were gone, a privileged pensioner on a ranch not far from the river that he had crossed as a young horse to become a member of our family.

Blue was not a big, powerful horse. Looking back, I judge he stood about fifteen hands and weighed about 750 pounds. He had a good head with a small star, his legs were straight, and he had a short back and muscled hindquarters. He was hardy and nimble-footed, a goat over rocks, and he seldom stumbled. He had balance. Now I think he possessed a strain of Spanish iron in his blood. He liked to run, although he never ran away with me, and, although he wasn't a race horse, he could run a long way. He wasn't gaited, no smooth running walk like my oldest sister's saddler had, but he could hold a steady trot by the hour in up-and-down country. He had bottom.

He also had a streak of independence, demonstrated now and then as if to remind me that he'd been foaled for loftier duties than fetching some kid here and there. Sometimes when I approached him with the bridle, he'd turn into a wild horse. Putting on a fierce display of head tossing and wheeling and kicking, with much snorting and wall-eyed looks. Then, after a while, cornered in the corral, his point made once again, he'd give up and assume his usual rôle.

He took me out of more than one foolhardy venture. Not long after the dam at the city reservoir broke during a flood, I rode Blue over there to scout around. At the time I was reading *Western Story Magazine* every week and fancied myself as a top hand with rope and a .22-caliber rifle, no less than the self-styled, fearless Mysterious Rider of the Osage Hills, who always rode a fast blue roan and was hell on outlaws and rustlers.

In the shallow pools below the broken dam, I could see catfish and bass and perch washed down from the lake. I made a mental note to come back before the pools dried up and get me a string of fish.

We climbed around the breached dam and followed a road that skirted the lake. Sight of the emptiness awed me. I drew rein. Blue and I stared at it for a long while. Under the hot afternoon sun the puckered face of the empty lake bed, dotted with tree stumps and clumps of washed-up brush, looked deceptively dry, safe enough to cross. If I crossed here, I'd save considerable distance, and I sure didn't aim to be late for supper. I was always hungry then.

I reined Blue over to the edge of the high bank and touched the spurs for him to go down it. He lowered his head, seemed to give everything a suspicious look, then flat balked. I spurred him again, harder this time. Still, he balked. I kept spurring. He'd never balked on me like this before. What was wrong? Why would he hold back? I spurred again. Grudgingly he went down the long slope of the bank.

The spongy footing should have warned me, because about halfway across, where the lake bed deepened, it happened all at once. Suddenly Blue bogged to his knees. I felt the quick catch of fear as he struggled to free himself and a greater, paralyzing fear that I'd never get him out of here and he'd die and it'd be my fault. I was frozen with fright and self-blame. After that, everything happened fast.

He humped up powerfully and broke out with hoofs sucking mud, only to sink down again, below his knees. He was fighting for his life, for both of us. If I dismounted, I'd bog down, too.

Once more he broke free. The green bank of the lake seemed far away. Now he bogged again, even deeper. It was the worst moment of my ten-year-old life. Blue was going to die here for certain, helpless, trapped in greasy mud, and it was my fault and there was nothing I could do to help him. We'd both die. I was crying, crying for him as well. I wanted to get off to help Blue, but I couldn't move.

And then, somehow, he seemed to find a hidden source of strength. He lunged free again. Like a bucking horse. Up and down. Like a wild horse. Hindquarters high, head down. Now head high, hindquarters down. I was thrown against his neck. I grabbed black mane and held on. Next, I grabbed the saddle horn.

Blue never let up, never hesitated, never seemed to tire. He moved faster and faster, and, moving faster, he wasn't sinking in so deeply. The green bank looked closer now.

The footing under us seemed not quite so soft. Alternately sinking and humping, we floundered some fifty yards more through the crusty mud to solid ground.

I slid down at once. Blue was heaving and trembling, greasy with slime. He just stood there, head down, blowing hard, front legs spread wide. I thought he'd never quit heaving. Mixed with my relief was a deep shame. In his eyes I thought I saw an expression of weary reproach because a fool kid had spurred him into treacherous footing against his wiser judgment. A heavier, less active horse would have bogged down to die.

That evening, when I shamefacedly told my father what had happened, he fixed me a look that equaled Blue's and said: "There are times when the judgment of a good horse is better than a man's. But a man has to be smart enough to follow it."

I just hung my head, grateful that Blue was alive.

On another wandering day, Blue and I saddled farther than we ever had before. A perfect summer morning, under a turquoise sky, with a gentle breeze moving like a current through the belly-high bluestem grass. I gave Blue his head. We left the familiar wooded hills near the ranch, crossed wide stretches of prairie, passed through more hills shaggy with stands of blackjacks and came to more broken prairie. We rode until it was all new country to me. That day, it seemed we'd already traveled a long way; now, in retrospect, probably not many miles. Blue trotted on in his usual confident manner. I had the feeling he knew where he was headed, so I just let him ramble where he pleased.

Of a sudden the prairie changed. It broke away and below us I saw a rocky ledge, plum bushes, and willows and the inviting shine of a limestone spring. It looked cool and clear in the speckled shade. In the tall grass around the spring, yellow grasshoppers crackled and whirred and jerked like jumping jacks. A perfect place, a secret place. Blue halted, gazing down at the spring.

I could hardly wait as I reined Blue down and around through the drooping willows to the spring. Then, side-by-side, we drank the cool water.

Afterward, while Blue grazed nearby, I took a fishing line from the saddlebag, cut a willow pole with my pocket knife, and caught fat perch as fast as I could feed them grasshoppers.

I rode away from there filled with the delight of discovery and the promise to myself to return there before long. But an out-of-state family vacation and visits to relatives changed that. It was late summer before I came back to the ranch, with me a friend from town. In confidence, I told him about the hidden spring, which I now called The Perfect Place. I was sure I could find it again. On foot, loaded with poles and lunch, we started out.

We hiked some distance in the direction I knew was correct, the way Blue had taken me as we wandered. But to my gradual puzzlement, I couldn't find the particular stretch of prairie that led to the spring. Somehow the rounded, wooded hills and the expanses of bluestem pasture didn't fit the picture in my mind. The ledge and the spring and the willows were out there somewhere, I knew, yet I couldn't find the place. As we hiked along, the odd feeling came over me that maybe I wasn't supposed to find it again, or that maybe, in my boy's imaginative mind, it wasn't quite real. Yet Blue had taken me there. Yet I'd caught perch there — plenty of 'em. And we'd both drunk from the pool and I'd dropped reins on Blue and he'd filled up on the lush grass while I cut a willow pole and knocked down yellow grasshoppers with my hat. That was real, I knew. Yet. . . .

The afternoon wore away in frustration. Disappointed, we turned back. My friend laughed at me and said the hidden spring was just something I'd dreamed up, that it wasn't real.

"It's real, all right," I told him. "I've been there on Blue."

"If so, why can't we find it?"

"Maybe we weren't supposed to find it."

He gave me a strange look.

I fell silent, not knowing what to say, troubled in a way I couldn't explain. But little by little as we trudged back to the ranch, sudden logic cleared my mind and I understood why Blue had found the spring and I couldn't today. A thirsty horse can smell water. And he *knew* where the spring was because he had watered there before. So he had headed there. That made sense. Yet why did the hills and the prairie look different today? Why?

Summer's end was nearing and it was soon time for school and no more wandering rides on Blue. Meanwhile, my father moved his horses to the old ranch not far from the Arkansas River. I never saw the hidden spring again. My afternoon there became a part of the haze of boyhood, forever mysterious and perfect and always to be dreamed and wondered about. As our family grew up and scattered, Blue, older now, was retired as a privileged hand.

The last time I saw Blue my father had turned him into the fenced yard at the ranch where the grass grew a mite higher that hot, dry summer. It was a Depression year. I studied him for a while before I went over and petted him. No head tossing and snorting and whirling away this time. Never a big horse, he looked smaller than I remembered. He'd lost flesh. The stout, short back was bowed a bit, but he wasn't sway-backed. Hell, no, he wasn't. He was just getting on in years, like some old-timers I'd seen, drawn down to leanness and stiffened joints, who rocked on the front porch and watched folks go by. He was crowding twenty-five by then. But his dark eyes seemed as alert as ever. Always a good keeper as they used to say, he went back to enjoying the thin grass.

"Blue looks pretty good," I said to my father, but I knew it wasn't so. My father didn't say anything. Why discuss the obvious? We ate supper.

When I came home again, a devastating drought had set in. Springs that had never quit running in the memory of the oldest settlers had gone dry. The well at the house was down to one bucket a day. A pall of blowing dust darkened the sky day after day.

To save the few head of cattle my father had left, he drove them to the river, shrunk to a scattering of shallow pools, and turned them loose. He was flat broke and the ranch would be foreclosed on before long, gone like the little ranch west of town. Like many others my age, I was working my way through the state university. Maybe I'd make a newspaperman, maybe someday I'd write a book about the Osage country and its people and its good horses.

I looked around. This time no blue horse cropped the yard's sparse grass or stood watching in the log corral down by the sheds.

My father had come out on the porch to greet me.

"How's Old Blue?" I asked forcing the question.

My father didn't reply for a little run of time. "I'd turned him out in the big pasture. There's a little water out there . . . a seep spring. And that's where I found him the other day."

"You mean . . . ?" I fiercely wanted to deny what I knew was all too true.

My father nodded.

"He was a mighty good little horse," I said.

My father nodded again.

No more was said. No more needed to be said.

Thinking about Blue, I felt an inarticulate sense of personal loss, and of inexorable change and of growing up. For Blue was my last tie with The Perfect Time, when everything seemed right and nothing was impossible, when the Mysterious Rider rode the blackjack hills on a fast blue roan and feared no man, and outlaws and rustlers took cover when he was about. In a way, I thought, it was fitting that Blue and the mortgaged ranch should go about the same time, since both had to go.

I know now that Blue wasn't a great horse as greatness is judged. He wasn't a fast, powerful horse you roped steers on at the 4th of July rodeo. He hadn't burning speed, nor a fancy, rocking-chair gait. He had none of those obvious talents. True, he was of unknown breeding, but so was the mighty Traveler, who was discovered pulling a scraper on the Texas & Pacific Railway and became the top Quarter horse sire of his generation, blessed with heart and speed.

To be candid, I know now that Blue was just another kid horse, endowed with character instead of spectacular performance. But I know, also, absolutely, that he was ever steadfast and brave, and had the right stuff when it counted, not once failing to bring his sometimes foolhardy rider safely home, and for that and much more I remember him still. I never had a better friend. . . .

So now, you prying members of the fourth estate, and you peeping-tom hosts of the tell-all tube, you know my roots and from whence I came, which is quite enough.

Adiós.

THE VANISHING RAIDERS

I

Out of the prairie vastness ahead, Laban Columbus Bushrod heard a single ring of sound, metal on metal, as he heeled the speckled gray mule up the crest of the long rise. And there in the glassy distance, under the great bronze eye of the Texas sun, near the shining snake of a looping creek, he saw a tiny settlement huddled on the hot plain as if forsaken — Jacksboro.

Again the familiar sound, rising and falling, the strokes of a blacksmith's hammer, and next he noticed the hooded blooms of wagons along the creek. Farther south, he could see a broad parade square and the flag flying there as a bird fluttering in the purring wind, and the neat buildings on all sides. He thought: *Fort Richardson*. He had come a long way, but his journey wasn't over.

Later, riding the dusty street, passing

adobe and picket buildings, smelling appetizing odors flowing from a grocery store's open doorway, he tied up to the pole hitching rack. Men lounged on benches by the door.

Starting forward, he felt heat race into his face. The loafers were showing amused grins over his chimney-pot hat and his extra long mane of brown hair and his butternut britches, which some folks called linsey-woolsey, and which hung high water above his ankles like stovepipes. But what galled him most was the funning way they looked at his raw-boned mount. With a stab of loyalty, he had a mind to tell them that Reuben was an Alabama mule and, in his prime, could plow as much cotton as any critter south of Huntsville, bar none.

In another moment Laban froze, knowing what was coming, as Reuben stretched his gawky neck, laid back his flapping long ears, opened his elongated jaws, and brayed with a fiendish grimace, loosing a trumpeting harshness that became a drawn-out honking, up and down.

As though an actor who had spoken his opening lines, Reuben stopped and faced his audience. The loafers laughed and Laban had to grin with them.

Hitching at his suspenders, he went inside.

For three cents he bought a handful of crackers and a slab of yellow cheese, then sat on a nail keg to eat his first meal of the day. Soon finished, he remembered he needed bacon and cornmeal, and, when the storekeeper had his order ready, he opened a drawstring purse and fished out his last coin — a ten-dollar gold piece.

He paused, thinking of his folks' hard toil and his own and the doing without so he could make the trip out West to search for work and also see his Uncle Gabe Bushrod at Fort Griffin — Gabriel J. Bushrod, it was — and handed the coin to the storekeeper. The keen blue eyes behind the silver spectacles lighted up like lamp wicks. The man's indifference vanished. "Don't see many of these out here."

Laban started to reply that it was all he had until he saw the eyes switch to a dubious glimmer. The man, he realized, was about to question his ownership.

"It's mine," Laban told him distinctly. "I earned it and more." He hadn't meant to sound uppity, but he did a mite, nevertheless, and his prideful tone mistakenly gave the notion there might be other gold pieces where that one came from, an unwise impression among strangers. The storekeeper turned away.

For the first time Laban noticed the man at the end of the counter. He looked lean and wizened and dirty, his unwashed face sparsely covered with a crop of grayish whiskers; his high cheek bones stood knobbed above the sunken valleys of his leathery flesh, forming a visage as wrinkled as a dried prune's. His lank jaws worked on a walnut-size wad of tobacco. The eyes squinting under the rider's broad-brimmed hat were a dull yellow. He stared at Laban without seeming to see him.

Laban felt a brush of chill. He looked away as the storekeeper said — "Here's your change." — and counted out $9.68.

"How far to Fort Belknap?" Laban asked him, folding the greenbacks and stuffing them in the purse, followed by the loose change.

"About forty miles if you follow the wagon road. Why not wait till a freight outfit goes through?"

"When might that be?"

"Week or so."

Laban shook his head.

"You can afford to wait if it means your scalp." The blue eyes fixed a closer exasperation on Laban. "See those campers on the creek?" When Laban nodded, he said: "They came in because of the Indian scare."

195

The merchant, Laban saw, was honestly trying to warn him of danger, and he felt somewhat mollified. "I understand and I'm mighty obliged to you."

"So you'll wait?"

"No, sir. I mean I'm goin' on, but I'll keep a sharp look-out."

"Boy, you're as stubborn as that ugly mule out there."

Going outside, Laban heard spurs jingling behind him. It was the whiskery onlooker. Laban untied the sack behind his saddle, tucked in his meager supplies, tied fast, and swung up.

Reuben was taking him westward out of town at an unhurried walk when a rider drummed up behind and drew even. Laban looked into the tawny gaze of the man who had left the store. Here in the blaze of mid-day sun he appeared even leaner and dirtier somehow, his gray chin whiskers stained a dull yellow that matched his eyes. But he rode a sleek bay horse and sat a new silver-horned saddle with flowers hand-tooled on the skirts. He wore a six-shooter and a rifle butt forward in a scabbard under his right leg.

"I'm headed for Belknap," he said curtly. "Want to ride along?"

Laban hesitated. "My old mule can't keep

up with your horse," he said, aware of a caution. "We'd hold you back."

"Never mind that. It's a lonesome stretch and I'm in no hurry."

"You don't know Reuben. Sometimes he takes a notion just to stop."

The rider's uneven mouth, a querulous trap in the bed of whiskers, squinched up; however his voice sounded friendly. "Where's your gun?"

"Don't have one."

"How do you reckon to fight Indians?"

"Don't . . . if I can keep from it."

The leathery jaws stirred. The man spat. He let go a short laugh, although Laban found no humor in it. "Say a war party rode up. What'd you do?"

"Reckon I'd try to make peace with 'em."

The man laughed hard, a brief, disdainful laugh. "You beat all. Why, you'd last about as long as a snowball in a hot skillet. Naw . . . you'd better tag along with me if you aim to hold on to your hair."

Again Laban hesitated. He had shunned strangers since leaving home; it was a good rule, his father said, and it had kept him out of trouble. Yet this stranger was offering him company — and protection — in Indian country.

"Much obliged," Laban gave in. "We'll try

to keep up."

They passed over a rolling swell and suddenly the village and the fort fell from view and Laban experienced a feeling of isolation. Ahead, the country pitched and tossed, long stretches of prairie turning brown under the June sun, and scattered patches of timber, and here and there a shaggy hill. *Handy look-out places,* he thought, *for Indians watching the wagon road.*

Now and then his companion would halt and gaze off, or he would pause to study cluttered tracks, halting so often that more times than not Laban was waiting on him.

"Man's got to look sharp in Indian country," the rider told Laban, who wondered if a body couldn't do the same without wasting daylight.

Toward mid-afternoon Laban spied a dark mass beside the road. Riding up, he scowled at the blackened ruins of two wagons.

"Indians," his companion said. "Happened last April."

They passed a stage station. The hostler came to the door and the rider waved.

On past, Laban said: "Guess the Indians didn't bother him."

"That man's a good shot," the rider said.

Not long afterward the horseman turned off the trail to a wooded draw. Laban saw the silvery gleam of a spring.

"We'll camp here," the rider announced, and began unsaddling.

Laban did not dismount. He was gauging the sun. "There's a good hour or so of daylight left. Why don't we go on some more?"

The man shrugged. "If you crave a dry camp, go ahead. Here's the only water for a long spell."

Laban came slowly down from the saddle, begrudging the lost time. He was untying his supply sack when he happened to see that the man carried no supplies; yet he was camping overnight. Of a sudden Laban felt a slap of guilt and his suspicion passed. By staying away from people on the trail, by riding alone, he had begun to distrust others without cause.

After that, he occupied himself unsaddling and slipping a halter over Reuben's long head and leading him to water. Next he took the mule out a way from camp, drove down an iron picket pin, tied one end of the picket rope to the ring in the pin and the other to Reuben's halter.

By now it was time to start fixing an early supper. Laban built a small fire, shielding its glow under a rock overhang in the draw. He cut a strip of bacon and fried it in the skillet, and, when the grease had cooled a bit, he stirred it in the cornmeal and added spring water. While the golden batter gurgled and firmed in the skillet, he cut more bacon and skewered the strips on a blackjack stick.

Engrossed, he glanced up to find himself being watched. "You're green," the man said, "but you don't cook green." A hungry look shone in his eyes. "I aimed to ride straight through till I saw you . . . gonna visit a sick friend . . . else I'd have food to share."

"You're welcome to this. I make pretty good skillet bread."

"There's a little coffee in my saddlebag. I'll get it."

"Fine," said Laban. He hadn't tasted coffee in weeks.

As the other tramped out to his picketed horse, walking pigeon-toed in his high-heeled boots, an insight came circling through Laban's head. If there was a sick friend in Belknap, why had he dallied so long on the trail?

The observation left him when he saw the lean man coming with a small brown sack and coffee pot. Laban watched him dip water into the pot and commence cracking and grinding the coffee beans on a rock with the butt of his revolver. When he had ground a handful, he dropped it in the pot, and presently boiling coffee smell fused with the tempting scents of cornbread and bacon.

Laban rummaged in his sack for tin plates and cups, halved the bread, and scooped out the portions on the plates, divided the bacon, and poured the coffee. His guest began eating at once, in wolfish bites. He was finished before Laban had half eaten.

"Greener," he said, swiping the back of his hand across his mouth, "that was right good vittles." He sat against a mossy rock, the firelight catching the greasy shine of his stained chin whiskers, his dull stare flicking over Laban. So long and steadily did he stare that Laban felt uncomfortable. Finished, he got up to move the mule's picket pin. Returning, he found his coffee cup full. His guest's was empty.

Laban looked at him. "You didn't give yourself any."

"Cook comes first, greener. Remember that." And he laughed in that humorless way of his.

Laban leaned back and sipped the black brew, lowered the cup, and sipped again. There was the faintest sweetness in it, almost lost on the tongue, which he hadn't noticed while eating, but, if anything, it tasted better than before.

Moments passed. He sipped some more. A breeze wandered off the short-grassed prairie, bringing the pleasant coolness and freshness of open country. A contentment spread over Laban. A well-being.

"Mister . . . ," he said, surprised at the laziness in his voice. "Mister . . ?" He let the last hang as a question.

"Out here, greener, you never ask a man his name."

"Well, mister, that sure is good coffee."

Idly he watched the haze of twilight thickening around him. Like a purple veil, he thought, growing darker and darker. He didn't mind. Never had he been more comfortable. He seemed to be floating through a dusky valley.

Across, the grizzly features were gradually blurring, dimming even while he looked. He thought of rising and spreading his blanket by his saddle; it was too much effort. He would make his bed later, after he had rested a while by the fire. There was no hurry. No hurry at all.

He sipped again. This time a strange revulsion filled him. His senses were beginning to reel. He started to set the cup on a rock; instead, he plopped it down and the cup turned over and spilled. He took a shallow breath, gazing about. Everything was dark — too dark — and he had no strength.

He struggled to rise. He could not. Trembling, he looked across the low glow of the fire and made out the grayish blur of the face, likewise staring. In fact, it was moving toward him, ever nearer. He opened his mouth to cry out, but he had no voice. He twisted to lift his arms, but his body would not obey.

Powerless, unable to cry out, he saw the whiskery features before him, now over him. Then Laban felt himself slipping into utter darkness. . . .

He came out of sleep with a vague sense of struggling, but when he focused his eyes he found the sun warm on his face, and he was alone.

He pushed up stiffly and discovered he was in about the same position he last remembered, near the fire, against the rocks. Except the coals were long out and the sun rode high in the sky. He wet his lips, aware of a sweet, sickish taste. A giant drum was beating inside his head.

A sharp sense of shock, and pieces of what had happened returned to him: the sweet-tasting coffee, the whiskery man. *Where was he?*

Laban swayed to his feet. Standing, head down, he saw his drawstring purse on the ground. He picked it up. It was open and empty. So was his food sack gone. Another fear grew. He scrambled up the rocky draw and looked. The bay horse wasn't there.

But his throat caught when he turned his head and saw his steadfast gray mule, the ugly face watching him, the old beast in an attitude of questioning.

Afterward, he rode, slumped and miserable, holding a hand to his splitting head. The silent, forbidding country through which he seemed to crawl swam before his eyes, more mirage than real in the glaring sun.

As best he could determine, Fort Griffin lay some sixty miles southwest, on the edge of the buffalo range. That meant a two-day journey without food. He willed himself to the long ride.

Deep into the afternoon, he saw shapes ahead on the trail. The canvas tops of two wagons, figures stirring. As he approached, he saw with relief that the figures were soldiers in dark blue uniforms, all grouped about the right rear wheel of the last wagon. One paced out, rifle at the ready.

"Halt there! Halt, I say!"

"Just goin' down the road," Laban said,

taken aback.

"You'll have to go around. Get along now."

The sentry couldn't be more than a few years older than Laban, and his high, nervous voice relayed a recruit's inexperience. An older man, ruddy-faced, wearing mutton-chop whiskers and bearing an air of authority, left the crippled wagon and bawled: "Good heavens, soldier! Can't you see he's just a boy? Let him pass on the road."

"Yes, sir, Major." Shamefaced, the sentry nodded for Laban to pass.

Starting by, Laban saw two soldiers pounding the iron tire of the wheel, which rested off the ground on a clumsy wagon jack; each time they drove the metal hoop snug, it slipped off at another place. Plainly the fello or wooden rim had shrunk.

The major tramped over, hands on hips, muttering impatience. Laban saw him turn and size him up. "You . . . you're a farm boy . . . know beans about fixing a wheel rim?"

"A little," Laban said, and slid down, glad to help. Stepping toward the open rear of the wagon, he happened to glance inside. A large wooden chest, strongly padlocked, squatted there. Otherwise, the wagon was empty.

"You can't do any worse than these green recruits," the major assured him. "Give him the hammer, soldier."

Laban tapped the tire here and there, gradually working it on. He scratched his chin and said: "Wheel needs soakin' so it'll swell up. Meantime, reckon I can whittle some wedges to pound under the tire. Might hold till you reach water. . . . Best thing'd be to heat the tire red hot . . . slip it on, pour water on it, let it draw up on the wheel."

"No time for that," the major said.

Before long the wagons creaked away, Laban trailing. The sun was sinking when a line of trees traced the course of a creek. Shortly, with Laban helping, the wheel lay soaking.

"Young man," said the major, "you are welcome to camp with us and share our rations. You live nearby?"

"No, sir, my home's in Alabama. I'm headed for Fort Griffin."

"I see. I suppose you have kin there?"

"My Uncle Gabe Bushrod."

A reflection entered the ruddy face. "Bushrod? Gabe Bushrod? In the freighting and stage business? Trades in buffalo hides?"

Laban nodded, full of expectation. Uncle Gabe must be a big man for the major to know of him. And then. . . .

"Ah . . . yes." The major opened his mouth to speak, but did not. He measured Laban an unfathomable look and went about his duties.

Twilight moved in muddy waves across the changing sky. The wind dropped to a mere murmur, lulling to the ear. Laban, on his blanket, caught the occasional drone of a recruit's tired voice and, steadily, the Army mule teams cropping the short grass. Dimly, around the camp, he could see sentries moving about. One stood guard by the disabled wagon.

Laban had eaten his fill of the detail's simple fare of salt pork and hardtack; now, his mind at ease, he thought of Uncle Gabe with a wondering anticipation.

Uncle Gabe had left home soon after the war, so Laban's memory of him was dim — a loud man, given to playing rough jokes. Laban's father, Jesse, used to say that Gabe didn't like to sweat for his bread, that he wanted to get rich quick; many were Gabe's schemes Jesse told about which never quite panned out. Except now, after so many years, his father said Gabe was making good out West. Times being discouraging at home, Laban could visit his uncle while he looked for work on the Texas frontier where prospects were bright.

He drifted off into a fantasy of sleep in which Uncle Gabe Bushrod, folks said, had just discovered gold way out West and bought himself a whole railroad that stretched plumb across the country and up and down it, too, and real gold cloth covered the train seats, and, when the locomotive came chuffing into Huntsville, puffing clouds of smoke that glittered like gold, there was Uncle Gabe, sure enough, on the engine's steps, in glossy-black high hat and checkered suit, and he twirled a gold cane with a gold head stout enough for a harness tug.

Yet, when the train stopped and Laban ran up to greet him and heard his uncle's booming voice, he drew back, bewildered, close to fright.

For Uncle Gabe Bushrod's face didn't seem to fit. It was like an ill-made mask of parts taken from other faces: the eyes too small, the trunk of a nose too large, the cave of a mouth too wide, the fleshy cheeks hanging in folds. And in the moment that Laban hesitated, the train puffed up and sped away, to vanish around a hill. Laban heard yells. Now shouts.

But although the dream had faded, gone, the yells and the shouts were real, resounding in his consciousness. Kicking off his blanket, he rolled up and rubbed his eyes.

A roaring smote his ears. Shouting and whooping. Hoofs pounding. Rifles popping. He smelled the hot scent of gunpowder. And through the first gray tint of dawn he saw figures struggling around the guarded wagon. A roaring red flash split the murk there.

A terrifying sensation plunged through him. Indians — feathered Indians were dragging the heavy chest from the wagon, whooping while they hacked at it with tomahawks. Other Indians setting fire to the wagons. The shouts, Laban realized, had come from the recruits. He heard them no more.

An Indian wheeled toward him, and Laban knew instantly that he was discovered. The Indian sprang toward him, tomahawk lifted.

Laban couldn't move. As if locked in a nightmare, he stared fully into the hideous face charging upon him. Seeing the streaks of war paint — red, yellow. The hawkish nose, the cleft in the chin — and the eyes a startling hard, hypnotic blue.

He rolled aside on instinct, at last, away from the swish of the descending tomahawk. Springing up, he sprinted for the creek, feeling the rush of wind on his face, his fear giving him strength and lending lightness to his flying feet. Behind him he could hear his pursuer in pounding stride.

II

Sprinting to the creek, Laban cut left and ran dodging through the timber and brush. His foot caught on a root. He stumbled and slammed into a tree and the impact flung him painfully against another, bounced him spinning. As he regained balance and straightened out running, he heard a *thunk* beside him and saw a tomahawk lopping off a sapling's trunk.

Hastened by a kind of fear he had never experienced before, he found within himself an unbelievable swiftness. Stride by stride, breath by breath, the sounds of pursuit slackened behind him, until, hacking for wind, he dared glance back. Not seeing his pursuer, he quickened his looking. Then he saw a figure leaving the timber. It was the Indian and he was running toward camp.

Laban listened. Not a sound reached him. Everything back there was so still, too still, although now he could see flames and smoke. It still seemed part of his dream. But it had happened and his life was still in danger.

He was trembling. A caution sent him across the shallow creek, to place it behind him. Several hundred yards away rose a wooded hill, conical, rugged, dense, secretive. Yesterday he would have hurried past it, wary of the menace it might conceal; now it meant a place to hide.

He could feel his second wind returning and the spring coming back into his long legs. He was well out in the open, going at a half run, glancing over his shoulder every few strides, when he saw a rider bob across the creek and quirt his dun horse to a gallop.

Laban broke running. Above the rushing *swish* of his bare feet through the curly short grass, he caught the growing drum of the horse. He ran faster still, and his chest began to burn. Ahead, the shaggy hill was looming closer. At the same moment he could hear the hoof beats more distinctly.

He heard a snapping sound around his head and the *crash* of a rifle behind him. He swerved, trying to make himself smaller, while the dark refuge of the hill massed larger and larger. With a final straining burst of speed, he tore into the first growth of trees and flung himself gasping behind a blackjack.

To his immense shock, he saw his foe racing to the foot of the hill. Hunkering down, Laban scrabbled backward several rods and looked again. The Indian was swinging off his horse. At once Laban started making his way around the hillside, through a scrubby growth of black-barked trees, over broken sandstone that cut his feet and past boulders, some as high as a man's head.

He moved like a hunted animal, drawing on all his senses, listening, feeling his course, reacting to each noisy movement his unseen tracker made tramping after him. He came to a knot of boulders and saw, between two, a hole large enough for his slim body, likely a coyote's den. An inner voice told him it was an obvious hiding place. He went on.

He passed an opening in the timber. After a time, he suddenly realized he no longer heard steps. He became motionless, and, when still he caught no sound, he knew that the man, like himself, was halted, listening, playing the same game.

And then, faintly, he heard the *tick* of loosened rock sliding downhill. On that signal, he began climbing rapidly, his intention to circle and come in behind. Again he halted, watching the opening he had passed. A shape materialized on the far side.

Limping faster, circling, Laban came to

the coyote den again. During an indecisive moment, he struggled with the notion of hiding there, and again an instinct warned him away. It looked too easy. He would be trapped if his pursuer looked in there. The dun horse at the foot of the hill was a better bet. He warmed to the thought. If he could get down there. . . .

His mind fastened on the chance. Before he could go downhill, a rustling reached him. By that he knew the Indian had doubled back on his own trail.

A near panic took Laban. He was already limping badly. He couldn't run. A thick blackjack reared craggily over his head. An old tree, broad and sturdy and rough-barked, its leafy foliage spreading a cool canopy over the coyote's home.

He listened another moment — and clambered to the top of a reddish boulder and grasped the lower limb and swung upward into the lacy greenery.

Squirming behind the trunk, he felt naked and helpless so high up. He had no more than settled himself when he heard the soft crush of pebbles, the crackling of brush. Those sounds ceased, and then, squeezing around the trunk, he saw low-growing bushes part and the Indian stepped out. He moved softly on moccasined feet, watching all about, rifle ready, the wind stirring his feathered headdress.

Laban held his breath. The man stopped, head cocked for sound, his hawkish nose tilted, his yellow-streaked face more hideous here in the full light. He brought his gaze closer in. Laban saw him find the coyote hole, saw him relish his discovery. Suddenly he got down on hands and knees and started poking with the barrel of his rifle.

A high whine rose from the den. He got up and appeared to shrug as a white man might, and focused his attention across the broken hillside.

Laban, face pressed to the tree trunk, peering with one eye, stood so long in that stiffened posture that he feared he would lose his hold and fall. His tension tightened as the Indian moved to the tree and paused under it; now Laban couldn't see him clearly or tell whether he was looking up or beyond. Laban pressed harder against the rough bark and his mind seemed to squeeze out of his straining body, to hang suspended over the hill, bright under the full rays of the morning sun.

An eternity later, it seemed, he heard the moccasins scuffing across the rock rubble. He exhaled ever so carefully, as if that sound might betray him. When he looked, the

Indian was striding downhill to his horse.

Only after the hammering roll of the hoofs beat back to Laban did he relax, sagging down in the fork of the tree, breathing in short gasps, the strength gone from his twitching leg muscles. Some moments and he slipped to the ground and limped down the west side of the hill, searching the prairie between hill and creek.

Feathers of smoke climbed above the creek timber that hid the camp. Watching, he felt his whole being gather into a black despair for the major and the little detail of recruits. It crept into his thinking that Fort Belknap was a few hours' ride to the west. His one choice left was to go there and bring help.

After the rocky hill, the prairie felt as balm to his bare feet so long as he avoided the clumps of prickly pear. Trotting and watching, he set a course to bring him in on the wagon road, and, when the smoke rose behind him, eastward, he slackened step, alternately trotting and striding.

He was more than a mile along the road when he heard a ruffling roll of sound from behind. Flattening down behind a spiny prickly pear, he saw, far out, a dark cloud of horsemen skimming over the brown prairie.

He crouched lower, fearful they had spotted him.

They kept on, not changing course. When they passed northwest out of sight, he rose and swung into a limping dog-trot, his mind heavily and darkly on the camp. There wasn't time to go back there now.

The morning burned itself out under the sun's bloody stare. Laban, shading his eyes, made out a cluster of stone buildings writhing in white heat this side of the winding red river. By now he was traveling on badly swollen feet, and, as he limped forward, he began to see that Fort Belknap, instead of an orderly post like Fort Richardson, stood in a shambles of neglect. Ghostly chimneys overlooked a wilderness of mesquite and sand.

He saw no person, but the flag floated over the parade ground, and, when he hobbled down the sandy road to the first dilapidated stone building, a trooper came in view, leading a horse.

"What is it?" The trooper halted, his unshaven jaw bulging. Although he had a mournful, ox-horn mustache, his brown eyes were twinkling and friendly, in them the patient knowledge of an old soldier accustomed to emergencies. On the sleeves of his unbuttoned blue jacket, between shoulder and elbow, he wore a sergeant's three V-shaped yellow stripes. Another stripe ran down the seams of his breeches.

Laban told him in a gush of words. It still seemed a bad dream.

The sergeant's sandy eyebrows flew up, forming a dubious arch. "Hold on, boy. You had too much sun?"

"I tell you I saw it," Laban replied, setting his jaw. "They'd 'a' got me if I hadn't run."

"You look tuckered, all right. Guess we better see the lieutenant." He tied the horse in front of a long, stone barracks, Laban hobbling after him and up the crumbling steps and inside and down a dim hallway. The sergeant entered a narrow room where a younger man, his hair a striking corn yellow, sat behind a plank desk.

"Lieutenant," the non-com said, raising his right hand in a vague salute, "this boy's got a story to tell."

The lieutenant traced a forefinger over the luxuriant semicircle of his tawny mustache. "Sergeant Huckleby, button your blouse."

"Yes, sir," said Huckleby, fumbling with the buttons. "Reckon it slipped my mind."

"Indeed . . . indeed," the lieutenant said. He looked frustrated and harassed, a conscientious young officer, perhaps a bit fuzzy, left to command a handful of cavalry troopers holding a run-down frontier post virtually forgotten in a lonely land. "Sit down," he invited, his brows knitting at sight of Laban's swollen feet. "I'm Lieutenant Nathan Carr. Now who are you and what's this cock-and-bull story?"

"It's the truth," Laban blurted. Leaning forward in the chair, he commenced the telling, sparing no details, his thoughts more controlled than when he had told Huckleby. His story finished, he breathed deeply and leaned back.

Carr fixed him with a questioning look. "What were you doing with the detail?"

Laban explained about the loose tire on the wagon wheel.

"And you *saw* Indians?"

"I did. Heard 'em whoop, too. They had tomahawks."

"Did you know what was in the chest they hacked open?"

"No, sir."

"Did you see them remove anything from the chest?"

"No, sir. I was on the run."

"Well, young man, that chest contained not only the Fort Belknap payroll . . . such as it is . . . but also Fort Griffin's. Not only one month's pay, but two . . . we haven't been paid in two months. Comes to approximately six thousand dollars." The sergeant groaned and the lieutenant turned to him. "Get eight troopers ready. I guess we can spare that many." He paused. "Is Ranger Emory back?"

"Rode in at noon."

"What did he find?"

"All he said, sir, was that he'd scouted northeast and north and there was no Indian sign."

Carr gave a mild snort. "Yet Indians attacked the payroll detachment." He began striding back and forth, hands clasped behind him, his sunburned features a study in perplexity and scowling concentration. "Present my compliments to Ranger Emory. Tell him I'll welcome his company to the site of the attack."

"Very good, Lieutenant."

Carr's expression stiffened, his eyes pecking. "Huckleby, you missed one button."

The sergeant began fumbling at his jacket. "So I did, sir. Guess I. . . ."

". . . guess you forgot again," Carr said crisply, and faced Laban. "Bushrod, you stay put till we get back. Your story will be included in my formal report. Meanwhile, Sergeant, see that he gets something to eat. He's as gaunt as a guidon lance. And see that he soaks those raw feet. A good soaking in soapy water will take out the swelling." He gestured them outside.

"Lieutenant," Laban said, thinking back, "mind lookin' around for my shoes at the camp? They'll be by my blanket and hat on the east side, if the Indians didn't take 'em. And look out for my gray mule. He's on picket . . . was, if the Indians didn't take him."

"We'll look," said Carr, amused.

The sergeant took Laban to the kitchen where the cook set cold beans and bread and buttermilk before him. While he ate, he heard Lieutenant Carr form the detail and clatter off eastward.

Afterward, sitting on a barracks cot, he soaked his feet in a wash pan of warm, soapy water until he dozed. He dried his feet and stretched out, yawning prodigiously. One moment he was staring up at the high ceiling, listening to the muted hum of the post in the stifling afternoon heat. The next he knew, he opened his eyes to the glow of lantern light. His bed felt cool to his touch and he was refreshed and content. At the end of the barracks several troopers chatted in low tones.

He dozed off, to awaken to shod hoofs chocking across the parade ground. The clatter stopped, changed to snufflings and stampings. A voice barked a command. The horses trotted off. Boots sounded inside the barracks. Laban heard the troopers shuffle to their feet. Carr's weary voice said: "At ease. Where's the boy?"

"Back there, Lieutenant."

Laban rose and stood by the cot, hearing the musical jingle of spurs, seeing Lieutenant Carr and a man wearing a high-crowned hat striding toward him. Dust coated Carr's blue jacket like talcum. A tired smile hovered along his mouth. He turned to the other. "This is Laban Bushrod."

"Howdy, Laban. My name's Enoch Emory. You've had a rough time." He held out his hand.

"I'm alive," Laban said, taking the rough hand. The Ranger stood a head taller than the lieutenant, and his stubbled face was as brown as a saddle seat. Although made of large bones, his body had a rider's lankness. He regarded Laban through interested black eyes, sun-wrinkled at the corners, lively and cheerful. His mouth was broad and tolerant. Silver spurs jingled on his high-heeled boots. He wore a cartridge belt and a long revolver hung in a leather holster, cut down, with the trigger exposed.

Carr held out a pair of box-toed shoes tied together, a brown blanket, and a chimney-

221

pot hat. "These yours?"

Laban took them eagerly. He spoke his thanks and hesitated, dreading to ask the rest. At which the lieutenant, slowly smiling, said: "Found your mule, too. Still on picket."

"He's too ugly for a body to steal," Laban said. "Though a mighty good mule. I'm glad the Indians didn't know that."

"Indians . . . ," Carr said in a musing way, and eyed Emory, who shrugged. Gravity entered his voice. "Bushrod, the entire escort was wiped out. Payroll's gone."

While Laban was not surprised by this time, a swift and grievous shock wrung him. His mind seemed to leap backward in time, and again he could see the major who had given him food, and the awkward young recruits tugging like store clerks on the heavy wagon wheel, later standing bravely at their posts, and he could hear their jesting voices dimly across the evening darkness.

"Indians . . . ," Carr said once more, rubbing his chin. "I should think Indians would have taken your mule, ugly as he is. He looks strong. Indians know stock."

"Maybe," Emory said, as though thinking to himself. "The Army mules were handiest. Laban's mule was a way off."

Carr cocked a condoning eye at him. "Do the Texas Rangers and the Army ever agree?"

"I remember one time we did."

"When was that?"

"When we agreed on who took your mount off the picket line . . . the civilian we caught riding it."

"If Indians took the mules," Carr went on, "why did we find them running loose north of the wagon road?"

"Maybe they got loose," Laban said, and saw the amusement on both their faces.

Carr pondered a moment. "Possibly . . . if the raiders were being pursued. Yet, when you saw them, there was no sign of pursuit?"

Nodding, Laban wondered what the officer was driving at.

"Most white thieves," Emory reasoned, "would be a little leery of taking Army mules. Those big US brands are like announcin' the Fourth of July. Maybe they drove off the mules like Indians would, then. . . ."

". . . let them go," Carr filled in.

"Why, Lieutenant," Emory said, "dogged if you're not beginnin' to think like a Ranger."

Carr ignored him. "There's another thing. Indians wouldn't take the payroll."

Emory pushed back his big hat. "Like a hound dog won't chase rabbits. Some Kiowa and Comanch' bands hold captives for ransom money. An' sometimes white renegades hide out among 'em, too. They sure know what money is!"

Carr became silent. Then he looked straight at Laban. "Bushrod, do you realize you are the only living witness to the massacre?"

Laban nodded solemnly.

"If the raiders were white men . . . and we can't be positive one way or the other just yet . . . they know you are alive. That means you are the only person who might identify any of them." His voice groped for a heartiness that, to Laban, sounded forced. "Bushrod, you'd better stick around the post a while. We'll talk some more tomorrow. Good night."

They tramped out.

Laban hadn't moved. He stood locked in spinning thought. Better for him, he saw, if the raiders were Indians; if so, being a witness didn't matter. He lay down, but his head still spun. And when, in the swimming lantern light, he saw the shadows of the troopers outlined on the wall — grotesque, oversized — a door seemed to swing open in his mind and once more he was pushing up on his blanket, not far from the hooded wagons, hearing the yells and shouts, seeing the struggling figures and the dawn light peeling away the murk — and charging out of it upon him, the paint-streaked face, the clefted chin, the flinty blue eyes.

A long time later he fell into a troubled, tossing sleep.

III

After breakfast, Laban went looking for his mule and found the gaunt gray hulk grazing, haltered, on the post picket line behind the commissary building. The speckled traveler looked no worse for his experience, unabashed in the orderly company of cavalry horses groomed and currycombed. Some rods away a trooper walked guard.

At Laban's step, Reuben flicked his unduly long ears, long even for his kind, and stared as if to make certain, and returned to cropping the short grass. Laban stepped across and patted the gawky neck, and, when Reuben gazed around at him, he stroked the ugly nose. Watching his friend grazing, Laban was both comforted and amused, for somehow the mule always reminded him of an old man enjoying his vittles of cornbread and milk.

Looking about, Laban located his worn-out saddle, saddle blanket, and bridle in a nearby pole shed. Coming outside, he wondered what he would do with himself while he waited at the post. Waited for what? For Lieutenant Carr and his handful of troopers to capture the raiders? To find out whether they were Indians or white outlaws? And how could so few troopers find the raiders, let alone capture them, in this vast country?

A chill knotted his stomach. The lieutenant wanted him to stay at the post because he was safer here, although only his pursuer had seen him up close — that in the dubious gray light of dawn. It seemed foolish to waste time here when he might be working at Fort Griffin.

He strolled past the picket line and paused, feeling aimless and discouraged. Yonder meandered the shallow Salt Fork of the Brazos, not unlike a piece of red ribbon flung between the flat on this side and the line of tumbling hills on the other. The deep ruts of the wagon road to Fort Griffin ran gouging to the river crossing and climbed and wormed through the jaws of a gap in the rounded hills.

"It always looks better on the other side of the river," a voice said behind him, and he jerked around. It was Enoch Emory, the

Texas Ranger. There was understanding in his tone.

"Reckon I could make it to Fort Griffin in a day or so."

"Time comes for you to go, buckaroo, I'll ride with you."

"When will that be?"

"Before long," Emory said, enigmatic about it.

"I can't wait long. I got to find work so I can help my folks. It's been mighty hard back home."

"Be plenty of work waitin' at Griffin. Buckaroo, you never saw such a place . . . hide hunters, cowboys, soldiers, tenderfeet from back East. Stores, hotels, livery stables, hide yards, blacksmith shops, harness shops." He was making it sound rosy easy, Laban thought, too rosy. "Meantime, don't wander off by yourself. Loaf around. Fatten up on Army grub."

"I been doin' that, all right," Laban said so earnestly that Emory had to smile.

By the end of the third day, Laban knew that he couldn't stay much longer. Each morning he had watched Lieutenant Carr and his little detachment ride out and return empty-handed, their dusty faces haggard with futility. This morning the

Ranger had ridden north. He was still gone.

Slipping away from the post, Laban also realized, wouldn't be the easy escape he had first believed. Twice a day troopers took the cavalry mounts and Reuben to the river for water; at night the stock was put on picket, under guard, either near the commissary building or behind the row of crumbling barracks, the fort being so run-down it no longer had stables. Tonight the guard grazed the stock behind the barracks where Laban slept.

Furthermore, every time Laban went to see about his mule, he was conscious of eyes. Friendly as they were, he was being watched, not only at the picket line, but also around the post and in the barracks — until he went to bed.

His mind was firming as he lingered over his supper. When no one was noticing, he stuffed biscuits inside his shirt, all the while eating more than usual, storing away the needed extra strength. Afterward, in the barracks, he took out the bread and placed it in his blue bandanna with the rest of the food he had been saving since morning: several strips of bacon, more cold biscuits, a slab of yellow cornbread. He retied the bandanna, laid it inside the folds of his blanket under the cot, and strolled to the other end of the barracks to listen to the troopers talk.

Darkness filmed the high windows when he left to go to bed, and the night was still and hot. He removed shoes and shirt and lay on the cot in his trousers, already feeling the faster drumming of his heart.

Time dragged. His chest was slick with sweat. His impatience raced. He heard the troopers yawn and, one by one, make ready for bed. A match rasped. The pleasing aroma of pipe tobacco smoke drifted across to Laban. At last, after some minutes, came what he was tensed for, the long, slow wail of "Taps" rising over the parade ground, the notes as sad and mournful as a mourning dove's call. The last lamp in the barracks pinched out. Save for the sallow glow of a late-climbing moon slanting across his cot, he lay in a well of darkness.

An hour must have passed before he sat up. From the other end of the barracks chorused a medley of snores. He listened a while longer. Those were weary troopers; most of them had gone out that day with the lieutenant.

Ears cocked, he pulled on his shirt and reached for the chimney-pot hat; carrying shoes and blanket, his food pack inside it, he tiptoed toward the barracks door. He passed one snoring trooper. Now, like a trap under his bare feet, a board creaked. At once a trooper stirred. Laban froze. He could see the man. He was the one nearest the door, and he was tossing and snoring. A second man turned on his side, sending a stiffening fear through Laban. He was expecting the second trooper, whose head was turned toward him, to awaken and sit up and find him outlined in the moon glow. He wondered what excuse he could give.

Laban held dead still, just watching, clutching his belongings. To his immense relief, the man flopped over on his back, snoring again, with the unbroken hissing of a steam kettle. Laban eased past him. But the trooper nearest the doorway still stirred.

Without warning, that man sat bolt upright in bed and began mumbling. Laban, motionless, hardly breathed. Now he crooked his head to see better. He watched, his breath suspended. Pale light bathed the trooper's features, revealing the bushy mustache, the tousled hair. He was staring straight at Laban, muttering. Yet his voice sounded blurred. He was, Laban gathered finally, talking in his sleep.

Laban moved fast, without sound. He inched open the door and was squeezing through and shutting it behind him when he heard a sleepy trooper mumble: "Ye're talkin' to yerself again, Tom. Go back to sleep."

Outside, Laban flung a quick look around. The moonlit parade ground was a pale bed of silver, the high wall of the barracks a dark cliff overhanging its edge.

He pulled on his shoes and tied them and slipped to the corner of the barracks. Peering around it, he saw the many blurred shapes of the grazing horses; at the farthest end of the picket line stood the grayish, high-backed frame of Reuben. About ten rods beyond, the sentry strolled at his post.

Laban's heart sank. He could not take his mule without being seen. He studied the horses again, his mind reaching out, and the movements of the sentry. How far he paced this way, how far he went the other direction before he turned back.

A tautness took Laban. Cold sweat cracked his skin. There was a way, but only one. He must work fast.

When the sentry turned his back, Laban eased to the side of the first grazing cavalry mount. It required but a moment to untie the halter rope to the picket pin. The horse, freed, began drifting eastward while continuing to graze away from the barracks. Before the trooper reached the end of his post, Laban had released four horses. Now he retreated to the end of the barracks to watch.

He saw the sentry pause, apparently an idle looking about, and about-face to resume pacing back this way. As yet the loose horses, although past the picket line, weren't straying fast enough. They would not be very far from the barracks, Laban saw, when the trooper took alarm. That meant Laban couldn't reach his mount unseen.

He picked up some pebbles and tossed one at the nearest horse. He heard the stone strike the ground, short. He threw higher. The startled animal shied away, drawing the others with him, their hoofs ruffling the night quiet.

Laban saw the guard, halfway along his post, appear to halt. But no more than an instant. Forthwith, he was striding for the drifting horses, his sudden action causing them to swerve north. Falling behind, the trooper ran wide to turn them back, and, when he did, boots pounding hard, the horses swung into a trot.

The loose mass was moving to Laban's left when he rushed down the shadowed flank of the barracks to his mule. He freed the halter rope and led Reuben south behind the barracks and east to the shed, bridled him, slung on blanket and saddle, cinched up, and led off toward the wagon road. Hearing horses running in the distance, he had his moment of self-reproach for the trouble he was causing. It might take hours to catch the horses, although being grain-fed, they wouldn't wander out of the country.

He went on doggedly, stumbling now and then in the deep wagon ruts. At the river's cool edge he swung up. A backward look revealed the dull eye of a lone light in the barracks. He caught a distant shouting. Against his face he felt the rising wind, weighted with the wildness of far-off places. He clapped his heels and the gray mule, after balking momentarily, stepped into the sluggish stream.

Daylight caught him following the rutted windings of the wagon road, breasting a heaving sea of ridge swells and grassy prairie. Already a hot wind was coursing out of the southwest, bringing flurries of reddish dust. He saw no movement; he heard only the wild wind.

It seemed strange, after traveling so far alone from home, that he felt more lonesome now than before he had met Lieutenant Carr and the troopers and Enoch Emory. All good friends, except they didn't

233

understand why he must find work at Fort Griffin. He doubted that his life was really in danger, even if the raiders were white men. On the other hand, he would know the hawk-faced man, whoever he was — renegade or part-Indian — should he see him again, anywhere he saw him. If so, though, wouldn't the man know him as well, having seen Laban, bare-headed, for as long as Laban had seen his face?

That sobered Laban and he locked up the realization in his mind.

As the light strengthened, he reined off and rode parallel to the trail, half expecting to see troopers dusting after him. But nothing happened. Toward noon a stage station — square picket house and pole corrals — materialized out of the dusty glare, almost an intrusion in this windswept emptiness.

Thirst burned Laban's throat and mouth. His caution told him to ride on, but his need drew him up to the place. A change of relay horses stood, tail-switching, in the first corral; otherwise, he saw no life. He rode to the open doorway and looked in.

"What're you snoopin' here for?" The rough voice jarred from Laban's left.

He whipped about. A man stood at the corner of the picket building, his shotgun covering Laban.

"Not snoopin'," Laban answered, stung. "Just want some water." He was aware of raking murky eyes and a mouth as hard as a slit in a board. The man's hair hung, long and greasy, and the prickly beard, also greasy, reminded Laban of tangled underbrush. He was thick at the waist, thicker at the chest.

"Why'n't you call out?"

"Wasn't time," Laban replied, dumbfounded by the hostler's hostility, and eyed the shotgun. "You can put that down. I'm not armed."

The hostler lowered the weapon. "Have to haul all my water. Just reckon you can find your own."

Disbelief ruffled Laban. "Whereabouts?"

"On down the road."

"I thought this was a stage station?"

"Is . . . for them on the stage."

"Meaning . . . ?"

"Been drifters prowlin' about. So you keep right on makin' tracks."

"I ain't no drifter."

"Makes no difference."

Laban reined the mule on, as bewildered as he was angry. He had met many rebuffs on the trail, but never had he been refused water. Down the road a piece, he glanced back. Squarely behind the station, between it and the corrals, he saw the rock wall of a dug well, a crossbar resting between two poles, and a bucket hanging from a pulley rope. From here the rope looked yellow-new.

The sun's hot hand pressed down upon him. The glittery land swayed drunkenly. Miles onward, the old mule threw up his graceless head and sniffed the wind, and by that Laban knew he smelled water ahead. Before long the ragged belt of a timbered creek slanted across the road.

Finding only a stagnant pool at the rocky crossing, Laban turned upstream to seek cleaner water. He rode through a snarl of brush and came to a widening pool fed by a seep spring trickling over reddish sandstone. He and Reuben filled up side-by-side, after which he took off his shirt and scrubbed himself to the waist.

Refreshed, he ate sparingly of his supply of cold bread and bacon, saving some for supper and breakfast, figuring he wouldn't reach Fort Griffin until late tomorrow. He was resting on the cool sandstone when he heard horses coming. Not walking or jogging or trotting as sensible horsemen would treat horseflesh on a hot day, but at a punishing gallop. Tying Reuben out of sight in the brush, he went forward and crouched down where he could observe the crossing.

Soon two streaks of dust appeared from the east, back down the trail that Laban had traveled. The riders did not slow up until almost upon the creek, whereupon they hauled on the reins and the sweat-flecked, head-tossing horses slid to rearing stops, a bay and a black, and fell to drinking the stagnant water.

Fine-looking horses, Laban saw. A shame their riders treated them no better. The black was two hands taller, but the bay had smoother lines. His dark tail and mane were long and silky, and the silver-horned saddle on his back increased his sleek handsomeness. The sight filled Laban with disapproval and pleasure, and, as he watched, he felt a stab of late recognition. He had seen the horse before — yes. At the same moment, the bay's rider shifted in the saddle and absently looked toward Laban's hiding place.

For a hanging instant of panic, Laban was staring straight into the man's face — seeing the wizened, grizzled features, the dull-yellow eyes squinting against the sun. Turning front, the rider grunted to his companion, flung up a hand in impatience, jerked up the head of his still-drinking mount, and spurred clattering across the creek, the bay's shod hoofs ringing on the rocks.

Laban half rose to stare after them, feeling the damp cold of recognition clean to his bones, for the man astride the bay had robbed him of all his money and food the first night out of Jacksboro. $9.68, to be exact.

He sank down, left strengthless, an odd feeling threading through him. Although not superstitious, chance had sent him and the grizzly-faced thief westward on the same trail. It was strange.

He minded a fresh caution after he crossed the creek and swung off the road, alert to all around him. It was funny, he thought. Here he was in wild country said to abound with Indians and buffalo, and he had sighted neither, and his main fear was of a white man, a petty thief.

That evening he spread his blanket in a mesquite thicket, rationed himself cold bread and bacon, and fell asleep with the comforting hulk of Reuben close by against the fading skyline, and hearing the unbroken rustling of Reuben enjoying his short-grass vittles. Once in the night he awakened, disturbed by a dream in which riders on bay horses chased him and from whom there was no escape. He sat up, shivering, tense, aware of a motionless shape but steps away. He shrank back, then he saw that it was Reuben, a sentinel gray ghost in the luminous moon tide.

Next day he found no water until he rode down the rocky road and saw below him a shallow valley, brilliant under a robe of sunflowers, cut by a bright, narrow stream.

Under the blue sky, on a stony bluff across the valley, the flag flew over Fort Griffin, its brood of stone buildings seemingly crouched together for protection. Watching, Laban became conscious of a persistent hum, and he turned his head and saw the tents and wagons on the flat, the people and stock stirring, and the clutter of the town strung from the foot of the bluff to the stream, which he knew was called the Clear Fork of the Brazos.

He watered Reuben and took a side road leading toward town and began passing numerous camps and mounds of buffalo hides stacked like hay. His nostrils prickled at the smells: the wood smoke, the rancid yet wild whiff of the piled hides. Heading for the tangle of shacks and tents at the lower end of the principal street, Laban thought of his Uncle Gabe Bushrod. Laban's father, Jesse, had said that Uncle Gabe was "well-fixed." That Uncle Gabe had a business all his own. That he freighted and such, and ran a stage line from Jacksboro to Fort Griffin, and bought and sold buffalo hides.

Laban entered the noisy, crowded street, and at once was caught in the shifting current of riders and wagons and men afoot. He passed a livery stable, a blacksmith shop, a gun shop, a saddle shop; onward, he came to a solid row of saloons and he could hear rinky-tink piano music and he saw many long-haired men who he took for hunters going in and out. He passed a large general store and another and at the end of the street, just below the bluff, he saw wooden signs that read: The Planter's House and the Bison Hotel.

Next, he rode up and down the short street at the foot of the bluff and finally drew rein, sorely puzzled and disappointed, having seen naught of Uncle Gabe's prosperous business. A pedestrian came by and Laban asked: "Sir, where is Bushrod's place of business? His freight and stage line?"

A tiny frown flickered in the man's face and went out. "The hotel clerk in the Bison sells stage tickets. That's where they pick up the passengers. Bushrod himself is likely at his office. That's out on the flat. On the road to Fort Phantom Hill. You'll see the sign."

He eyed Laban with considerable curiosity and was still doing so as Laban rode off.

He found the sign over a rambling picket building, or *jacal,* the timbers being set on end and daubed with mud between. It read:

Bushrod's Freight & Stage Line
We Buy Hides

Hills of buffalo hides rose on both sides of the place, and behind it Laban saw several empty freight wagons and a scattering of sheds and corrals holding horses and mules and oxen. A warm expectancy hurried him. He tied Reuben to the hitching rail and went inside. Two men looked up from their card game. One a solid-bodied man, with trickily tobacco stains at his bearded mouth corners, the other middle-sized and gray and stooped, who jumped nervously at Laban's sudden entrance.

"Is Mister Bushrod in?" Laban inquired.

It was the big man who spoke, after a pause. "What you want?"

"He's my uncle. I've come all the way from Alabama to see him."

"What's your handle?"

"Laban C. Bushrod. The C stands for Columbus. Jesse Bushrod is my father."

The meaty face was expressionless. The

241

matter-of-fact eyes sized Laban up and down. With a shrug and a look of resignation for his companion, the man raked back his chair, stepped past the wooden counter, and disappeared through the doorway into the rear of the building.

Laban heard the indistinct murmur of voices back there, voices that ceased. Boot steps approached. His heart picked up momentum as he waited, taut, excited, shuffling his feet, while his whirling mind sought to piece together the confused image he had of Uncle Gabe.

The boot steps sounded just beyond the doorway. Laban leaned forward, his eyes intent. Suddenly a man stood there and Laban felt his expectancy drop away.

IV

The man in the doorway did not fit the picture that Laban had laid away in his mind, someone about the height and build of his father, someone tall and angular, stooped from working in the fields.

Instead, Laban saw a man short and round, his moon face beardless and pink, his mouth a cherry red, his white teeth as even as palings in a picket fence. Except the eyes didn't seem to go with the rest of him. Cool and quick, they were, between brown and yellow, flecked with glints.

And then that impression faded as the man came out, a wide smile wreathing his well-fed face. He held out a plump hand and his congenial voice melted the last of Laban's hesitancy.

"You're Laban . . . Brother Jesse's boy. I'm glad to see you!"

"Hello, Uncle Gabe."

Gabriel J. Bushrod's colorful get-up would have been outlandish back home, although on him, Laban thought, it looked just right: the buckskin jacket and wide-brimmed hat, the black string tie, the silver-buckled belt, the light blue pantaloons, and the polished Wellington boots.

"My boy . . . my boy . . . I remember you well. What brings you here?"

"Work," Laban said.

The slightest scowl, vanishing even as Laban noticed, ran across his uncle's face, and Gabe Bushrod was saying: "Brother Jesse must've misunderstood my letter. Although prospects are fair out here, there's no work for a boy. The frontier's no place for you. Mighty dangerous at times. Indians all around. You're welcome, though."

Laban spoke fast. "Oh, I didn't come to live with you, Uncle Gabe. Just rode in. Came by to see you first. I'll find work on my own. I can do purty near anything . . . handle mules, milk cows, pick cotton, dig taters, chop firewood, cut posts. I can even cipher some if I have to. Papa says I'm good at figures . . . well, good enough to add to and take away and divide and come out right."

"Fine, my boy. Fine. That's a manly way to look at the world." He tucked in his cherry-red lips and stared reflectively at the glossy toe of his right boot. "Fact is, since you're on the look-out for work, there's no better place in the West right now than Fort Worth."

"Where's that?" Laban asked, let-down.

"Southeast from here. Hundred miles or so. It's on the boom. Big cow town. Big shippin' point for buffalo hides and bones."

For a moment Laban's mind bent under his bitter disappointment, then sprang back. He shook his head. "I'll look around here first," he said, turning to go.

"Work's hard to come by in Griffin," Gabe Bushrod said, his tone discouraging. "Town's full of drifters and hunters. Not the buffalo there was last year." Laban was near the door when he heard his uncle's voice again. "Hold on, my boy. You broke? You need anything?"

Laban swung half around, fighting the

wrongness here, fighting the gnawing in his stomach. He saw his uncle slip his hand into a pocket and hold out a silver dollar. In the plump palm it looked as bright as hope itself and also, somehow, humiliating and cheap. Laban swallowed and said: "I've got money enough. Don't need a thing. I'm obliged to you." He went out in ragged step, unable to define the feeling he had, as if Uncle Gabe wasn't glad to see him and wanted to shoo him on elsewhere, out of town.

Riding past the camps toward Griffin, smelling the appetizing scents from the noon cooking fires, he felt the juices start in his jaws; for a flash he was tempted to ride over to the nearest men eating their dinners and ask if he could sit in. But he rode ahead, annoyed with himself, thinking it was bad to be so hungry you lost your manners and your pride as well.

When he came to the livery stable on the street, he dismounted where a man stood in the entrance, and asked: "You happen to need a hand around here? I can handle stock."

"You're the third by here today. Sorry, son."

"Much obliged just the same."

He rode upstreet, past the gun and saddle shops, through the reek flowing from the rowdy saloons. Seeing the first general store, he tied up there and entered, wondering what he should say to a town merchant, feeling his confidence sag. He'd felt at home talking to the livery store owner, a man used to handling animals; this was different.

Hearing the drone of voices, he saw two clerks waiting on shaggy hunters purchasing powder and lead. At the rear of the store a lumpish man was grimacing wryly over the pages of a thick ledger. He glanced up at the *clomp* of Laban's heavy shoes.

Laban opened his mouth to speak. Nothing came out.

"What is it, boy?"

"I . . . ah . . . is there," Laban squeaked out the hard-coming words, "any work I might do for you?"

The merchant's wryness retreated, giving way to a scrutiny that was not unsympathetic. "I turn down grown men every day. Business is bad. Hunters not haulin' in the hides they used to." Laban thanked him and was leaving when the other said: "Come back in a few days. There's a load of freight due."

He passed on to the other general store and inquired, and again there was nothing for him. He went out and stood in front, only vaguely aware of the passing riders and creaking wagons, struggling against a hollow desperation. Well, Uncle Gabe *was* right. Work was hard to find in Griffin. And suddenly he looked down, in the hopelessness of one who had reached an end in a strange land.

A vagrant breeze blew dust along the street. With that stir, Laban smelled cooking meat and beans and coffee. He raised his head and turned and saw a sign: Cowboy Café. Inside, he could see a rough counter and several tables and customers. Hungry as he was, a sense told him that now wasn't the time to ask. He pulled his attention away and started off, choosing to walk around rather than wait here.

He idled to the end of the street where it bumped against the base of the bluff on which the fort stood; turning right, he saw a creek beyond an alley and he stopped at the head of the alley and glanced down its cluttered length. A white-haired man, an apron around his waist, limped out the rear door of the Cowboy Café, gathered wood chips off a woodpile, and went back inside. The woodpile, Laban saw, had plenty of long saplings, but no pieces cut stove-size.

His mind turned on that, and after a while, when he entered the café and saw the man in the apron wiping off the counter,

Laban said: "I'd like to work for a meal."
Instantly he saw refusal forming in the long
face, and Laban spoke faster: "I can chop
wood."

"Most drifters would rather wash
dishes . . . it's easier."

"Your woodpile is low."

"How d'you know?"

"I looked."

The pale old eyes showed surprise. "If you
mean *work*, hop to it." He hooked a thumb,
gesturing out back.

His mood lifting, Laban waded through
the ravening smells in the kitchen and out
to the woodpile. He dragged an elm trunk
over to the chopping log, picked up a
double-bladed axe, rested his left foot on
the trunk to steady it, and commenced
chopping.

Sweat dripped off his forehead and nose
and ran down his chest. He skinned off his
shirt. It felt good to be doing something.
Every few minutes the café owner would
come to the doorway and look. He never
spoke. Laban split the larger chunks into
fours, pausing only to stack the pieces near
the door and drag another long length to
the pile.

He was still chopping when the old man
limped outside. His eyes shifted from the

stack of cut wood to Laban. "A whole rick," he said, although careful not to show his pleasure.

"I'll cut some more," Laban offered, resting on the axe handle.

"Enough there to last me a week," came the gruff reply. "Come in and eat your dinner."

It seemed that he would never fill the gap inside him. He ate buffalo steak and gravy, sourdough biscuits, and beans and rice, liking the sweet, gamy taste of the wild meat.

When he had finished, the proprietor said: "Reckon you earned your supper, too. Be back before eight o'clock. I close early."

Feeling more comfortable now, Laban mounted and decided to ride out on the flat; maybe he could find an odd job, even though he realized his chances were slim. He rode by camp after camp without stopping, seeing that all had idling, able-bodied men. Turning back, he saw the dark mounds of the hide yards spread out on the upper end of the flat. His expectancy waned when he saw no wagons bringing in fresh hides.

By late afternoon he had made the rounds of all the business places in town without success. Maybe he should go to Fort Worth after all, like Uncle Gabe urged. He ate supper at the café and got up to leave. The proprietor motioned him to wait.

"You keep me plenty of firewood chopped up, my place swept out neat as a pin . . . you've got two meals a day here. There's a shed across the alley you can sleep in."

Laban could do no more than stare at him for a moment. "I'm mighty obliged, Mister. . . ."

"Folks call me Panhandle." Unwavering gray eyes looked out from a craggy face. He was tall and skinny and his white hair, combed straight, came out behind like a duck's tail. He wore cowboy boots and was so bowlegged, what with his limp, he seemed to walk in a crouch. "Broom's behind the door. Now get to work an' don't stir up too much dust. This ain't no barn."

"You bet, Mister Panhandle."

The old man, starting off, pivoted around. "Listen, sprout. Don't get the notion I'm tender-hearted. Why, when I was your age, I could take the kinks outta any bronc' in Texas, an' you know how big the Lone Star state is. Did, too, for a long time, till a spooky one fell with me, busted me up." He glared at Laban. "Hop along now. I'm too busy to waste time gabbin'."

Later, Laban rode to the creek to water his mule, returned, and tied up behind the shed. Tomorrow he would manage for a picket rope. Inside, he found a board bunk, wash pan, two candle stubs, and an empty wooden bucket that he filled at a well behind the shed. He spread his blanket on the bunk and lay down, in his ears the raucous murmur of the town. A restlessness invaded him and he went to the doorway to look across the creek. Deep twilight was settling over the river valley in purple waves. A southeast breeze routed the last of the day's heat.

Impulsively he slapped on his hat and strolled around to the street, watching the changing sky, at ease with this frontier world that had seemed so hostile until he met Mr. Panhandle. This end of the street was silent. Toward the river the saloons glowed with light, men crowded in and out, and their voices lifted above the jerky music. Horses lined the hitching racks. Laban heard a *whoop,* followed by a shot. Nobody on the street as much as turned in that direction, nor did the music pause.

His rambling eyes noticed a poster nailed on the wall of a shack. Laban read:

$500 REWARD
Wanted
(Dead or Alive)
Duff Fallon, *alias* Red River Jack, *alias*

251

Rattlesnake Monte, alias Brazos Bill:
wanted for murder, horse and cattle theft
in Young and Shackleford Counties.
Description: dark hair, Roman nose, steel
blue-gray eyes; stands six feet, four
inches, weighs about 225 pounds. This
man is extremely dangerous; has a
violent temper; is known to ride with
renegade Indians.
Any person having information as to his
whereabouts notify the Texas Rangers
at once.

Signed,
Enoch Emory
Texas Rangers
Fort Belknap, Texas

Seeing Emory's name was like a warm hand outstretched in the twilight. Sometimes at this hour Laban's thoughts turned irresistibly to his people and home. He found himself letting down, caught in a web of homesickness. Knowing that wouldn't do, he drew straight and put away that weakness and walked on down the street, forcing himself to take further note of the town. A little way on, he pressed his back against the front of a darkened store, satisfied to avoid the noisy crowd.

A single shot sounded at the lower end of

the street. A horse was running. Laban saw the rider racing upstreet, whooping and firing his handgun over his head. The milling crowd parted like a wave as the rider dashed through. In front of Laban, he wheeled his horse and, drawing another six-shooter, went charging and shooting back down-street as before.

As the last gunshot sounded, the street regained its rowdy voice and the same rackety din prevailed. A figure limped up to Laban. It was Panhandle, who glowered his disapproval. "This is no place for a sprout after sundown."

"Just takin' in the sights," Laban said.

"Same sights you saw in daylight." Scorn spread into Panhandle's gravelly voice: "I would swap this hull dad-burned town for one good, clean cow camp." He swung on, his boot heels striking hollow beats on the boardwalk.

Two booted men jingled out of the saloon next door and halted in the outthrown light near the hitching rack. One spoke, his voice loud and blurred: "Seco . . . let's punch the breeze for camp."

"Too early," the other said. "I aim to look around town."

He shouldered away, and Laban's senses jumped alert. He would know that curt,

253

unfeeling voice and those gray-dirty, grizzled features anywhere, for they belonged to the man who had drugged him and robbed him that night, camped west of Jacksboro, and who Laban had seen later on the trail between Fort Belknap and Griffin.

It was abruptly too much for Laban. A righteous hot anger burst in him. A hard determination. Before he quite realized it, he was striding over and facing Seco and hearing his own tight, unnatural voice: "Remember me? You stole my money that night in camp. You owe me nine dollars and sixty-eight cents . . . I want it back!"

Seco leaned away, taken by surprise. A snarl creased his leathery face. "Go on, you fool kid. I don't know you." Yet Laban saw recognition flare in the yellow eyes. Seco started to turn.

Laban grabbed his arm. "You do too know me!"

He expected Seco to face him, to deny again. Therefore, he was unprepared for the snake-like swiftness, for the blinking suddenness of the long-barreled revolver in Seco's hand. Laban tried to dodge. The barrel followed him, ever faster. Too late, Laban flung up a protecting hand. Pain splintered through his head, and he felt the strength going from his legs in one empty moment.

He was falling, dropping off into a bottomless world without light. . . .

Somewhere high above him, hazily, dimly, all but lost, he thought he saw a cone of light, as if he lay in a deep well and that was the sky up there, so far away. He struggled toward it painfully, only to fall back; everything before him became black. When he opened his eyes again, the light was still there. It seemed a little brighter this time. His breath coming in tortured gasps, he staggered up and groped toward the wall. Sharp rocks bit into his hands. He reached upward and caught hold, lifted his right foot, found a niche in the rocks, and started climbing. For a measureless interval the light stayed as distant as ever. He kept on. Often he had to rest, hugging the rocky face of the wall. His strength was nearly gone when, to his wonder, he emerged into strong, yellow light — real light.

A face swam out of the uncertain glow. The worried features of Panhandle.

"Where am I?" Laban asked, his voice trailing off.

"On your bunk. Now cut out your gabbin'. I was comin' back down the street when I saw that galoot pistol-whip you." Panhandle growled his courage. "He got away 'fore I could lay hands on him."

That didn't matter now to Laban. His head was whirling and he was drifting away on a cloud of softest down, while Panhandle's craggy face grew dimmer and dimmer. . . .

After that, whenever he opened his eyes, Panhandle was there; later, Laban sat up and touched hands to his throbbing head, feeling the thick layers of bandages.

"Gettin' hungry?" Panhandle asked.

"Kinda," Laban said, squinting up against the pain.

"Good sign," the old man said. "Now see if you can hike over there to the door an' back."

Laban leaned forward to rise. The room spun. He sat back.

"Try it again," Panhandle said gruffly.

Laban wobbled up. His head thundered, but his vision was clear. Weaving, he reached the door and looked out. The timbered creek, the hills rimming the valley — all seemed to float in a beckoning soft haze of warm sunlight under the blue arch of the sky. He had the sensation of being gone on a long and dangerous journey and, humbly, of being allowed to return. He went back to the bunk, his walk steadier.

"Good thing you've got a hard head,"

Panhandle barked, although he sounded relieved.

By the next day, Laban felt strong enough to go looking for work.

In front of the general store where he had first stopped, two men grunted and sweated while unloading barrels and boxes from freight wagons. Laban quietly joined them and tugged and carried a box inside. He was wrestling with another to the tailgate when a burly freighter demanded: "Who hired you, boy?"

"Nobody. I just figure you needed some help."

The man wiped a shirt sleeve across his beaded forehead. "Well, that's plain. What you figure you're worth?"

"A man's wages."

"A boy gettin' man's pay?"

"I can do a man's work."

"Show me."

Laban lifted and heaved and tugged and toted until sundown, when the unloading was finished. The freighter paid him $1, and Laban trudged to the shed and washed up. After supper, he swept out the café. Back in the shed, he lay down to rest a short while. He awakened to find the morning sun gliding high.

That afternoon he made fifty cents cleaning out the livery stable, an opportunity that the proprietor's painful back made possible. Next morning, astride Reuben, passing a small hide yard, Laban spied a lone man wearily tossing buffalo skins off a wagon onto an elongated pile.

"Need a hand?" Laban ventured.

"There's five hundred hides on this wagon."

"Some heap. I can see that."

"Bull hides," the man said for emphasis. "Average fifty pounds apiece." He gripped a stiff hide and flung it upon the pile. "Takes a man," he stressed, and eyed Laban up and down. "If you can earn your salt, I'll pay you a dollar to finish up."

Laban dismounted, tied Reuben to a rear wheel, and climbed aboard the furry load. He took hold of a hide, surprised at the flint-like stiffness and weight, and tossed it on the pile. It landed askew. He jumped down and righted the hide and clambered up and tossed another, which came down about right.

At that, the owner got down, stuffed and lighted his pipe, and rested against a front wheel to watch.

Throughout the rest of the week Laban did odd jobs around town. By then he showed a profit of $7, five of which he mailed home. He began to feel a certain order and confidence in his new life, the elation that he was making it on his own.

Today, replenishing Panhandle's stove wood supply, he dragged a sapling over to the chopping log and swung the axe. It bit halfway through and stuck. Lifting the long handle to free the blade, he paused in the middle of another swing, his attention fixed on a roundish rider coming up the alley on a high-headed sorrel gelding.

A nameless feeling whipped through Laban, for he didn't want to see Uncle Gabe Bushrod. But there wasn't time to go inside. Uncle Gabe waved in recognition and Laban leaned on the axe and waited, seeing the moon face light up, hearing the rolling voice:

"Laban, my boy! Where you been keepin' yourself? I've looked all over. Got a job for you."

"Job?" Laban rubbed his chin, searching for the eagerness he couldn't find.

"You bet. A good 'un . . . at man's wages." The clean-shaven, pink face was beaming. "Think Gabriel J. Bushrod'd let his own kin be in need if he could lift a little finger?"

"I don't need a thing," Laban said. "Everything's jim-dandy."

"Ah, good boy. Good boy. You're a true Bushrod. Went out and made good on your own. I like that. Shows spine. Shows spine. But the job I got in mind beats this all hollow."

"What is it?" Laban asked, in the grip of an obscure caution.

"Riding, my boy. Riding."

"My mule's purty slow and old."

"Forget that old scarecrow." Laban ruffled up. Uncle Gabe, seeing, showed an amending smile. "I mean you'll ride blooded stock . . . the best."

Laban turned it over in his mind, feeling the point of his reluctance dull. Hadn't Uncle Gabe been right about the lack of work in Griffin? Hide hunting was falling off; the buffalo herds were thinning out. All Laban had found was an odd job here and there. Most of all, steady riding at man's pay meant he could help his folks sooner, in the way he longed to. Of an instant the last of his hesitation dissolved.

"When do I start, Uncle Gabe?"

"Right away, my boy. Right away. Come out to my ranch first thing in the morning."

"Your ranch?" Nobody in the Bushrod family had ever owned land.

"East across the Clear Fork. Take the first trail south off the wagon road." Gabe Bushrod whirled the gelding and tore down the alley, out of sight in moments.

He rode a fine-looking horse, Laban mused. As fine as the bright bay that Seco mistreated. Laban picked up the axe. As he lifted it for a swing, an insight delayed him. Why would Uncle Gabe hire him, a green kid? Why would he pay man's wages? And where would Laban ride in Indian country? And why?

It was kind of strange, now that he thought about it without hurry. But he had given his word.

V

Next morning Laban rode east across the Clear Fork and, following Uncle Gabe Bushrod's directions, reined off on the first trail south. He covered several miles and saw no living creature. The trail seemed to be leading him nowhere, into a low huddle of hills. Passing through them, he saw buildings and sheds hugging the brown earth and a vast outscatter of corrals, all empty except one holding a band of saddle horses.

A windswept place, bleak and harsh to the eye, dulling his anticipation. Save for the desire to help his people, he wondered whether he should have come here.

Hardly did he reach the picket house

when Uncle Gabe stepped out under the overhang, his spurs jingling, so abruptly that Laban knew he had been watching. His uncle's hearty voice was as a genial wind blowing away Laban's doubts.

"Welcome, my boy! Welcome. Come in."

Laban dismounted and untied his blanket roll. A ranch hand hurried up and took Reuben's reins. At his uncle's sweeping gesture of invitation, Laban entered the house.

"Here it is, my boy," his uncle said, gesturing. "My poor little ol' ranch. Nothing fancy like town, but it's home to me."

Laban took a circling look. Except for a rifle over the fireplace, the walls were bare and the furniture was crude. A man's house.

"Wanted a little place of my own," his uncle was saying, almost wistfully. "Where a man can sit back and enjoy his sunset years when he's too old to sweat out an honest day's work. Once the country quiets down, I'll go into the cattle business. Too many Indian scares now."

He showed Laban to his room, and left. Laban put down his blanket roll. The room was as bare as the shed behind Panhandle's café. Beyond the window, spread the great tangle of stout pole corrals. A heap of corrals, it occurred to him in an absent way, for a little ranch.

Drifting back to the main part of the house, Laban found his uncle gone, and he sat down and glanced around for something to read. There wasn't, he saw, a single book or old newspaper or picture in the room. He rested there a while, his mind running free, and got up and walked outside. All his young life he had toiled hard; now, unoccupied, he felt an eagerness to look around.

Another picket structure, longer and lower than the house, made like cowboy bunkhouses Laban had read about, caught his eye. In the shade there, five nondescript men lounged and smoked and talked, among them Gabe Bushrod. Laban strayed that way. He hadn't gone far when he saw his uncle rise and come toward him in his round man's rolling gait. He was smiling broadly as he approached and he laid one hand on Laban's shoulder, and before Laban knew it he was headed back for the house.

"Be time for dinner directly," Gabe Bushrod said genially.

After the noon meal, which Laban ate with his uncle in the house, Bushrod put on his wide hat, crimped it at a jaunty angle, and said: "Got some business chores in town. You hang close."

Laban felt the urge to ask about his riding job, but Uncle Gabe was jingling out the door by then. Watching from a window, Laban saw his uncle and the others saddle up and dust for town. Laban shrugged mentally. Uncle Gabe was a busy man, what with a stage line and freight business and the ranch to look after. Be time enough this evening to talk about riding. As he mused, Panhandle's parting words came back to him:

"So you're gonna ride for Gabe Bushrod, an' he's your uncle?" The old man glared down at the lunch counter, scrubbed as clean as an old woman's washboard. Gruff as his voice sounded, his usual bite was missing. He pinned on Laban a look that brushed concern. Laban saw it fleetingly, and then Panhandle wheeled, limping back to the rear room, where he slept, and limped back, *clinking* a pair of light spurs. "Man needs jinglers if he's gonna ride." Something gone by, yet fierce, glowed in the rheumy eyes. Waving aside Laban's grateful thanks, he turned his back to busy himself in the kitchen.

Laban became restless as the idling afternoon wore on. He wandered to the corral where the speckled-gray shape of old Reuben stood, looking as indestructible as the bleak, surrounding hills, and on to a larger corral, its hinged gate swung open. Heavy posts buttressed the pole enclosure; it showed a much used and battered appearance, the vertical post braces leaning outward as if sprung by lunging horseflesh.

He inspected two more corrals, drawn by their size and sturdy construction. A thought spun up: *Uncle Gabe must buy and sell a heap of horses and mules . . . no doubt he needed a big number for his stages and freight wagons. But why didn't he keep extra stock here?*

Laban poked along. From a hilltop south of the ranch house, he spied the winding shine of the Clear Fork; way out, he could see a dark mass. His blood raced. Buffalo! A distant *boom* rode in on the wind, and after it more deep-throated *booms,* and he saw puffs of white smoke, miniature blooms, and the dark mass moving off. In a bit, the bellowing rifle sounds ceased.

He picked up a flat fragment of gray rock and threw it with all his might, watching its sailing flight, seeing it drop, fading faster, blurring, and hearing the dim *tick* as it fell to earth. Picking up another piece, he turned in a different direction, to his right, and threw, and, as his eyes followed the downward course of the rock and it struck, something attracted his attention. A rocky ledge on the opposite slope, and the dim, pale trace of a path leading to it, and under the ledge an opening. A coyote or wolf den, and immediately he felt a yearning to explore it.

Long-legging down the hillside, he understood how he had missed seeing the place until now. To a body coming from the ranch, the ledge, southwest, was hidden from view by a hump in the uneven slope.

He came to the path and turned along it and topped the humped rise, seeing the ranch house not far away. It dropped from sight as he descended the other side. The path, plain enough from the hilltop, ran dimly through rocks and short grass. His pulse was quickening. He wasn't ready for the path to drop so fast. It dipped steeply, past a spur of the ledge, and down to flatter footing, there to broaden and run straight to the opening under the ledge.

Laban did not know why, but he was shortening his step and aware of a strangeness. It was the path. Here below the ledge, which he saw was an eroded bank of a little stream, now summer-dry, the path was as plain as a cow track. He dropped to one knee, his gaze fixing. In the grayish dust lay the unmistakable print of a cowboy boot, the long, broad sole and the small boot heel.

An oddness, a wrongness, deepened in him. He rose and moved slowly onward, seeing the den — yes, the opening was big enough for a den, maybe larger, maybe a cave. He was within a dozen steps of it when he heard a slight sound above and behind him, then a heavy voice calling down: "Boy! Where are you?"

Glancing upward, he recognized the ranch house cook, a lanky, shaggy-browed man who Uncle Gabe had called Mitch. He held a rifle. He was puffing hard, blowing out the ends of his tobacco-rusty, handlebar mustache, and had to catch his breath before he continued. "There's Injuns skulkin' 'tween here an' the river . . . come on!"

He held a look on Laban, who, for a moment, sensed that Mitch expected him to make argument. But Laban, after a glance at the den, turned and climbed the path to where Mitch stood. Laban looked toward the river. He saw no Indians. Neither, it crossed his mind, had he sighted Indians from the hilltop and he could see a long way from there.

Mitch seemed to read his thinking. "Think a greasy Injun's gonna stay in sight forever? They disappeared in them trees there where the river bends." A keener look, and Mitch said: "Stay outta this place. Rattlers thick down there."

He hurried back, looking over his shoulder at the river, and Laban followed. At the house, Mitch handed Laban a rifle and told him to watch sharp, and they took positions in the yard. Laban saw no motion. An hour later Mitch shrugged. "If they's comin' here, they'd hit us by now. Just the same, Gabe will send the boys down there to look."

Short of sundown, Gabe Bushrod and the crew rode in. Laban saw Mitch go out and talk to them, making gestures. Bushrod, nodding, took the entire outfit in a rushing ride toward the river, fanning out as they went. Laban lost sight of them in the timber. No shots came back.

Early darkness was near when his uncle came to the house. He looked dusty and tired. His cool eyes, glinting brown and yellow in the lantern light, acquired a severity.

"My boy, it's not safe roamin' these hills by your lonesome," he said, shaking his head from side to side. "We found enough Indian tracks at the river for a whole tribe."

"I got restless, Uncle Gabe. When can I start riding?"

A quicksilver smile replaced Gabe Bushrod's sternness. Playfully he poked Laban's shoulder, took a hitch at his silver-buckled belt that had slipped below the melon-shaped bulge of his middle. "My boy," he boomed, "you took the words right off the tongue of Gabriel J. Bushrod, you did. In town today I finally located just the horse I want for you."

"A horse?" Laban was thinking that Uncle Gabe, with all his stock, shouldn't have to go looking for another saddle horse.

"Not just *a horse*. This one's special. A stocking-footed sorrel. Quick as a cat. Easy to ride. Like sittin' in a rocking chair. Now you rest easy. Eat your supper. I'll take the boys out for another look-see upriver. Man can't sleep with the Indians around."

Far into the night, it must have been, a drumming invaded Laban's slumber, a growing clatter. Vaguely, half awake, he knew he was tossing and struggling to shut out the intrusive noise that continued to rise in rolling waves.

He sat up, thrown awake, startled. Through the open window poured the drumming rumble of many horses. He went to the window and looked out into the yard. It seemed to float in moonlight. Down by the corrals he could see the dark, swerving knots of horses. He could hear their *clicking* hoofs.

He drew around, his head churning. On bare feet, he stepped into the hallway and down it to his uncle's room and looked in. Moonlight streamed over the empty bed, over the unwrinkled blankets.

Wondering, Laban started back to his room. At that moment the rumbling racket grew louder. He stopped, listening, curious. Obeying an impulsive wish, he hastened on through the silent house, opened the front door, and let himself outside. When he stopped, he stood behind a shed midway between the house and the bunkhouse. Men's voices reached him, voices mixed with the nervous whistling of penned horses circling inside the corrals.

The voices ebbed and there fell a pause, when he caught just the quick-footed horses, then, gradually, the tinkling cadence of spurs and boot steps as riders moved heavily toward the bunkhouse. He saw them and flattened against the shed's wall, recognizing the round figure of his uncle among them.

"Plenty time for coffee," a man said curtly, and Laban tensed at the familiar voice.

"Not as much as you think, Seco," a strong, compelling voice answered. "It's fixin' to light up pretty soon." Laban had not heard the voice before. In the pale glow of the moon, the speaker loomed above the other riders. His wide, hat brim cast shadows around his face.

"Time enough," Seco snapped.

"Just don't forget who gives the orders."

Seco did not reply.

The riders jingled on to the bunkhouse, and, when a lantern glowed there, Laban slipped back to the house, more bewildered than before. Why would Uncle Gabe hire a man like Seco? Why would the crew drive horses at night? It had to be because of Indians. And who was the man who towered over the others, the man with the deep voice?

Laban lay down, troubled. Later, he heard Uncle Gabe come in.

He blinked awake to dazzling sunlight warm on his face, and he realized at once that it was late. He dressed and, thinking of breakfast, left his room. Passing Uncle Gabe's room, he glanced in and saw it was empty. Yet that would not be unusual at this hour. Yet that emptiness brought upon him a faint intuition, and suddenly he rushed back to his room and over to the window and looked out.

The corrals were as lifeless as though he

had dreamed of the penned horses circling and whistling in the moonlight.

It was early evening of the next day. Laban sat in the kitchen finishing his supper. Across from him sat Mitch, as inscrutable as a slab of sandstone, the only member of the crew left on the ranch.

Horses clattered outside the house, and Gabe Bushrod's voice boomed: "Laban, my boy, come out here!"

Laban did not rise. He felt uncertain, puzzled. He met Mitch's pointed stare, and Mitch said: "He's callin' you . . . better go out there." Laban obeyed, for he was going out anyway, walking slowly.

Uncle Gabe held the reins of two horses. He groaned and held a hand to his stomach.

Laban was alarmed. "What's the matter?"

"Just feelin' poorly. Never mind." Gabe Bushrod then, with a show of ceremony, placed one set of reins in Laban's lax hand. "Never let it be said that Gabriel J. Bushrod failed to keep his word. Here's your horse, my boy . . . the one I promised you."

Laban couldn't speak. His eyes widened on the horse, a compact sorrel gelding with stocking feet and pointed ears, his reddish-brown coat as glossy as satin, the long sweeping tail and the graceful blond mane hanging like silk. An irregular white blaze marked the handsome face and one eye looked glassy. But, if anything, the big patch of blaze and the one off-color eye made striking differences that Laban liked, as if nature had made certain that a body, once seeing such a horse, would never forget him, for the rest of the little sorrel was perfect.

Still, Laban delayed, uncertain whether he should accept.

"He's yours," Uncle Gabe said. "I'm giving him to you to keep. His name is School-boy. See that new saddle on him?"

Laban saw, and he stared at the reins he held, without knowing why he hesitated. Was it because of the way Uncle Gabe had acted that first day in town? When Laban had sensed that he wasn't welcome? Now all this. It was too much for him to understand.

"Take some of the squeaks out of that new saddle," he heard his uncle suggest.

Laban was thinking of still another thing. He stopped himself just in time from asking: *Does Seco ride for you?* To ask would have told his uncle that Laban was spying the night he saw the horses and overheard the crew. Acting on something far in the background of his mind, some instinct he must trust, instead he said: "A fine-looking horse, Uncle Gabe. I'm proud to have him and I'm obliged to you." He stroked School-boy's nose.

"You start riding in the morning," Gabe Bushrod said, his tone changing.

Laban dropped his hand from the velvety nose. His uncle meant it. Laban would earn his keep.

"I'll be ready. What do I do?"

A sliver of time passed. Finally Gabe Bushrod said: "Ride to Jacksboro and back."

"Jacksboro?" A quietness stole over Laban. He stood a mite straighter, surprised, thinking of what had happened to him and Reuben, of the men like Seco who preyed on travelers taking the Jacksboro-Belknap trail. Maybe he and Schoolboy wouldn't be so lucky a second time.

"It's a long way," he said uncertainly.

"Just do what I say and you'll make it fine." His uncle's voice sounded as cheerful as usual. His eyes, however, had a tense and searching quality, and, when he spoke again, he seemed to pick his words with extra care. "I'd go myself but I got the miseries and the crew's gone. There's a letter in Jacksboro I want you to pick up for me. A business letter. . . . Be greenbacks in it from an old friend. That money's important to me, my boy . . . important enough I can't trust it on the stages, which can't run regular no-how on account of the cussed Indians . . . and nobody would expect a boy to carry money. Now, would they?"

Laban had to admit that made horse sense. He rubbed his cheek bone with his left forefinger. "I don't have a gun," he said, thinking of Indians and the likes of Seco.

"There's a new saddle gun in the house," his uncle assured him. "If you see any Indians, just turn Schoolboy loose. I promise you he can throw dust at any scrub Indian pony." Some of his light-hearted manner lessened. "Don't tell any white man you meet what your business is. He might try to rob you. Don't even tell a Ranger, if he asks you, or any yellow-leg trooper. They might stop you . . . take you to the post . . . figure you're too young to ride the trail." All banter left his round face. Worry squeezed into his eyes; *funny,* Laban thought, touched, *they now looked a pious, beseeching brown instead of yellow glinted.* His uncle spoke in a still softer voice that brushed self-pity. "I've got to have that letter back here in four days. . . . My boy, my business is in a desperate way. That's why . . . if you thought . . . that first day in town. . . ." He hung his head. He let go a painful sigh and groaned from deep within him. "If I don't get that letter, I could even lose my poor little ol' ranch, here, where I aim to finish out my days, whatever Providence has in store for me. And I'm gettin' no younger. My boy, can I trust you to do this one last thing for me? Can I?"

Laban's sympathy burst forth. He nodded agreement at once, unable to resist the pleading face. Unimportant was Seco's presence on the ranch or the mysterious horses and their disappearance or where the crew had gone. For Laban was a Bushrod, and a Bushrod man always helped others.

"I'll go," he said. His voice sounded strained, unlike his own.

"Ah, good boy. Good boy. In the morning, I'll tell you the rest."

VI

Daylight crouched behind the streaky eastern grayness. Laban, mounted on Schoolboy, looked down at his Uncle Gabe Bushrod. A saddle gun slanted, stock forward, in a short leather scabbard under Laban's right leg. An ample supply of jerky and biscuits bulged his saddlebags, a blanket was tied behind the cantle of his stiff new saddle, and a canteen hung on a strap from the saddle horn.

Gabe Bushrod pressed both hands to his

generous middle and a low groan escaped him. "Man can't ride the ridges when he's off his feed. Remember, now, follow the trail as long as you can keep a sharp look-out all around. When that oak timber and mesquite starts to hem you in, hit for open country a while, then swing back on the trail. That way no cussed red devil is gonna jump you in close. If some try it, let Schoolboy throw dust in their feathers."

Grave and silent, Laban thought his Uncle Gabe made the ride sound as easy as falling off a log, which wasn't so, he knew. Nevertheless, Laban wanted to help and he had given his word and he was going to Jacksboro, hell or high water.

"Now about that letter. . . . Go to Daley's Blacksmith Shop. Ask for Daley. Tell him Gabe sent you. He'll give you the letter. That's all there is to it, my boy."

Gabe Bushrod stepped back. He seemed to avoid Laban's eyes, and for that one moment the moon face was free of the grimacing pain. But when Uncle Gabe brought his gaze back, Laban saw the pained look again.

"I don't figure you'll see any red devils," his uncle said. "We've chased 'em hard around here. Good luck, my boy. Watch sharp. Trust your horse."

Laban barely touched spurs to Schoolboy's flanks, and the eager sorrel, nodding his handsome head, glided away, taking Laban off in his smooth running walk. Last evening, riding the little gelding for the first time, Laban had found himself aboard a mighty good horse. Alert, quick, easy to ride, Schoolboy hardly required reining. A mere pressure of his legs, Laban discovered, turned the horse, thus leaving Laban's hands free, and, when he dismounted and dropped the reins, his horse stood without straying.

All the warm excitement and pleasure of that first ride swelled in Laban again, dispelling the nature of his dangerous ride. Only one question remained unanswered — could Schoolboy run as fast as Uncle Gabe said?

In a short time, Laban was riding through the gap north of the ranch and approaching the Jacksboro trail. There he turned east. Night sounds lingered. Insects hummed. A coyote slunk across the road. He jerked at a sudden series of rushing cries. A moment and he expelled his breath in relief. It was only a late-hunting nighthawk swooping low over the road, uttering shrill *peenks* as it zigzagged after insects. Schoolboy had ignored the sounds.

Daylight found Laban traveling into the

rising sun. About an hour afterward, he spotted the first stir of motion ahead. Being in open country, he did not yet leave the trail. Dark-clad horsemen coming toward him. White men. Troopers. A detail of seven. He sighed his relief.

As Laban swung over to ride past them, the lead trooper held up a delaying hand, and Laban recognized Sergeant Huckleby, his blouse unbuttoned, the ends of his sandy mustache drooping in a mournful ox horn.

"It's you . . . the fool kid that turned the mounts loose an' skedaddled," Huckleby said. Laban said nothing, and the sergeant asked: "Pass anybody between here and the Clear Fork?"

Laban shook his head. "Been trouble?"

"Army dispatch rider robbed last night other side the stage station."

"I reckon Indians are bad hereabouts, too," Laban said.

Huckleby swept him an old soldier's puckered frustration. "If it was just Indians, you can bet we wouldn't have to scout up and down this road ever' day like we been lately. Where you headed?"

"Jacksboro."

"Hmmm." The sergeant scratched his cheek in reflective strokes. Another question came and passed in his sun-reddened eyes. "Bet-

ter steer clear of strangers. Somebody might take a powerful likin' to that dandy horse." He grunted a command and led the detail on down the road.

So steadily did Schoolboy cover ground and the hours glide by that the square picket house and the corrals of the stage station came in view sooner than Laban expected. Remembering the hostler's unfriendliness, he would have ridden on except he wanted to water his horse.

He rode up, his jaw set. Again he saw the man, standing, this time, in the doorway, and again the man held a shotgun. Nearer, Laban read the stiff unwelcome in the hostler's stance, in the way he watched, in the unyielding, greasy mouth.

Laban halted, uncertain how to begin. He was about to speak when he saw the hostler stare at Schoolboy, saw the unfriendly eyes blink and change, saw an astonishing alteration come to the bearded face. The man was actually smiling, or trying to — a forced smile — and he lowered the shotgun and invited — "Step down." — as though he wasn't used to being agreeable. "Help yourself to water out back."

Nodding his thanks, wondering at the switch, Laban rode behind the house to a watering trough near the well and got down.

While the sorrel drank, Laban looked about. It was a littered place: tin cans, broken bottles, bits of rotten harness, a worn-out boot, the bones of a stage wheel — all on a rubbish heap. But the stage teams in the first corral looked well kept.

He took a lengthening look, noticing the size and sturdiness of two additional corrals farther back, both empty, the hinged gates swung open. He wondered why they interested him so. Still watching, he suddenly understood why. They were sturdy copies of the corrals on Uncle Gabe's ranch.

"See somethin'?" queried a voice that was friendly yet not friendly.

It was the hostler. Musing, Laban hadn't heard him walk up. "Just resting," Laban said, and climbed to the saddle. He waved his thanks and swung out upon the broad trail, puzzling over the unexpected hospitality.

While the miles fell behind, the spreading swells of summer-yellow grass glittered in rippling waves under the smoky barrel of the sun. The little sorrel saddled eagerly across the prairie world, ears flicking, watchful, nostrils flared to the grassy scents, the beat of his small hoofs as unbroken as the roll of a drum.

Now and then Laban recognized a stretch

of prairie, a shouldering ridge, a mesquite-dotted flat. Up ahead the floor of the rolling prairie was wrinkling and humping toward the red-hued Salt Fork of the Brazos.

Schoolboy's easy gait, the warm sun, the whispering wind, the glimmering face of the land — Laban began to feel a light drowsiness under their lulling spell. The rutted trail crooked around the knob of a hill and ran toward a clump of post oaks, poised to climb the backbone of the ridge guarding the river.

Something among the trees, a shifting movement, held Laban's eyes. He thought, late, of the open stretch to his right, but, as he whirled his horse, he saw two white men riding out of the oaks. Men in high-crowned hats. He held up. Looking closer, he felt a swift recognition. One man was Enoch Emory, the Texas Ranger.

Emory waved and spurred over. An incredulous smile spread over his saddle-brown face. "You? Where'd you run off to?"

"To Griffin to find work." Laban sounded apologetic while not meaning to.

"Looks like you found some," Emory drawled, his approving gaze on Schoolboy. Although Laban could see questions behind the steady eyes, he sensed it wasn't this soft-spoken man's way to pry into a body's business. And Laban offered no further explanation.

"Meet anybody on the road?" Emory asked, casual about it.

"Some troopers."

"Where you headed, buckaroo?"

"Jacksboro."

Emory raised an eyebrow. "Long ride," he said, curious, but no more. "Don't make a fire tonight."

"Been Indians around?"

"None spotted . . . but that means nothing a-tall." All the while he was thoughtfully studying Schoolboy. "Wonder where I've seen your horse before . . . and maybe I didn't. Mind tellin' me how you came by him?"

Laban told him, leaving out the purpose of his ride. That was Uncle Gabe's private business, Laban decided, and he had no right to tell others. As he finished, he saw the brief search of Emory's eyes.

"Remember, buckaroo . . . no fire tonight," the Ranger said, and reined upriver with the second man.

Laban crossed the tawny river and swung past the fort, the only visible life there the flag whipping high over the parade ground and the wooden-like figures of the scattered sentries. He thought of Lieutenant Carr, who, like Emory, had been kind to him, and passed on into open country.

Evening was sketching the sky a purplish haze when he reached the burned Army wagons, the bones of their frames reminding him of blackened skeletons in the fading light. A shiver passed through him as the scene blazed up again in his mind, and also a seated fury for the senseless violence that had happened. Well off the trail, on a little grassy rise, he saw the raw scars of the mounds where the payroll escort lay. At that moment the wind stirred the grass over there and imparted a sense of movement, of life's mystery going on.

He experienced a depthless loss for those men, and then he looked north, seeing the odd-shaped, conical hill where he had found uncertain refuge, pursued by the hawk-faced raider, marveling at his escape. Alone, scowling and secretive, as shaggy as an old hermit, a landmark for wary travelers, the hill had another face as well. It came as though he really saw it for the first time, on a thrusting suddenness, stamped across his mind: the image of a wooded island floating on a yellow sea. Or, instead — the picture still forming, still changing as he noted the hill's broad base and its forest of masts — a ship drifting broadside. A ship on the prairie sea. From there a man could see wagons approaching east and west of the trail for several miles. From there riders could rush upon a wagon train within a minute or two. Had the Indian raiders lurked there before attacking the Army wagons that blood-curdling morning?

The hill wakened an unease in Laban. Eyes could be watching him now. A coldness moved over him and he sent Schoolboy away in the ground-eating running walk, and, just before full darkness came down, he rode into a clump of mesquites off the trail. There he unsaddled and picketed his horse, ate his cold supper of bread and meat, with the saddle gun across his knees, while he watched the blurring land.

He could not recall a night on the trail so still, yet he did not feel alone. At intervals Schoolboy would drift over and smell of Laban, rolled in his blanket, then go back and graze. On toward morning, very late, Laban heard his little horse lie down and sleep.

Soon after daybreak Laban stepped to the saddle. The sun was hiding this morning and the air felt sticky. He came to the stage station where he remembered Seco had waved at the hostler. Laban saw him working on the bars of a corral. He glanced up as Laban drummed by, glanced once, and turned back to his work. More quickly, he turned and sent out a follow-up look. It was keen and questioning and expectant, as if he wondered why Laban didn't stop.

Before noon, under a cloudy sky, Laban marked Jacksboro's few buildings mustered loosely on the hot plain. At the same moment he saw his destination, he felt a pleased discovery. Since yesterday morning Schoolboy had covered some eighty-odd miles, with time out to camp. He could, Laban knew, have come faster.

Laban located Daley's Blacksmith Shop at the east end of town. Stepping into the gloomy interior, breathing the cindery smells, he paused to watch a brawny, leather-aproned man pound and turn and shape a cherry-red horseshoe upon an anvil. The smithy cooled the shoe in a tub of blackish water and strode over to a tied saddle horse, lifted the left front hoof, held the shoe in place, drove the nails, which he took from his mouth, and twisted them off with his light hammer, filed and smoothed the hoof with a rasp, and stood up.

He drove his glittering glance at Laban. "Well . . . ?" he spoke.

"Mister Daley," Laban said. "Gabe Bushrod sent me." Talking in this roundabout manner gave him the uncomfortable sensation of wrongness, or being a conspirator.

"Who be you?"

"Laban Bushrod. His nephew."

The smithy shrugged. "Didn't know Gabe had a nephew."

Laban was stumped. How was he going to prove he was? He said: "You'll have to take my word for it."

"I don't have to take your word for anything, hear? What're you ridin'?"

Laban pointed outside where Schoolboy was tied.

Daley was a large man, formed of big bones, big hands, big feet. He cast out the impression of a bear as he lumbered to the doorway and looked out. Instantly Laban saw his doubts end.

"Back here," Daley said.

Laban followed him to a crude office. Daley opened a drawer and took out a wax-sealed envelope, which he handed Laban, who removed his hat to place it inside. He felt the absence of bulk in the envelope, which Uncle Gabe had said would contain money. But it wasn't that reason he hesitated. It was his increasing dislike for everything — the purpose of the long ride, the secrecy, and Daley. He brushed the feeling aside and walked ahead of Daley to the shop. There Daley, without a word, using a pair of long tongs, picked up a cold horseshoe and held it in the glowing coals of the forge, his back turned on Laban.

Daley's powerful torso, his hairy, thick-set arms, the smoky smells, the shop's gloom, the forge's pulsing eye. For a count Laban doubted the reality of what his senses relayed to him. He went out quickly, glad to leave the place and Daley behind. He had no wish to dally in town when half the day remained. The thought foremost in his mind was to finish his ride, to return to some everyday chores. First, thinking of his horse, he bought corn at a livery stable and fed and watered Schoolboy, rested him an hour, and swung out of town, riding away.

Off southwest, he began to watch the changing sky, the low hedges of clouds banking there. His skin felt clammy, and there was a near stillness that Laban, accustomed to the steady wind, did not like, and the trail led him head-on toward the darkening clouds.

For a while the sullen sky seemed unchanged, just hanging in the southwest. He traveled through a breathless stillness, and presently he saw the clouds darkening anew and moving. He rode on in the humid heat, aware that Schoolboy's sides dripped with sweat.

Now thunder rumbled in the distance. Schoolboy nervously flicked his ears and quickened his smooth gait, taking Laban down a slope and up a rolling rise. There, staring off, Laban saw the clouds boiling like pitch, and the wind pushing against his face felt as moist as a dripping hand.

He had no choice except to forge ahead, for he could see no sheltering timber nearby and he was afraid of timber in a storm, for trees drew lightning. Suddenly a cannonading thunder crashed and Schoolboy shied, yet steadied as Laban brought him back on the trail. The little horse trembled, went forward.

Before many moments, Laban could feel the wind flinging rain-shot against his cheeks. He tugged on his hat brim. He heard a dim roaring overhead. Schoolboy shied violently and Laban grabbed leather; in that instant his hat flew off and he saw the envelope, like a leaf driven by the wind, go flouncing over the yellow prairie.

Reining, spurring, he raced after it through the slanting rain. The envelope was a mere white blur, fluttering here, now there, now right, now left, like a wounded bird. In another moment it climbed swiftly, soaring away, almost but not quite gone from sight. After a bit, he saw the envelope flounder to the ground. But just as he rushed up and dismounted, the wind gusted again and took it sailing away.

He lost all sense of time and direction as he raced here and there, trusting his horse to watch underfoot while he strained to see through the driving green of the rain, and, spotting the envelope once more, running Schoolboy after it again. He was on a treadmill, seeing the pale note disappear almost, only, when he galloped there, he couldn't trace its fluttering flight this time. The envelope was gone from sight, lost in the swirling, greenish world. Exhausted, soaked, he saw the spiny tangle of a mesquite thicket, poor enough refuge at best. He rode in and dismounted, holding his horse on short rein, grateful for the scant shelter of the low, wind-whipped trees, determined to wait out the storm. When it passed, he would commence searching again. Schoolboy turned tail to the wind, patiently bearing his punishment.

It seemed to Laban, miserable and worried, that he clung in the thicket for an age, his horse at his shoulder, before he noted a change in the wind; it was dropping at last, the rain letting up. Some minutes more, and past him, eastward, he heard the thunder marching on, even that rumble dimming. A longer pause and the sun broke through. Leaving the mesquites, he discovered that he was northwest of the trail, beyond the stage station that he had passed during his confused chase.

He mounted and glanced back at the thicket and turned perfectly still, aware of an incredible lift of relief, seeing the envelope caught in the fork of a branch, swaying in the wind. He rode back in, leaned from the saddle. A gust fluttered the envelope. A little more and it would fly free again. He let go the reins to stand up in the stirrups, pawing through the wet branches with his hands, and snatched the envelope as it quivered, ready to vanish.

His grab crumpled the paper, but he had it fast now. It was soaked limp and he saw that he had broken the wax seal. He slipped it inside his shirt and rode out to search for his hat, which he found after a circling search. Back at the thicket, he stripped off the saddle and wet-smelling saddle blanket, untied the soggy sleeping blanket behind the cantle, and skinned out of his sodden shirt and hung it on a limb to dry, and laid the letter on the crown of his hat in the wet grass.

The sun bore down and the spongy prairie became a steamy bright glittering like glass, and the rain-washed air had the sweet pungency of drying buffalo grass. Laban turned the blankets again. Before long, impatient, he saddled and donned his shirt. Bending to pick up the letter, he noticed the tip of the envelope flap had curled up. He tried to smooth and press it down; the flap merely sprang higher.

As it had been in the blacksmith shop, the thinness of the envelope flagged his attention. He bounced it lightly in the palm of his hand, weighing it. Had the greenbacks fallen out? He didn't think so. A peek inside would tell.

He opened the envelope and found a single sheet of paper. The blood rushed to his heart as he unfolded it. There were no greenbacks, just the piece of writing paper and on it four pencil-scrawled lines. A compelling sense seemed to force his eyes over the words:

Ship plows
the sea
Fireworks
light the sky

He read it that once, rapidly, a second

time with a consuming concentration, wondering and puzzled. Still immersed in thought, he folded the letter and slipped it in the envelope. Where were the greenbacks Gabe had said would be inside? And it wasn't a letter at all. It was just a sort of riddle. No more. Holding the letter, feeling the hot sun over his body, he felt a shiver run up his backbone. And all the strangeness that had stalked him since Seco had robbed him, and since that terrible nightmare around the Army wagons, seemed to rise up again and surround him.

Suddenly shaken, he went to his horse.

VII

Laban's strange feeling persisted as he rejoined the trail to Fort Belknap, as he mulled over the words and wondered why he, alone, should carry the message — for it had to be a message. *Ship plows the sea.* What could that mean, away out here on the broad Texas prairies in June? Red River wasn't close. If it was, you couldn't take a steamboat, let alone a ship, up to Indian country. *Fireworks light the sky.* He thought of wind and rain and lightning, maybe, of skyrockets and comets.

A chill grazed him. Everything was out of place, odd, mysterious. Did Uncle Gabe, to

293

protect his business, have to send puzzling messages back and forth? If so, what if somebody stopped Laban and searched him? On that precaution, he removed his right shoe and slipped the envelope inside.

Darkness swooped down when he was still east of the post, in the vicinity of the burned Army wagons and the peculiar hill. He could not shake the somber perception that yesterday and today, when passing this dreadful place, night was coming on each time. Onward he made his fireless camp, picketed, ate, and lay down, listening to the soft roar of the wind in the grass.

Sleep was a drug, a troubled drifting wherein he dreamed that he was riding Schoolboy and, from the rear, he caught the rush of a horse coming like the wind itself. He looked back and swayed with fear. It was the hawk-faced man on a huge, dun-colored horse whose great eyes blazed and whose flaring nostrils spewed smoke. . . . Laban loosened rein and spurred. School-boy shot away. Behind Laban the dun's hoofs clattered closer. . . . Laban looked back. The dun was almost upon him. . . .

He awoke in a cold sweat, relieved to hear the comforting stir of Schoolboy grazing. Laban lay back. The frightful dream lingered. Sleep evaded him. Finally he saddled and rode into the filmy night. Daylight wasn't far away.

Passing the fort, he was conscious of an insight as he thought of his friends there. He was lonesome. He longed for the sound of friendly voices. He was weary of wondering what a thing meant or did not mean, or waking up half scared.

Dawn was creeping in when he started through the jaws of the ridge overlooking the sheeny thread of the river. There was no warning. The rider blocking the trail seemed to grow out of the red earth. Instinct sent Laban jerking for the saddle gun. A ringing voice stayed his hand.

"Hold on there, buckaroo!"

Laban relaxed, feeling a little foolish. Out of the murky light swerved Enoch Emory astride a snuffy bay horse. "You made fast time," he said, approving and curious.

"I didn't make any fires," Laban said seriously. Emory's laugh floated back. A soft laugh, yet underladen, still curious. "I'll swear I've seen your horse before." He shook his head in a puzzled way and gestured in the direction of Fort Griffin. "Well, stay on the look-out."

"Indians again?"

Emory shrugged, a yes or a no. Starting on, Laban met Emory's searching interest, and suddenly the Ranger held out a detaining hand. "Buckaroo, you've been ridin' too hard. Be Fourth of July in a few days. Ride into Griffin . . . have yourself some fun. Gonna be a big celebration there."

"I'd like that, you bet."

An even keener attention built in the Ranger's brown face, marked by a certain reluctance. "If you're in trouble, if you need help. . . ." He left the rest unfinished, as if waiting for Laban to complete it.

"Everything's fine," Laban said. "Much obliged." He rode on then, remotely troubled. Because everything wasn't fine. He knew that, he sensed that. Only he had to find out for himself and not lean on his friends. Down the trail a way a last moment sensation akin to fear rolled over him, that he was going back where he knew not what might happen. Something lumped in his throat, and he swung around and waved.

Emory waved back. He was still there, watching, when a bend in the road took him from Laban's view.

Nearing the stage station, Laban held straight to the road, wanting no more of the hostler's doubtful hospitality. He was past when he heard a shout, and, looking over his shoulder, he saw the man in the doorway motioning him in. Laban saddled on faster.

Around mid-afternoon he rode up to the ranch, and Schoolboy seemed as fresh and eager as ever. Laban watered and unsaddled him, dumped a ration of corn in a feed box. In the next corral Reuben observed him solemnly. Laban climbed over and stroked the old traveler's nose and noted that his trail-worn friend was fattening up a little.

Only a few saddle horses were up, which told Laban the crew wasn't back yet. At the house Uncle Gabe met him at the door. The moon face put on its wreathing smile. "Ah, you made it a day early. Good boy. Good boy. Lean the saddle gun over there in the corner."

"I got your letter soakin' wet in a storm," Laban began, "and the seal came loose." A weariness gripped him. He took off his shoe, drew out the envelope, slipped the shoe back on, and handed the envelope to Uncle Gabe.

Gabe Bushrod looked pleased as he fingered the creased letter. A haste came over him and he turned his back and Laban heard him open the envelope; during a drawn-out space his uncle stood, motionless, head bowed, reading. A rustle of paper. Laban tensed, set for his uncle to ask about the money.

Gabe Bushrod faced around. Now, if

Laban asked about the money or the message, Uncle Gabe would know that he had looked inside.

"Good work, my boy," Uncle Gabe said, the moon face lighting up. "How did you like your horse?" The ghost of an expression flitted behind the cool eyes. The yellow flecks were glinting there again.

"Best I ever rode."

"Remember, he's all yours." Again that flecking look; in it Laban thought he read satisfaction. "See any Indians?"

"Not a one. I kept a sharp look-out."

"Meet anybody on the trail?"

"Some troopers. Two Rangers."

"Scouting for Indians, I reckon?"

"Nope. For a robber that held up an Army dispatch rider."

Gabe Bushrod pursed his plump lips and swiveled his head from side to side. His voice became outraged. "Robbers on the trail . . . as if Indians don't make times hard enough for a decent citizen. Good thing you rode a fast horse. Just in case."

Laban felt inclined to remark that the cavalry sergeant and Emory hadn't acted worried about Indians. A new awareness caused him to hold his tongue. With such a generous and valuable gift as Schoolboy, far more than a body would expect, went a strong measure of loyalty to the giver. A certain protective silence as well. Laban had already discovered that while talking to the Ranger.

But before he could keep the horse he had to know about Seco. He could feel his mouth working.

"What is it, my boy? You all right?"

"Uncle Gabe," said Laban, stumbling over the words, "does a man named Seco work for you?" He was prepared for his uncle to hem and haw.

"Why," Gabe Bushrod said, neither blinking nor hesitating, "I believe there is a new hand . . . a drifter by that name. You know him?" The brown-yellow gaze reflected an open innocence.

Laban nodded bitterly, sensing that he dare not say when and where he had seen Seco on the ranch, that night the horses jammed the corrals.

"What about this Seco?"

"He robbed me. I met him on the way to Fort Belknap, when I first came out here."

"Robbed you!" The moon features showed heat. "Did he harm you?"

"Not then. But he took all my money . . . nine dollars and sixty-eight cents. Later, when I hit him up for it in town, he pistol-whipped me."

Gabe Bushrod made a chopping motion. "Seco's through here!" Crossing to a roll-topped desk, he racked it open, and turned with a money sack. From it he counted out greenbacks and change. "Here's your money, my boy. Next time you'll know not to trust every Tom, Dick, and Harry. I'll take it out of Seco's pay when I send him drifting."

Laban murmured his thanks, turned to go to his room. A step and he was facing around at the sound of his uncle's voice, feeling the charged tone: "Only time Seco's been on the ranch since you came was the other night when we drove in some horses . . . horses I bought to sell in the eastern settlements. That's where the crew is now."

Meeting his uncle's gaze, Laban discerned something unfound before — a stoniness beneath that genial surface that contradicted the rounded softness of the man.

"How did you know Seco was on the ranch?" Gabe Bushrod asked.

Laban delayed, knowing he had talked himself into a hole. But hadn't Uncle Gabe just mentioned his horses? "I heard the horses that night," Laban told him straight. "I went outside. I heard somebody call Seco's name." And then he realized, also, that was a mistake.

His uncle's voice hardened. "Go clean up for supper."

Going stiffly to his room, standing by the window and looking out and not seeing, Laban struggled to sort out the flogging questions. *Why wasn't money in the envelope? Why wasn't Uncle Gabe angry? Was there really supposed to be any money?* He sat down on his bed and stared at the floor. A conviction redoubled. A sense. He was trapped here, same as a prisoner.

He awoke, wolf hungry, stretched, and sat up. Sunlight was a golden arm reaching into his room, rousing his lulled senses. He felt at peace with the world, and then yesterday's events swarmed back and he groped again for the answers that were no nearer now than then.

"Gabe's gone," Mitch told him at breakfast. "He left you some chores to do."

Outside, Laban saw the crew hadn't returned. He chopped wood, pulled nails from scrap boards, pried rocks out of the trail to town, and, in the afternoon, rode Reuben to the river to cut poles for the corrals. Facing the ranch while he chopped and trimmed, he could see Mitch keeping him in sight from the yard. Any other day, he reflected, Mitch would have warned him about Indians.

Snaking a rope around some cut saplings, Laban dragged them off behind his mule. He chose the easiest way back, a circling route south of the ranch, and, as he idled along, the mystery of the message pestered him again. *Ship plows the sea.* He'd read about big wagons being called prairie schooners; maybe that was it. Even so, what did it mean? *Fireworks light the sky.* The only fireworks a body saw were on the 4th of July, always.

Equally puzzling, why had Uncle Gabe looked so pleased when there was no money in the envelope? When he needed money to save his business and ranch?

Starting up the gentle slope below the house, he saw the angling scar of the path that led to the ledge and the den or cave from which Mitch had called him that day of the Indian scare.

Knowing that Mitch waited, Laban rode to the corrals. There he yanked out the weak and rotten poles, laid like rails between the double upright poles, and cut the new ones to size, and slid them in place. That done, he saddled to the river for another load. When he was ready to leave, the crimson disk of the sun was sinking and Mitch no longer watched from the yard. At this hour he would be inside fixing supper.

Laban's blood rushed faster. A knowing came. He could ride out of here. He could be out of sight before Mitch missed him, saddled a horse, and gave chase.

The moment fluttered away. Old Reuben was brave, but he couldn't run fast enough to scatter dust. And if Laban did escape, he'd never unravel the puzzling message, or the secret of the cave, if any, or all that was wrong at Uncle Gabe's ranch, and he wouldn't see Schoolboy again.

He hurried, expecting Mitch to come out of the house at any moment, and reached the slope. At a point where the rise hid him from the house, he slid to the ground and in long strides made his way to the dry streambed. His breath came faster when he saw the cave's black mouth. It drew him plunging up the slant to the rocky path and along it. He halted, his heart racing. The cave was larger than it appeared from a distance. His scalp tingled as he saw fresh boot tracks in the dust. He cast a final look around and ducked inside, and at once he smelled dampness and a strange muskiness like old leather. A little way in, he stood still. The musky smell flowed stronger, almost rank. Although he could see but dimly, the cave was widening before him.

By now he could stand erect. His right foot bumped something — a wooden bench, it was. He felt around and touched a slender, upright object, cool to his hand — a candle. He brushed a tin cup and picked it up. It gave off a light rattling sound — matches. He scraped one aflame across the bench, looked up — and flinched back, startled.

Eerily, beyond the tiny yellow cone of light, he could see things hanging on the rough wall that resembled the hides of animals and the plumage of birds. He stiffened. The match burning his thumb and forefinger broke his rigidity. He dropped the fiery stub, the light pinched out, and he struck another match and, resisting an edge of fear, forced himself to move nearer.

Meaning crashed through him and a giant relief. The feathers were attached to Indian headdresses and leather headbands. And what he had taken for hides — also hanging from wooden pegs driven between rocks — were leather buckskin leggings and buckskin shirts, and buffalo-horn headdresses and red calico shirts. *Enough gear,* he thought, *for a dozen Indians on the warpath.* He examined a pair of fringed leggings. The buckskin felt soft and pliable, not crinkly and dry and old. Lighting more matches, he fingered the feathered war bonnets, one by one, a buckskin shirt, and another legging. He began to frown, wondering. Even his unpracticed eye told him these garments, although durable, were crudely cut and sewn.

Farther on, squatted a round-bodied keg, a cluster of wooden handles thrusting up from it. He pulled one out — a hatchet, hammerhead and broad blade — and hefted it in his hand. And for a mere instant, in his mind's eye, he could see the whooping figures hacking at the heavy chest outside the Army wagon. With a shudder, he dropped the hatchet.

The match he held burned down and he turned to see the entrance and ducked outside, sunk in thought. Would Indians hide their war gear here?

It was getting late. He hurried back to his mule and dragged the poles to the first large corral. Mitch strode down from the house.

"What took you so long?" Suspicion whetted his voice and the fear, Laban thought, that he had kept negligent guard.

Just as Laban was about to tell Mitch of his discovery, a tiny voice of caution seemed to speak. "Had to fix my load," he said. "Rope kept slippin'."

"Time for supper."

"Good . . . I'm hungry." Mitch wasn't a bad fellow, Laban decided. He was just following orders.

Laban did not see his uncle that day or the next, and, while he went about his tasks on the third day, he had the bewildering helplessness that other persons now determined the order of his life, directing him from one unnecessary chore to another.

Once he saddled Schoolboy, Mitch appeared as if shot out of a gun. "You ain't finished diggin' post holes for that new corral."

"Thought I'd take a little ride."

"Ride your mule."

"What's wrong with Schoolboy?"

"Gabe said to keep him fresh."

"You mean," Laban flared, "Reuben's so poky you figure you could catch me if I run off, don't you? Well, he's faster'n you think."

"A real track burner, eh?" Mitch scoffed, ridicule seeping into his tone. But he had made his point: Laban *was* a prisoner.

Laban unsaddled and resumed digging post holes. That afternoon he rode Reuben to the river to cut more saplings. On the way back, coming where the slope hid him, he slid down and trotted to the cave for a quick look.

Everything was just as he had left it. But this time when he examined the costumes, a new meaning guided his eyes. He was looking for beads. He had read that Plains Indians sewed trade beads on their dress-up belongings, but he didn't know about clothing worn on the warpath. Although he inspected each piece, he saw not a bead. Just as he was leaving, he found three terrapin shells. One held red clay, and he knew Indians used clay for war paint. His doubts weakened. What had happened, then, he reasoned, a war party had cached its finery here and not come back, maybe scared off by Rangers or troopers.

On the following morning he heard the ruffling of horses on the trail. Resting calloused hands on the post-hole digger, he watched the crew pass the house. Uncle Gabe rode in front. A rider on a spirited, long-legged dun gelding sided him, a rider whose jutting chin was noticeable from here and who towered over Uncle Gabe. Laban didn't remember seeing the man earlier at the ranch. He looked and did not find Seco's wizened shape and felt immensely better. True to his word, Uncle Gabe had sent Seco drifting.

The crew dismounted at the bunkhouse. Soon Uncle Gabe and the new rider came out and led their mounts to the corral next to where Reuben was and hung their saddles and blankets in a picket shed.

Laban began digging again, his efforts half-hearted, not looking up until the two men were leaving. At that very moment, as if to display his mulish indifference, Reuben chose to arch his ungainly neck and flap his ears and wall his eyes and let go a disdainful trumpeting.

Both men checked up. Laban, grinning, heard his uncle laugh. The other man was staring at Reuben, an intensity in his interest, a questioning. "Where'd that bag of bones come from?" he muttered.

"Like to buy 'im for a pack mule?" Gabe Bushrod jested, enjoying the other's annoyance.

"That ugly critter?"

Laban decided the new man had no sense of humor; most folks laughed when Reuben brayed. There was a tight-lipped air about him, a suggestion of strength and violence, barely contained. And that voice? For some unaccountable reason its deepness pressed on Laban's memory, although heard in just those few words. He tried to place it and could not. It was possible he was overworked and jumpy and just thought he had.

The two left the corral, and the tall man,

after playing his attention over Reuben again, tramped off to the house. Gabe Bushrod, with a wave, called out — "Ah, my boy, you are doing good work . . . good work!" — and hurried on.

Questions jumped to Laban's throat, but there wasn't time to speak. Uncle Gabe was going on to the house. He was, Laban saw all too well, avoiding him.

An uncertain rebellion roused him. He longed to get out of here. Everything about the ranch and the crew was wrong. He leaned on the digger, slowly coming to grips with himself. He guessed he had better quit acting like a fool kid. He glanced at the sky, noted the ten o'clock sun, and, with a lifting of his slim shoulders, went to a pile of posts he had cut, dragged one to the hole he had just dug, upended it in the hole, and straightened it. Head down, he began foot-tamping the reddish earth around the post.

A hackling up and down his spine warned him first. A feeling as subtle as May wind rustling through short grass, yet as sharp as the jab of a Barlow pocket knife. He turned.

The new rider stood at the corner of the shed, his gaze flicking over Laban, his wide hat brim shading his dark face. Then he opened the gate and paced deliberately to the gate that opened on the corral where

Reuben stood. The man stopped. His attention on Reuben settled to a close prying. A longer moment and he paced outside, straight to Laban, who waited, his left hand gripping the post.

"Gabe's nephew?" the man questioned, brief. His voice seemed to rise from the depths of a bottomless cavern.

Laban's fingers tightened on the rough bark. It was, he realized, the same voice he had heard argue with Seco the night of the horses.

"I am," Laban said, nodding. The sweat beading his forehead was as cold raindrops. He had no breath. He was staring into eyes as blue and as hard as a six-shooter's muzzle, into a face as craggy as a rock slide, braced by a broad nose beaked like a hawk's and a jutting chin cleft in the middle. Laban tried to tear his gaze away, tried and could not. The boring eyes seemed to hold onto him. Neither could he speak.

A breathless moment, and suddenly the man turned away. Laban stood nailed with fear. But as the tall figure disappeared around the corner of the house where Uncle Gabe had gone, Laban felt a panicky alarm. Shock ripped through him. It was as though, swimming upward through deep and murky water, he had burst into the harsh reality of cold, clear light. That hawkish face burned his vision, seared there everlastingly, for he had last seen it rushing toward him through the grayish mists around the burning Army wagons and soon thereafter on the odd-shaped hill.

He threw down the digger and sprang to the corral gate, inside, past the haltered dun gelding, and bridled and saddled Schoolboy, and led him out through the corral holding Reuben, away from the house. One last glance for his mule, looking forlorn and left behind, and Laban hit the leather, traveling south, free.

Later, circling northeast, he found himself heading instinctively for Fort Belknap and his friends. It wasn't long until he reached the trail. He swung in, feeling relaxed and carefree. The open trail beckoned under the bright shield of the sun. But he hadn't gone far until he detected an encroaching cadence, the racket of hoofs behind him. An inescapable dread chilled him. He looked backward and saw dust and something ahead of that dust, a bulk that formed a running horse and a rider crouched over the horse's neck. Big man, big horse.

Laban went colder. It was the racy dun gelding coming like an angry wind. This time not in a dream vanishing with awakening. It was real.

He lurched forward and gave Schoolboy his head and the little horse shot away, keen to run.

VIII

Laban felt Schoolboy's muscles bunching, felt the eager sorrel stretching out, fairly skimming the rough wagon road, fox ears back, silky mane flying. Wind hummed around Laban's ears. Objects along the road rushed past — a hunk of reddish rock, a gnarled mesquite.

Low in the saddle, Laban glanced back again. The dun was falling behind, now coming up, a charging blur, now losing ground as Schoolboy held the burning pace without switching stride. Still, the dun held on. Schoolboy took him easily over and down one grassy swell after another. Under the fevered sun the open land shimmered and beckoned, looking more imagined than real.

When the little horse swept to the next crest, Laban took another look, hopefully expecting to see his pursuer quitting. But back there the dun clung, doggedly eating up the distance in those long-legged strides. Fort Belknap was thirty miles or more away, and Laban eased up to save his horse and see what would happen. At once the dun racer drove nearer, running gamely, showing his iron, and so Laban urged his horse faster, and once more the dun faded, although never quitting, always in sight.

After a while, with both horses tiring, the see-sawing race settled down to a game of endurance and heart, and the distance between the two stayed about the same. When the dun closed up, Laban let Schoolboy out. When the dun fell back, Laban eased his horse off the pace, to a gallop or fast trot or the effortless running walk.

For an interval nothing changed. Laban could feel his horse moving stronger, gathering his second wind, ready to fly again. He nursed that eagerness, he held Schoolboy in, he humored him, spoke to him, saving that steadfastness.

Patches of scrub oak dotted the way as the land commenced to knuckle up, to rise and dip more. Suddenly — quite suddenly — Laban saw dust spurt on the road to his right and heard the mean whine of a ricocheting bullet and the dim *pop* of a rifle behind him. Startled, he swerved his mount the other way and ducked a look. The dun was charging, in a final surge to end the race. And almost together Laban heard the *whee* of a bullet and the *crash* of the rifle, closer than before, and saw the bloom of white powder smoke.

Clapping heels and Schoolboy in a dead run, he gave to his white panic. If he stayed on the road, his horse might be shot and killed. Off the road lay the scattering oaks. He reined for them, and in moments timber rose between them and pursuit.

Laban set a course roughly parallel to the road. To his dismay, he saw broken sandstone and gullied dips ahead. Schoolboy had to slacken stride. But there was smoother footing southwest. Laban rushed that way, letting his horse run as he wished, pell-mell. The open country seemed to wave him on. In the passage of a moment he tasted the temptation to go for a far-off ridge rimmed in blue haze, an impulse he willed down about as quickly. He'd better keep working toward Belknap, instead of trusting unknown country and maybe losing himself.

Pausing, he saw the dun bobbing this side of the scrub oaks. The rider didn't hesitate. He forced his horse, high-stepping, into the cruel rocks and down the first punishing gully. For a moment Laban pitied the animal. He pressed on and shortly he heard a shot, a wild shot, but close enough for him to catch the bullet's *whing*.

Dipping below the lip of a rise, he lost

sight of his pursuit; angling north, he picked up the eastward trail again. It wasn't very long until he marked the coming-on shape of the dun, like a brown bur. Yet by going off the trail, even by circling the rocks and gullies, Laban had added about 200 yards to his lead.

Climbing the backbone of a long-running ridge chain, he saw that it was an arm of the one swimming in haze far to the southwest, which he had almost headed for after detouring the rough places off the trail. From this vantage he could see the ridge's offside, a treacherous jumble of up-and-down country, broken, shaggy with cedars, eroded, slashed with wicked draws and cañons. Had he ventured there, he would be blocked off by now, hemmed in. As that perception steadied in his mind, a hard certainty came — there was no easy way out.

Thereafter, all sense of time seemed lost. The morning was burned out. The sun was a smoking-hot muzzle pointed straight at him. His neck ached from the constant swiveling to watch. It pained him to feel the labor of his hard-used horse that never faltered, that always responded when the dun threatened. He rode miserly, a gallop, a trot, a walk, running when he must. Once he dismounted and led Schoolboy for a while, and, when another ridge rose ahead, he got off and walked to the top, his mind occupied by a deeper dread that the real race was yet to come.

He wondered why his enemy didn't charge in for a long-range shot now and then. Whatever, the dun never fell far behind. Horse and rider made a brown streak of dust, hanging back there like the tail of a kite, only Schoolboy's steady swiftness keeping Laban out of rifle range.

Laban kept hoping for sight of a cavalry detail prowling the road. Nothing broke the heat-glazed emptiness at all. Nothing. He was alone. Again the absolute knowing crossed his mind — there was no easy way.

Coming to the creek where, hidden, he had watched Seco, a day that seemed long ago, hardly real, Laban watered Schoolboy at the stagnant pool and swept ahead. Farther on he recognized with relief the first signs that told him he was approaching the stage station — a little round-topped hill, a twist in the road. Fort Belknap wasn't far now.

He looked back and was astonished to see the dun coming dangerously close, running with the wind. Laban sensed there was to be no hanging back this time. The rider had saved the dun as he had saved Schoolboy, each waiting for the finish.

A mere touch and Schoolboy scooted out, tired, as brave as in the morning, willing, Laban knew, to run without urging until he dropped dead in his tracks. He crouched lower, hunkered for the spiteful bullet sounds. Schoolboy took him flying through a series of snake-like windings of the rutted road, leaping a washed-out place, scrambling over a rise. Thereon the road ran as straight as a schoolmaster's rod for a long stretch, and, where it turned, dodging toward the river, the stage station appeared to wait for Laban, tranquil, secure. He felt a bursting elation. The hostler would help him. The hostler had a gun.

A shot cracked behind Laban. A second. A short pause. Then two more shots. He heard no bullet sounds. Looking back through the fog of yellow dust, he saw the dun just coming in view, in a tired, weaving run.

It was only as Laban faced forward that the wrongness of the shots filtered into his thinking. *Why had the rider fired back there when he couldn't see Laban?*

It didn't matter. Laban glued his gaze on the hostler, who was stepping from the station's doorway to watch the road. It was encouraging to see him cradling a long-barreled weapon, likely that big shotgun. Laban waved. The hostler didn't wave back. He was shading his eyes against the sun.

Laban flung around. The dun was running in the ragged stride of a used-up horse. Front, Laban waved jerkily. The hostler ran to the middle of the road and swung about. Something in the blocking way he stood there, legs braced, weapon ready, hinted at trouble. But by now Laban had no time to change course.

In a telescoping rush, he glimpsed the greasy shine of the bushy beard, the trap of the grim mouth, saw the shotgun tilting up — right at him. And in that split second the meaning of the shots seared his mind: they were signals. He saw the hostler motioning him to pull up.

Staring into the metallic eye of the shotgun, Laban instinctively reined up a trifle. But then an unbearable feeling took hold, and, without thinking, he dug in his heels, low like a jockey, and sent his horse plunging straight toward the menacing figure.

Sorrel horseflesh streaking out, the sodden *thud* of Schoolboy's shoulder connecting, and the man's lifted scream of pain, the *boom* of the flung-back shotgun thundering in Laban's ears — all this together, it seemed, and the log of the hostler's body spinning away, the loose shotgun flapping downward, and Schoolboy running free as a wild horse.

Laban touched his face, glanced at his hand. He saw no blood. His ears rang. He looked back. The hostler lay writhing in the dusty road. Beyond, the game dun was still coming, the rider raking with spurs. But the dun was wobbling. Schoolboy had broken him at last. The race was all but won.

Not long afterward, Laban passed through the gap in the ridge above the copper-hued river, saddled down the road veined with wagon ruts, and splashed into the warm waters of the shiftless Salt Fork. On the farther side he watered his horse and rested. He turned for a final look. It jolted him to see movement so soon, the familiar horse and rider bulking in the jaws of the pass, the dun racer's head down, beaten, but there, a reminder. And then the rider drew away.

Laban's elation withered. A coldness enveloped him, an unfinished dread, which he took with him on his way to the fort.

The same Sergeant Huckleby, his blouse still ajar, intercepted Laban as he crossed the parade ground toward Lieutenant Carr's

319

headquarters. Huckleby blinked in recognition, and, when Laban said he wanted to see the lieutenant or Ranger Emory, the sergeant gestured to the north.

"They're out on a little scout. Be back in the mornin'." His horseman's knowing eyes trailed critically over the sweat-dripping Schoolboy. "Walk your mount till he cools off. Stable him and come to the barracks."

Laban dismounted, and unexpectedly the ground seemed to sway away from him and Sergeant Huckleby's wind-burned face became not one but a whole crowd of shivery Hucklebys. He lowered his head and slowly everything settled back in place and he led Schoolboy away.

Laban moved in an unreal haze. Dust powdered his nostrils and ears. He couldn't think, his eyes were swollen from the sun glare, his neck stiff, his body sore, and he felt himself riding yet, bent low in the saddle, before him Schoolboy's mane flying, head bobbing, the landscape flashing by.

The sense of unreality followed him at sunset while he watched the fragment garrison of some fifteen troopers ride forth on the hard parade, while Sergeant Huckleby barked the roll call, while the bugler sounded "Retreat", and the flag began to descend.

At ten o'clock next morning Laban stood in Lieutenant Carr's headquarters, his story told.

Carr, freshly groomed, brushed an imaginary speck from his spotless jacket sleeve. "You say this man resembles the Indian . . . if it was an Indian . . . who tried to tomahawk you the morning the payroll escort was wiped out?"

"Yes, sir."

"You're certain?"

"Dead certain," Laban replied, wearied by the repetition.

The lieutenant continued in a voice as matter-of-fact as an official report. "Yet the attackers were Indians, presumably . . . that is, they acted like Indians . . . and the man on the dun was a white man?"

"I'll tell you who he is," spoke up Emory, who had been toying with the rowel on his left boot, ". . . it's Duff Fallon!"

Carr gave a start. "Fallon . . . the outlaw?"

"Fits Laban's description to a T. He was after Laban because he's the only living witness who can testify that Fallon took part in the payroll massacre. . . . What's more, Lieutenant, it could be those Indians were nothin' but dress-up Indians, wearin' the suits Laban found in the cave."

"But Fallon has been known to run with *real* Indians," Carr insisted. "Some of the wild bands off the reservation, hasn't he?"

"He's been known to do a heap of things, all on the shady side," the Ranger said dryly.

Carr bounded out of his chair. "You see what this means . . . about the Indian suits in the cave? You are implying that one of Shackleford county's most honorable citizens . . . Gabriel J. Bushrod . . . is providing a haven for these scoundrels."

"I can't honestly say that," Emory said, turning considerate eyes on Laban. "Maybe he's in the dark about the whole business."

Listening to the echo of his own fears, Laban felt sickened. Even if Uncle Gabe wasn't involved, Laban had brought that suspicion down upon him, his very own kin.

"Sometimes," Laban began, his tone halting and defensive, "Uncle Gabe hires drifters. Could be that's how Fallon came to be at the ranch."

"He's a drifter, all right," the Ranger said. "Has to be . . . can't afford to stay hitched very long. Why he's run with Indians sometimes."

"Then the raiders could've been real Indians?" Carr reasoned, his brows stitched in thought.

"Maybe . . . but that brings us back to the

Indian suits." Emory shrugged inconclusively.

"There's nothing to stop us from riding to Bushrod's ranch and taking Fallon into custody."

Emory showed a creased smile, in it a vague reluctance.

"Since when did the Texas Rangers start letting a lone outlaw buffalo them?" A goading smile flecked Carr's face.

"I reckon about the same time the Army started lettin' a little dab of Comanches run bluff on 'em," Emory replied, equally bantering. "What bothers me, Lieutenant, is why Fallon hangs around where he's a wanted man. You can bet your bottom dollar where there's bees, there's some honey close by. I want to corral the whole shebang . . . outlaws, Indians, whatever they are. Gabriel J. Bushrod, too, if he's guilty. . . . If we jump Fallon now, the whole outfit may leave the country. If there is an outfit."

"But where's the honey?"

Again Emory shrugged; thoughtfully he spun the wheel on his spur.

No one spoke for so long — Carr stroking one flank of his waterfall mustache; Emory absently tinkling the rowel — that Laban felt the powwow was over. He kept thinking of his uncle, his own kin, the same as accused with murderous Duff Fallon, a known outlaw. His mind wavered between suspicion and loyalty, and he could not forget Uncle Gabe's generous gift of Schoolboy, and yesterday Schoolboy had saved Laban's life. Laban had to speak up:

"Uncle Gabe's been mighty good to me. Gave me food and shelter. Gave me the fastest horse in the country. Put me to work."

Emory took off his high-crowned hat and ran fingers through his thick, black hair. "About that lightnin' horse. I've shore seen his majesty some place, and it wasn't on a race track."

"But you don't know where, do you?" Laban pointed out.

"Nope. As for work, buckaroo, you mean like ridin' to Jacksboro?"

"Uhn-huh. And when I delivered the message and there wasn't any money in the envelope, he didn't say a word." Not till now did he realize that in all the long telling he had failed to mention the message.

Both men looked startled. Carr roared: "Message . . . money? What's this?"

Laban, shamefaced, explained down to the last detail.

"Ship . . . plows . . . the . . . sea . . . fireworks . . . light . . . the . . . sky. . . ."

Emory appeared to roll each word around in his mind. "*Hmmm.* That means big medicine of some kind. Would the Army have any notions, Lieutenant?"

"Would the Rangers?" Carr flung back.

"Looks like we're buffaloed again. What say, we all take a little sashay over where the payroll wagons got burned?"

"Why so?"

"I can't seem to think inside a building. I need fresh air. Some things don't tally right, Lieutenant. Why'd the raiders attack the train at that spot? How'd they know the payroll was in the wagons? They *knew*."

With the lieutenant and the Ranger and a few troopers, Laban toiled through the blinding afternoon glare, his mind shifting back and forth from Duff Fallon to Uncle Gabe. The detachment passed the scene of the attack, scouted down the road a piece, and returned to the skeletal ruins of the wagons.

Laban said no word, haunted by his vivid memories. All but he and Emory went poking around the hulks of the blackened wagon frames. The Ranger interested himself in the surrounding country, facing one direction, then another.

"Nothing new here," Carr said presently. "We've gone over every inch of the camp."

Emory looked off again, preoccupied. "Dawn is always a good time to hit a camp. Shore. But I keep comin' back to that hill yonder."

"It's obviously a landmark," Carr said, smiling his amused tolerance.

Laban, likewise, was eyeing the hill, the shutter of his mind open, reaching out, fixing. "It looks funny. Like it floats."

Carr ceased his banter. Laban became aware that the lieutenant was turning slowly toward him and saying: "Go on."

"Just reckon this place fetches me the haunts," Laban said, and fell silent, brooding.

"I believe you were about to say something more, Bushrod."

As if an unconscious part of himself formed and released the words without effort, Laban said: "Other evening when I rode by here . . . the trees looked more like masts stickin' up . . . the hill like a ship. . . ." He broke off, ready to disregard what he had said. "Reckon it was just the light."

"You said like a *ship*," Emory murmured in the quietest tone Laban had ever heard from him. "I wonder. . . . Now if a man stretches his imagination a little, that hill *does* look like a ship, and all the prairie around it could be the sea. . . ."

He left it there. Laban said no more, nor did the lieutenant. Soon they mounted and rode away in silence.

Afterward, they were standing outside post headquarters. Emory's eyes on Laban bore remembering sympathy. "Fourth of July comin' up. Too risky for you to ride over to Griffin." He looked at Carr. "How's the Army's firecracker supply, Lieutenant?"

"I'd planned a modest celebration. You know, dinner on the grounds." Carr coughed politely. "A short but impressive oration by the post commander. But since we haven't seen a paymaster in more than two months. . . ."

The Ranger became absolutely motionless. His brown face changed, wholly absorbed. He stared point-blank at Carr and swallowed rapidly. "Know what day this is? It's the First of July."

"I'm quite aware of that," Carr said, amused.

"When's the next payroll in from Fort Richardson?"

"Not in time to bring fireworks for any celebration. It leaves there the morning of the Fourth."

Emory slapped his thigh. He raised his voice. " 'Fireworks light the sky' . . . that's it! They'll try to take the payroll on the

Fourth of July. Where? Laban had it savvied at the wagons . . . 'ship plows the sea' . . . near that hill that looks like a ship!" He wheeled, both jubilant and grim. "Laban, there's gonna be a celebration, after all . . . some *real* fireworks!"

IX

Beneath the swaying canvas cover of the jolting Army wagon, Laban felt the smoky heat banking around him and smelled the dust fuming up between the chattering floorboards. Past Sergeant Huckleby, lolling in the driver's seat, he saw the wrinkled brown floor of the prairie dipping and gliding away.

He sat on a wooden bench, flanked by troopers holding seven-shot Spencer repeaters. Additional troopers sat on the other side of the wagon and more rode under cover in the two trailing vehicles. The sides of the wagon covers were rolled down. But a moment's yank on leather straps and up the canvas would go and the troopers inside, crouched and ready to fire.

He could see the small advance guard; behind the last wagon trailed the rear guard detail — to watching eyes from afar just another undermanned escort from Fort Richardson plodding toward Fort Belknap.

It was, he remembered, the 4th of July. And he would not be here had he not convinced a reluctant Lieutenant Carr and Ranger Emory that he be needed to identify Duff Fallon, the outlaw.

He could still hear Carr's serious voice: "Under one condition, Bushrod . . . that you stay put if anything happens." His even features hardened. "Besides, you'd be safer with us should Fallon decide to chance a raid on the post. He knows where you are, and I'm taking half the garrison with us because Fort Richardson is down to one company."

At noon Carr, riding alongside the lead wagon, ordered a rest, and Emory swung back with the advance. His long arms hung out the sleeves of his unbuttoned, high-collar cavalry jacket and he wore his black wool hat tipped back on his head.

"You Rangers dress no neater than our raw recruits," Carr chided him.

"How d'you yellowlegs stand these oven suits?" Emory demanded, running a forefinger inside his collar.

"We do . . . the year round . . . and buttoned."

Emory's good nature disappeared, replaced by a puckering worry. "I don't like the sign, Lieutenant. Not one bit."

"What's wrong?"

Emory reached into his saddlebag and held out an object. Laban, leaning forward, saw an old moccasin, a hole in the stiff sole, the buckskin upper hanging loose, and fringes, some broken, some tipped with silver, running from the lace to the toe.

"Comanch'," Emory said. "You can tell by the fringes. They trade with the Mexicans for the silver." Carr examined the moccasin and handed it back, his lean face growing grave. "Twice this mornin'," the Ranger went on, "unshod tracks have crossed the trail. Last one just a mile or so back."

"Possibly just a horse-stealing party."

"It's a big 'un, whatever they're after." The Ranger swept a look ahead of the train. "Another thing. We're movin' too fast. Let's slow down."

"And invite an attack?"

"Wasn't that the idea, Lieutenant?"

"Certainly. But remember, we have the Fort Belknap payroll along. It's my responsibility. I'd feel safer getting it there in daylight."

Laban glanced to the heavy oak chest under Huckleby's seat, stout-hinged, padlocked.

Emory was in one of his reflective moods. "Wonder if we don't need to put out some extra bait, Lieutenant?"

"Good heavens, man! Isn't the payroll bait enough?"

"I'm thinkin' about *where* and *when* we put it out. Make it look easy pickin's. Dangle it in front of 'em a little. Savvy?"

A mule threw up its long head, rattling bit and bridle. A trooper coughed. Carr's mouth under the golden banner of his mustache turned grim. "You mean make camp for the night?"

"You're gettin' warm, Lieutenant."

"South of the hill where the first attack occurred?"

"Lieutenant, you savvy fast."

Carr pulled on his buttoned jacket. He tipped his head downward in thought, deep thought. When he looked up, a tight little smile scurried across his face. "Emory, are you aware that the rear axle on the lead wagon is in a treacherous state of disrepair? By the time we fix it and creep along the trail, I dare say it will be about time to bivouac. Savvy?"

Emory's answer was to come down off his horse, smacking and rubbing his hands. Lieutenant Carr dismounted and Sergeant Huckleby left the wagon seat, and presently Laban heard, underneath, the first aimless taps of the time-killing tinkering and puttering and occasional pounding. There was much strolling back and forth between the wagons, much standing around and gesturing toward the maligned axle. The troopers in the wagons stayed out of sight.

An hour or more passed. Emory and Carr conferred briefly by the lead wagon. Huckleby climbed to the seat and the mules jangled out.

The long hours of afternoon faded. The hot wind husked off the short grass, breathless, spent, and a drowse as still as time seemed to grip the silent country.

Once more the Ranger rode back to the lieutenant by the wagon, and above the grind of the wheels and the rumbling of the wagon bed over the ruts, Laban caught the tail end of Emory's words. Something about "sign" and "Indians" and "just passed", and he saw the Ranger's face ridged in trouble.

The sun was a sinking crimson ball when Lieutenant Carr signaled the wagons to form circle for the night. Laban put an eye to a peephole, and, as through the glass of a telescope, he saw the lone hill standing guard over the plain. He dropped back to his seat on the bench, waiting as the taciturn troopers waited, for dark to come, when they could escape their stifling canvas cell.

A waiting without end before Laban heard the guard details building fires and the rattle of cooking utensils. And, finally, the evening coolness came lifting over the camp, gently stirring the heavy wagon covers, and he dragged in the hungering coffee and bacon smells.

At full dark Lieutenant Carr's crisp voice reached him. The troopers climbed down from the wagons to stretch and eat their meals in the long shadows away from the cooking fires, now down to glowing coals. Laban joined them. Around the camp the dark glove of night had a thousand invisible fingers. At intervals Laban heard the muffled calls of the sentries and the stampings of the mules and mounts, hobbled, on double picket ropes tonight, nibbling the short grass.

Just past the camp circle lay the skeletons of the burned wagons, remindful and eerie in the vague light. Seeing them raked up the vividness of that early morning darkness, that nightmare, the cries, the shots. He saw it all again, clear-cut. Over there the major's wagon. Over there the wagon with the money chests. Over there he had picketed Reuben and spread his blanket.

Lieutenant Carr's calm voice broke his fixation. He was posting the troopers under and around the wagons, most of them facing north toward the hill. That told Laban it was time for bed. On impulse, he took a blanket and spread it under the lead wagon's front wheels. He had no more than done that when the clomping tread of high-heeled boots sounded behind him, and Emory said — "Back in the wagon, buckaroo . . . stay there." — and passed on.

Picking up the blanket, Laban climbed up and made his bed by the money chest, which it occurred to him provided a strong bulwark. He closed his eyes and felt the tension of the long day recede from his tight body; in an instant he was drifting toward the brink of slumber. And then, like a clanging bell, his mind awakened, a flurry of images striking it — the mysterious hill, the message, if it really meant that, and Duff Fallon and Uncle Gabe.

Whenever he considered his uncle, mixed emotions tore him. No, he decided fiercely, it couldn't be true. Maybe Uncle Gabe loved money more than anything else in the world, as Laban's father, Jesse, had once remarked, but Uncle Gabe wouldn't take another person's life for money. No.

Restless, wide-awake, he sat up and looked out. The moon was up, big and yellow-bright as a pumpkin. Here and there he could see the dark forms of the guarding troopers, the huddled stock.

He lay back, unable to quiet his thinking. He shut his eyes and saw again, as a picture pasted across his mind's eye, as he knew he would see it the rest of his life, the burning wagons, the paint-hideous face growing larger before him.

Sleep did come at last, a light fitful dozing, baleful faces and crashing sounds streaking it.

When he opened his eyes again, he saw, after several moments, that daylight was but a stroke of time away. A reminder throbbed in his mind: whatever was going to happen, if it was, would come all at once.

He lay there, as if his active mind were detached from the hulk of his inert body, waiting, waiting, and he seemed to wait a very long time. Tense, cold, listening, he saw the night murk change ever so slightly, flushed a rose pink, and next, in a streaming swiftness, a flood of dove-gray light struck, spilling across the silent camp. He sat up, sensing, knowing, his dread building.

It began as a single, curdling whoop, high-pitched and savage — *Yee . . . haaa . . . haaa-haa!* And on the heels of that wild quavering, the ripping of rifle shots and horses running. Laban was somehow prepared for that — but not from where the sounds broke, south of the camp instead of the north, not from the direction of the hill. The answer crashed in one pulsing flash. The raiders were attacking from the weak side.

He saw red streaks splitting the shredding light. He smelled the rank and bitter scent of powder smoke. He heard Lieutenant Carr roaring a command, after which he saw and heard troopers running to take up positions on the south.

He sat hunched forward, clutching the top wooden side board, rooted there by an awful suspense. He had the feeling of a spectator, apart from the confused din, sensing a strangeness. Why didn't the raiders rush the camp?

A noise penetrated to him, a close-up drumming of horses coming in a sweeping rush. It came from behind the wagon, from the north side. It sent a cold hackling up his back.

He flung about. He saw nothing wrong, although he could still hear the horses over the firing. He waited with suspended breath. The hoofs ceased. In sudden shock, he saw the feathers of a headdress rising above the wagon seat, followed by a paint-daubed face.

A numbing fear lumped in the pit of his stomach. His throat suddenly contracted. He couldn't move, even as he saw the Indian, groping under the wagon seat, take hold of the payroll chest.

Something snapped in Laban, an intolerable feeling. Without thinking, he lunged and drove with his doubled fist. The blow took the intruder fully on his paint-smeared face. He gave a surprised cry of pain, driven back, but not falling. His headdress toppled and under the streaks of red paint Laban recognized the wizened and whiskery face of Seco.

Laban hit him again. Seco fell backward off the wagon. Laban tore after Seco, scrambled to the wagon seat, looked, and pulled back, grasping what had happened. While the firing swelled to the south, a handful of raiders had slipped in on the north side.

Seco was sitting up, shaking his head.

Leaping down, Laban landed near a swirl of struggling figures. Sergeant Huckleby was wrestling a short, round Indian for possession of a tomahawk. They tussled from side to side, swaying, as though in the embrace of a bear-hugging dance. Another raider ran up, swinging a long-barreled handgun. Huckleby cried out and reeled down. Now the raider started toward the wagon.

Instinctively Laban turned to block his way — and for the tick of a sinking moment he looked into the old nightmare face, as merciless as fate itself, the hawkish nose, the frightful paint streaks, the dented chin. The shiny snout of the handgun glinted, coming up. Laban raised a fending arm.

"Laban . . . get back!"

A round shape bolted in front of him. A roar filled Laban's ears. Oddly he felt no pain, only the jolt of the plump figure wilting into his arms.

Fallon rushed for the wagon; Laban saw it was Fallon. Across the camp rose the full-voiced battle shouts of the troopers running this way. Laban, rising, saw Fallon hesitate and wheel toward his horse. Laban clutched at him. Fallon slammed him aside and ran on, Seco scrambling after him. They pounded away.

Laban looked down at the man moaning on the ground, shocked to recognize the moon face of Uncle Gabe Bushrod, painted up like a medicine-show Indian, a face that looked tragically comical save for the twisting pain.

"Uncle Gabe," Laban said, and put his

arm around him.

He was still holding his uncle when he heard the troopers around him, saw the Ranger and the lieutenant, and Huckleby wobbling to his feet. It reached Laban, finally, that the firing had stopped moments ago.

A gesturing trooper shouted. Northwest, Laban saw two streaks of dust, Fallon and Seco racing their horses. Out from behind the look-out hill streamed Indians — real Indians, Laban saw — their ponies in a dead run, yelping like coyotes as they angled to cut off the two white men.

Carr barked an order. Carbines banged. Nothing changed. The Indians were beyond range.

Fallon and Seco turned west. The swift Indian ponies shortened the gap in surges, closed it suddenly. Open-mouthed, Laban saw a wave of bronze-bodied riders roll over the pair. A savage, whirling tangle, and Fallon and Seco disappeared. A brief pause in the violent milling, and the war party veered north, leading two riderless horses.

Laban turned his head away, feeling sick, looking down into the farcical face, pale between its stripes of yellow war paint. Gabe Bushrod groaned.

A voice said: "Let the surgeon get in there."

Laban watched them carry Uncle Gabe to the lead wagon. Low voices mingled. An orderly hurried to a wagon and back with dressings. Once, faintly, Laban heard his uncle's subdued voice.

A while longer, then Emory drifted back to Laban. He wore a thoughtful, hesitant expression. "Your uncle's told us everything. He was more or less just a front. It was Fallon who gave the orders. . . . A clerk in the Army paymaster's office at Fort Richardson was passing word to the blacksmith. Whoever rode Schoolboy always picked up the message. I know now where I saw that horse . . . in Jacksboro."

"But why did Uncle Gabe send me? Why not one of the crew?"

"Because things were mighty hot, and all Fallon's wild bunch are wanted men. After you came on the scene, the Rangers and the Army started stopping every rider that passed on the trail, although how we'd have figured out that message, I don't know. Maybe not. Gabe was smart. He knew we wouldn't stop or search a boy."

"But the money? Uncle Gabe told me there was money in the envelope with the message. Money to save his ranch."

Emory smiled faintly. "That was to make it seem important to you. To give it a reason. There was just the message."

Laban nodded gloomily, understanding. He could see it all now. Almost all. "The horses I saw that night at the ranch . . . what about them?"

"Stolen. Fallon's bunch moved 'em at night, sold 'em in the settlements along Red River. For instance, that stage station west of Belknap was another holdover place. So was the station this side of Jacksboro."

Lieutenant Carr came around the wagon and motioned for Laban, who ran across.

"Your uncle wants to see you," the lieutenant said.

Gabe Bushrod struggled for breath. He looked even more ludicrous, the zigzag yellow lines on his clownish face in contrast to the bandages binding his chest. Yet, when he spoke, his whispering voice carried a suggestion of its old confidence:

"Don't say a word, m'boy . . . just listen. See, I thought you'd run off. Fallon told me he tried to *catch* you. . . . Your Ranger friend told me what Fallon really tried to do. If I'd known that, I'd. . . ." Anger bubbled up through his pain. "Believe me, boy?"

Laban could only look at him. Uncle Gabe

had done some terrible things. How could you believe him?

"Speak up, boy . . . speak up!" Gabe Bushrod stared up at the wagon cover, his face in strain. "Been no Indian war parties around here for 'bout a year. All there was, we made up . . . till this morning, when that real war party showed up. Otherwise, I wouldn't've sent you after the message. . . . Believe me now?" He tried to raise up, fell back.

"Don't talk any more, Uncle Gabe."

Gabe Bushrod stretched out a desperate hand. "Believe me? Do you, boy?"

Just then the surgeon appeared. He inclined his head for Laban to leave.

Stepping back, watching the grimacing, clownish-streaked face, Laban became aware of an absolute truth. Submerged until now, it lighted up his mind.

"Uncle Gabe," he said, hurrying a little. "You gave me Schoolboy and Schoolboy saved me from Fallon . . . saved me same as you did just a while ago, when you took the bullet Fallon meant for me. I believe you."

Gabe Bushrod seemed to be smiling behind his hideous yellow mask.

Laban turned and walked out from the wagon, knowing the long nightmare was over at last. Yet, also, he sensed that he had

found a new beginning in new country, and
an even deeper awareness. He was a man.

ABOUT THE AUTHOR

Fred Grove has written extensively in the broad field of Western fiction, from the Civil War and its postwar effect on the expanding West, to modern Quarter horse racing in the Southwest. He has received the Western Writers of America Spur Award five times — for his novels *Comanche Captive* (1961) which also won the Oklahoma Writing Award at the University of Oklahoma and the Levi Strauss Golden Saddleman Award, *The Great Horse Race* (1977), and *Match Race* (1982), and for his short stories, "Comanche Woman" (1963) and "When the *Caballos* Came" (1968). His novel, *The Buffalo Runners* (1968), was chosen for a Western Heritage Award by the National Cowboy Hall of Fame, as was the short story, "Comanche Son" (1961).

He also received a Distinguished Service Award from Western New Mexico University for his regional fiction on the Apache frontier, including the novels *Phantom Warrior* (1981) and *A Far Trumpet* (1985). His recent historical novel, *Bitter Trumpet* (1989), follows the bittersweet adventures of ex-Confederate Jesse Wilder training Juáristas in Mexico fighting the mercenaries of the Emperor Maximilian. *Trail of Rogues* (1993) and *Man on a Red Horse* (1998), *Into the Far Mountains* (1999), and *A Soldier Returns* (2004) are sequels in this frontier saga.

For a number of years Grove worked on newspapers in Oklahoma and Texas as a sportswriter, straight newsman, and editor. Two of his earlier novels, *Warrior Road* (1974) and *Drums Without Warriors* (1976), focus on the brutal Osage murders during the Roaring 'Twenties, a national scandal that brought in the FBI, as does *The Years of Fear* (Five Star Westerns, 2002). Of Osage descent, the author grew up in Osage County, Oklahoma during the murders. It was while interviewing Oklahoma pioneers that he became interested in Western fiction. He now resides in Tucson, Arizona, with his wife Lucile.